These Foolish Things

MODERN ROMANCE CLASSICS
General Editor Michael Levien

This series presents outstanding twentieth-
century novels by British and foreign writers
whose central themes are love and romance.
Other titles are in preparation.

PUBLISHED

MICHAEL SADLEIR These Foolish Things
ANDRÉ MAUROIS The Climates of Love

Michael Sadleir

These Foolish Things

PETER OWEN · LONDON

ISBN 0 7206 0670 5

PETER OWEN PUBLISHERS
73 Kenway Road London SW5 0RE

First published 1937
This edition published 1986
©The Estate of Michael Sadleir 1986

Printed in Great Britain by
A. Wheaton & Co. Ltd, Exeter

Oh, how the ghost of you clings! These fool - ish

poco cresc.

things Re-mind me of you.

By kind permission of Holt Marvell, Jack Strachey and Boosey & Co. Ltd.

CONTENTS

SALLY darling, you remember those last twenty minutes before the boat sailed; and our standing side by side, your hand on the top rail and mine over it, and the strangle of misery which clutched the two of us? Of course you remember. At least I must believe you do—*must*, Sally, because otherwise nothing means anything any more. I can hear all the noises that went on about us—the scuffle of the passing crowd behind, the snatches of talk and laughter, the banging and creaking and restlessness of a big steamer ready to sail; most clearly of all, perhaps, I can hear the noise of the rain, as it drummed, drummed into the sea—out of sight but horribly within hearing—and how we stood there staring into a streaming darkness.

Some time during those twenty minutes you said to me:

" Niki—I don't even know who taught you about love." And I said: " You did, Sally." And you said: " No, I got the fruit; but I didn't plant the tree. Nor train it. Who did that? " And I said: " Not any one person, I think; there were several." And you said: " Some were unkind, weren't they? " And I said: " Perhaps a little, but I deserved most of what I got. Anyway how did you know? " And you said: " Oh, I could tell almost right away. That wet day in Paris I knew. How I hated them." And I said: " Don't hate them. None of them mattered once you were there." And you said: " Leave me out, my dear. We have lived our love story and it is the only memory I shall keep for always." After a pause you added: " All the same, I'd like to have known what happened before. I wish I'd asked you. I nearly did the time when . . ."

Then the hooter went, and everything was forgotten as in the sharpness of death. For the last time I kissed you, for the last time felt your shoulders quiver under my hands. Perhaps

I

you crossed to the shore side of the boat, peered down on the gangway, and wondered which of the huddled rain-blurred figures jostling their way ashore was your ex-lover. He did not, could not, look up. But once under the quay-side shelter he hid behind a pillar; from its shadow and that of his own misery gazed up at the sheer side of the liner, and from the crowd who clustered along the rail, tried for the last time to pick you out.

Oh, Sally, that pouring night in Cherbourg! I stayed by the dock, watching the ship swing away into the darkness, its lights gradually mist and grow faint. Between you and me the curtain of the rain drooped and drooped, and at last fell, finally and for always.

And then what? Indeed I hardly know. It is cruel how vivid and accurate is my memory of every detail to the moment of your going, how confused and uncertain since. I recall streets more or less deserted, and the rain sizzling on the pavé, and the slap-slap of my soaking mackintosh against my legs. I know that I found myself in the mournful acreage of the Place Napoléon and that, standing by the statue, I made out by the light of a distant arc-lamp the foolish inscription about the " Merveilles de l'Egypte." Later—but how much later who shall say?—I was leaning on the zinc of some bistro or other, leaning heavily and telling myself that I would drink you out of the extreme foreground of my mind. I'd tried to do that once before, and not only out of the foreground of my mind—right out of it. I think I told you; and what a failure it was, and how ill I felt next morning; and we laughed together, little dreaming it would happen again. Was I more successful this time? In a sense " yes." I had this " foreground " idea so wedged in my head, that I came to see nothing in front of me but a vast proscenium arch, with a single powerful footlight which beat upwards on you—on YOU, Sally, the foremost, indeed the only figure on an immense stage. And you kept changing, in every respect changing. . . .

You became a summary kaleidoscope of all the Sallies I had known and worshipped, from the moment of our first meeting in Alice's drawing-room in the Rue la Tremoille to the enchanted anguish of our last night together in this now hateful Cherbourg. " Our last night together "—the night before the day on the evening of which you sailed away; the night before the day at the very end of which, propped against the sloppy counter of a second-rate bar, I was burning my vitals with cheap Calvados and torturing my brain with variations on the theme of Nevermore. I wanted to drink that huge, haunted stage into blackness, to extinguish the footlight, to obliterate every imaginary you, just as darkness and rain had so lately obliterated the real thing.

And for a little while I succeeded. I have no memory of leaving that bar or of finding my way back to the hotel. I do not even recall taking the key from its hook or mounting the wide shallow stairs which seemed to sag towards the well and quiver as one trod on them. But once in the room—our room that had been—recollection returned. No one could have been near it since we left for the boat. The litter of paper and oddments over from your packing still strewed the floor. The espadrilles, which at the last moment you decided to leave behind, lay forlornly on a chair. Your powder-box; your broken kirbigrip; your crumpled packet of cigarettes—these and other pitiful little relics were scattered here and there. I remember closing the door behind me, leaning a little crazily against it and, my hand still on the light-switch, surveying under the hard glare of the unshaded bulb in the middle of the ceiling this worse-than-emptiness—this room so full of what had been you, so bare now of everything but what you had left behind. I remember being fiercely glad—in the heart of my desolation— that we had chosen this obscure, utterly French, rather melancholy hotel for our last sojourn together, instead of going to the great cosmopolitan palace whence most American travellers depart. To have crawled back, drunk with brandy and misery, to view the débris of my love-story in a setting of pink eiderdowns and white paint and shaded lights would have been wrong. You always hated the standardised luxury of international hotels, international bars, international pleasure-haunts; and this high sombre room, with strips of carpet on its polished floor, its ludicrous little wash-basin, its twin walnut beds, its cumbersome wardrobe which threatened to fall forward every time the heavy door swung open, with—above all—its central unshaded light which seemed to cast no shadow, yet left the place a mass of shadows—was suitable enough as a vault in which to bury the dead among my memories.

Just so far, as I have said, I remember what happened that night. But thereafter is nothing until next morning; until the grey light of another wet day came chinking through the curtains on to your empty bed; until I realised that my head was like a burning wheel and the future a waste of ashes.

ᔥ   ᔥ   ᔥ

It must have been nearly noon when I made my way downstairs again. I had packed my bag (if you can call " packing " what was merely a kneading together of crumpled incompatibles), swallowed a cup of tepid coffee and taken a final farewell of our final privacy. My head still ached, but not so savagely as on waking. I had in an exaggerated form that vague, irrelevant feeling characteristic of a hang-over. How often we had shared that feeling—and enjoyed it. Do you remember Charbonnières, on the hills above Lyon, and our wild evening in and about the Casino, and the host of friends we made, most of them couples who had probably never seen one another before, but were already as fond and intimate as after a liaison of three months? We were enchantingly vague next morning and floated through the woods in a maze of laughter. That was a happy hang-over; but the Cherbourg variety was all of the other thing. I concentrated sufficiently

to tell the bureau that I had vacated the room, that the luggage
was ready, that I would return for it and my bill in time to catch
the five o'clock express.   I then wandered unhappily into the
street.

The rain had stopped and the clouds had broken.   Rather
watery sunlight shone on a town which cannot surely be so
detestable as I thought, but must, none the less, be a place of
very moderate attraction.   I slumped into a café chair and drank
some really hot café-cognac.   Then fumbled my way back to
the docks.   The embarkation-shed was deserted and barred.
I could not even re-visit the pillar from behind which I had
watched your boat depart.   You were already miles out to sea
and here was I, denied access even to the dock from which you
had sailed.   I had a horrible feeling of being locked into Cherbourg, as though those great doors through which we had both
passed last night, out of which I had later crept alone, were the
only exit from this ill-favoured town.

I turned on my tracks, and after a little exploration found
myself clear of the docks and on the shore of the bay from which
the harbour opens.   You never saw anything much of Cherbourg by daylight, Sally; and although you did not miss much,
you must share what I saw because, loathe the place as I do, we
had our last night there and it must rank as one of *our* places.
As I stood looking across the bay toward the open sea, the town
lay at my back and a little to the right—a saucer of smoke,
behind the warehouses and cranes of dockland.   A circle of low
hills surrounds the basin in which the place lies, repeating the
curve of the bay.   They looked pleasant enough in the
strengthening sunshine of a morning after rain, a chequer of
irregular fields, with little woods and occasional farm-houses
scattered up and down.   But between the friendly countryside
and the shore of the bay lie barracks like grey boxes; banked
fortifications, grass-covered and probably obsolete; the be-
ginnings of concrete breakwaters, from which jetties run out
ending in castellated forts and studded with pill-boxes.   It

seemed characteristic that Cherbourg, which had already cut me off from re-living my last sight of you by a shuttered shed, should now interpose useless defences between me and a kindly rusticity. Nor was this all. Overhead an aeroplane zoomed; in the bay lay a couple of dark green destroyers. So not only landwards, but skyward and seaward also, the way was barred. Cherbourg was a dead end indeed, with no escape save backward into France.

I trailed toward the town again and, after eating something somewhere, sat in the sun outside a café and thought back and back, until the memory of our times together blurred me to inward tears. Then the hotel and the bill and the bag and the station.

The five o'clock does not stop between Caen and Paris. It rocked and screamed through the falling darkness in true *État* style. At eleven o'clock, St Lazare. I carried my bag to the little café at the end of the Salle des Pas Perdus, and told myself that now the show was really finished. I sat in a sort of trance. My proscenium arch loomed again. I could see the lights darkening—first on the empty stage, then about the house. At last there was only one light left—just under the stage, where the conductor sits. It seemed that a darker shadow than the rest flitted from the wings and hung for a moment over the orchestra-pit. The light was very faint, but I could just make out your face. Your lovely mouth smiled sadly, and I think your eyes were full of tears. Then the last light went out and the vision faded; the noise of the station crowded in on me once more, and I was on a hard chair under the arc-lamps of St Lazare, with the theatre crowds jostling toward their suburban trains, and the huge clock already a fraction past the half hour and on its way to midnight. In less than thirty minutes the utmost possible prolongation of the love-story of Sally and Nicholas would be over—your love-story and mine. Another dead end, this time with no way out at all. At that moment there came back to me—as clearly as though you were once again speaking them—your last words on board. "I'd like to have known what happened before. I wish I'd asked you." In effect you had asked me, Sally; and I decided, when I could face up to the job, to write this book for you. Now that it is written, I wonder if you will ever read it?

I: MYSELF WHEN YOUNG

THEY say that a man's attitude toward women is conditioned in advance by the child's feeling for his mother. Maybe; but I cannot help suspecting that the theory is one of those convenient generalisations which can neither be proved nor disproved. Every apparent exception can be ingeniously explained away; and inasmuch as the conditioning is permitted to work by opposites as well as by analogies, the psychologist, if he be skilful, gets you every time. Consequently, I am quite prepared to be claimed as a perfect example of the mother-governed male, although frankly I do not recognise my qualifications or believe that in my case the doctrine has much of relevance.

My mother was, of course, the centre of my childish universe, and the trust and affection given to her were instinctive and complete. But, side by side with this trust and this affection, developed, as I grew into adolescence, a tinge of fear. She was a woman of great practical capacity, of the highest moral principle, and of a certain severity of outward mien, which I now recognise to have been a blend of personal shyness and traditional puritanism, but in youth mistook for an over-zealous policy of discipline. I had friends whose parents not only gave them more pocket-money (and they were folk in circumstances similar to ours) but also allowed a liberty in theatre-going, visit-paying and so forth far in excess of anything permitted to me or to my brother. I was first puzzled, and then a little ashamed, by this apparently unreasonable difference between my independence and theirs; but it never occurred to me to challenge my mother's authority because, as I have said, I was in my heart of hearts frightened of her. Do not misunderstand the nature

8

of this fear. It was not a fear of hard words, still less of physical correction; for she was the most self-contained of creatures, with a wonderful power of serene silence. It was the inevitable awe felt by fallibility for virtue, the embarrassed sense of inferiority with which a specific moral weakness confronts its counterpart.

I suspect that among my qualities is neither that of great moral courage nor that of instinctive sensual self-control. And it was precisely in these two qualities that my mother excelled. If she believed a thing to be right, no respect for persons nor nervous qualm prevented her saying so. As for controlling her own tendencies to self-indulgence, her mastery of them was so complete, that it is not disloyal to suspect them of only very moderate development. Certainly an instinct to push pleasure away from her just because it was pleasure, was inherent in her nature; and the effect of continuous self-repression, on a temperament never very warm or volatile, can only have been to reduce still further its liability to temptation.

The sense of being more closely under control than many lads of my age and kind developed the more quickly because, in this matter of instinctive puritanism, my brother was more thoroughly than I our mother's son. Consequently I had not even the consolation of sharing with one of my own generation a subterranean grievance against the despotism of our elders. He was four years my senior, and for long enough the difference in our ages made any contact over questions of spare-time amusement impossible. But by the time I was sixteen I was more or less aware that no help could be expected from Geoffrey in evading—still less in defying—the rigid control exercised by maternal principles. My brother was no more aggressively austere than my mother; he simply lacked that particular form of youthful curiosity about life which expressed itself in foolish ragging, in visits to musical-comedy or music-hall, in crude flirtations with shop-girls, or in kisses on the stairs during the private-house dances of pre-war middle-class suburbia. When I

B 2

was at Oxford, and he had already started in the publishing office he now helps to control, we went about together as much as circumstances allowed and were always good friends; but even then I had a queer sense of being on my best behaviour, of avoiding certain topics and certain jokes, of using, as it were, about two-thirds of myself, and keeping the other third scrupulously in reserve.

Originally, of course, this tendency was part of the protective colouring of adolescence. But shynesses and obliquities belonging to that shyest and most oblique of all the ages of man, are more than apt to become permanent—as in my case they bade fair to do, until I found you and, with you, freedom to be myself.

For this nervous suppression of one element in my character I often paid indirect penalty. Perhaps penalty is too strong a word. Let us say, rather, that my consciousness of never being all of myself at ordinary times has driven me to a pretended complaisance which, though it may have convinced comparative strangers, left me more self-critical than ever. And I still cannot help being conciliatory, ready to see another's point of view, prompt with offers of service, willing to regard as bygones things not really gone by, although in the very moment of being so I often long to be otherwise. Often I want to seem stubborn and difficult, and am fearful lest the facile amiability which I despise in myself make me contemptible in the eyes of others. Perhaps it does; and perhaps also, in so doing, it has damaged me. But on one occasion—and at an important moment—my reluctance to assume that my way of doing things was right and another's wrong, did me a vital service.

තු   තු   තු

You will wonder what all this has to do with a possible parallel between my attitude toward my mother and my subsequent relations with women. Not a great deal, I am afraid;

but sufficient, perhaps, to justify my having written it down. It is relevant on general grounds, because sooner or later I would have had to assess my adolescent self for your benefit, and why not sooner? More particularly it is relevant, because, so far as girls were concerned, my mentality was to develop on exactly contrary lines to those planned by my dear mother, but absolutely in accordance with the quirks of my own nature. It began with timid adoration; went on to trustfulness and pliability, both of which were abused; and had arrived—when you came on the scene and shattered the basis of my cynicism— at a state of mind toward women, half-desirous, half-resentful, which drove me to take pleasure where I found it and let romance go hang. That I got to this state could, I suppose, be remotely ascribed to the emotional secretiveness of my 'teens, and to my devious avoidance of contact with family unsympathy.

If that proves that my attitude to my mother conditioned my after-attitude to women, all right. But it seems to me to stretch the point rather.

Ꙩ   Ꙩ   Ꙩ

My mother took an unfavourable view of wild oats. She regarded them as unnecessary and undesirable, and laid her plans to frustrate them. No doubt, from the angle of her own unassailable integrity, she acted rightly; but in her strategy— at least so far as I was concerned—she was at fault. Up to a point her policy succeeded admirably, for never were 'teens more innocent of oats. Indeed I doubt if I kissed a girl before I was eighteen or nineteen; and when I think back at what I now recognise to have been invitations to dalliance from half a dozen young persons of my own age, but took at the time to be mere kindly condescensions from a genus always alarming and usually aloof, I have to smile a little ruefully. I was a case, with a vengeance, of " If youth but knew! " Certainly I had a mild attack of the familiar adolescent hobby for postcards of actresses, which I carried about in my pocket and stuck on the walls of my school study. (They cut film-stars and Goldwyn girls and what not out of the picture-papers these days, and certainly get more of a view for their money; but the principle is the same.) I also, for a short period, bought surreptitious copies of *The Winning Post*, and chuckled with exaggerated satisfaction over the not very subtle jokes on the first page of that painstaking weekly. I remember one to this day about Twin Beds, which convulsed me for days with experienced merriment. But these excesses were as much conformations to type as anything else, and my personal record of romantic adventure is pitiful—nothing less.

There was a girl in Switzerland—at one of those winter-sport places above the Lake of Geneva—who spent nearly a fortnight trying to get me going. Poor soul! She was not a particularly alluring girl, as I recall her; one of that too-familiar British type, with a thin pointed nose, a mouth like a circumflex accent, and an excited provincial voice. But she did try. And the pathetic thing is that I thought she succeeded. I had so little idea of what was expected of me, that I imagined I was head-over-ears, and saying my piece well enough to fill the house twice over, just because I pulled the girl's *luge* up the hills for her, and danced two out of every three dances with her, and had tea with her in the lounge instead of upstairs over the family spirit-lamp. I even took a minute and rather bad snapshot of her, of which I kept a print in the back of my watch. I repeat—I had no idea whatsoever that this was not the way to conduct a regulation amour. I now realise that there was every excuse for the young lady becoming at first distraite, then pettish, and finally otherwise engaged. But not then. I was hurt, Sally; bitterly hurt. "Here am I" (I thought) "the plaything of a selfish wanton!" 'Plaything' is particularly good. The soap-box on wheels which serves the slum-baby for a motor-car was nearer reality than I to the kind of temporary gallant poor Phyllis wanted. And there it ended. I went home to England; so, presumably, did she. I never saw or heard of her again.

My next outbreak was hardly more desperate, though considerably more protracted. Circumstances (that is a diplomatic way of saying the limitations of my normal holiday existence) kept me to the dissipations of outer-suburbia. These included dances, tennis-parties, boating-parties, picnics and even progressive games. I plunged into this whirlpool of gaiety, and soon developed an infatuation for the daughter of a retired colonel. I can still see her round, pretty, foolish little face quite clearly, but nothing else about her. This, perhaps, is not surprising, because I do not think I ever noticed anything else. Partly I was too frightened to look; mainly I felt no urge to do so. I was still at that stage; barely hatched out. Of course one had not the facilities of a later period for a study of legs, but I might at least have got a line on her feet, or hands, or general carriage.

I do not think she ever had the least idea that she had inspired a fledgling passion. I was too self-conscious to show any sign of special eagerness to be with her, still less to breathe a word of admiration or endearment. So it is not easy to see how she could have drawn any very flattering conclusion from our occasional meetings. Nevertheless I managed to get great emotional satisfaction from a passion one-sided and unavowed.

I procured some beautiful heart-throbs by bicycling round and round the group of houses in one of which she lived, on the chance that she might come out into the garden and be visible over the fence. And every small dance was a thrill, thanks to the uncertainty whether she had been asked or, if asked, whether she would come. I have just said that my infatuation was unavowed. So it was, to her who caused it; but it was not absolutely concealed from the whole world. I was so full of ardour and excitement that I just had to confide in someone. With the impenetrable stupidity of my inexperience, I disclosed the secret of my fancy to a girl of my own age, whom I had known since small childhood and regarded as a sister. That she hardly regarded me as a brother I only came to understand long afterward; and it still puts me to shame to think of the naïve clumsiness of my avowal—to her of all people, and of the patient sympathy she showed toward my futile aspirations. Whatsoever she could do to bring me into contact with my divinity, she did. And there was nothing cynical about her help. She just wanted to please me. And the fact that the whole affair was trivial to absurdity, cannot detract from the fine quality of her self-abnegation.

This amourette had a comical ending. I suppose, as the months went by, I got a little braver and my attentions became faintly obvious. I still do not recall their making the least impression on the young woman herself; but they must have put into her father's head an idea which he lost no time in implementing. He wrote me a note, asking me to go and see him. I had never been inside his house, for the Colonel and his daughter were not officially part of my mother's acquaintance; so an invitation to the lady's home was a terrific event. With no misgivings, and no particular curiosity save as to whether she herself would be visible, I obeyed the Colonel's summons. There was no sign of the girl; the father received me in his study. For the first time I felt a twinge of uneasiness. Nurtured on Victorian fiction, I could not help wondering whether the stage were set for an enquiry as to my intentions. The fact that boys of seventeen have no intentions and, if they make themselves a sentimental nuisance, are subjected, not to enquiries, but to a kick in the pants, did not occur to me. Increasingly flustered, I tried to imagine how young Lochinvar or Rupert of Hentzau would deal with this particular brand of military inquisition, but decided that no useful analogy could be drawn from the answer, even if I could think of one. I need not have worried, for the very next moment the Colonel announced that he had decided to invite me to become the local scout-master.

When I got home and considered this disagreeable suggestion, I found myself in something of a dilemma. The activities of a scout-master had no lure for me. Indeed I felt strongly that

to prance round familiar suburban roads in shorts and a wide-
awake, followed by a handful of urchins all badges and cords
and ribbons, would be shame-making beyond the reasonable.
On the other hand, to become, as it were, second in command
to the Colonel (for the scout-troop was of his creation and he
their Panjandrum) would inevitably bring me into frequent
contact with his household. This was obviously desirable;
I could have wished that shorts were not essential, for my calves
—though adequate—were not prize-winners; but I told myself
that one must not be pernickety and that there would be intervals
of mufti. So, after a day or two of conflict, love conquered
indolence and vanity and I accepted my commission—only,
about two weeks later, to be finally and irrevocably scored off.
For then the Colonel, with a guile unsuitable in a simple soldier,
blandly remarked that he was particularly glad I had taken on
the management of the scouts, as now without a qualm he could
complete his preparations for moving house. He was leaving
our suburb for good, and taking his daughter with him. The
troop, with perfect confidence, he consigned to me. Never
can a lover so remote from any degree of love's fulfilment have
been left carrying so many babies.

                    ∽   ∽   ∽

Up to a point, as I have said, my mother's method of keeping
her younger son unspotted from the world succeeded admirably.
That point had now been reached. No doubt, if I had continued to live a placid outer-suburban life, going after Oxford
was over into a London office and gradually settling into normal
English manhood until the war came and swept me and my
kind away, I should have developed (or failed to develop)
more or less along the lines she preferred. Poor darling! She
was a typical English woman, and liked her men-folk to grow
up in body but not in mind. This feminine preference still
persists and is supported by logical, though unavowed, reasoning. Not only is a mentality of prolonged boyhood easier to

acclaim on grounds of wholesomeness, but it is also much easier to control. And to control her male belongings has been for nearly a century the proudest service a really nice woman can render, alike to her God and to the tradition of British respectability.

But my mother's excellent intentions were defeated (oddly enough) by the return from the United States of one of my father's brothers, and the defeat (more oddly still) was turned into a rout by my own susceptibility to light music. Both processes were sheer bad luck for her and unpredictable into the bargain. She could hardly have foreseen how influential this fortuitous reappearance of Uncle Nick would prove to be; nor can she be blamed for having no premonition of the part to be played in my emotional education by a popular waltz tune. Yet both the one and the other did its work quickly and thoroughly.

II: UNCLE NICK

UNCLE NICK was younger than my father by two years; and it might, of course, have been mere coincidence that since my father's death (which had taken place nearly ten years before the time of which I am writing) we at home had heard speak of him far less than previously. I know now, however, that my mother did not like him, and indeed never liked him, and that his virtual obliteration from family conversation was the completion of a process begun many years earlier. At one time he and my father had been close friends; then came my father's marriage, and forthwith the comradeship was exposed to the relentless pressure of virtuous womanly disapproval. It endured for three or four years without manifest weakening (I deduce this from the fact that I was named after Uncle Nick, so that my father's fondness for him must still have been articulate at the time of my birth), but then began to sag, as on one side home-influence worked ever more persistently against it.   The departure of Uncle Nick to America in search of fresh air and a fortune finished it.   Thereafter I have a small boy's memory of letters on the breakfast table—letters bearing the long pictorial stamps of the Columbus Commemoration Issue (followed by an interval of dull presidents, followed again by the satisfactory and eventful designs of the Trans-Mississippi series)—and of my father reading and chuckling, and now and again quoting an excerpt to my mother in a voice which even then struck me as vaguely apologetic.   And then my father, who had gone to Scotland to lecture and caught cold on the journey, suddenly developed pneumonia and in three days was dead.   There was a period of fluster; of bewildered unhappiness; of unwelcome, if muted, control by all manner of relations.   But in time the disturbance and the sorrow of this tragic happening died away, and were replaced by new and urgent trivialities of developing boyhood.   When next I became conscious of a tranquil home life and once again took notice of the standard preoccupations of our household, Uncle Nick had ceased to exist.   Indeed I might have forgotten him altogether, but for overhearing a remark of my mother's as she stood in the garden with some long-separated female friend, not far from where I was busy in the shrubbery uprooting an unwanted elder-stump.

" . . . And of course his poor brother heard nothing until it was all over? " the friend said.

" I daresay that was all for the best " replied my mother. " Nicholas' presence would hardly have improved matters. Although I am bound to say " she added, with characteristic fairness, " he wrote me a very nice letter."

When, therefore, during my third summer term at Oxford I suddenly got a letter from the Carlton Hotel, announcing that my " affectionate Uncle, Nicholas G. Dering " was coming on the following Saturday and would I show him round in the afternoon and dine with him in the evening, I felt something of the excitement which attends the opening up of a room long sealed, in which there is some reason to anticipate the discovery of a skeleton. I was prepared to disapprove of Uncle Nick, partly because my mother disapproved of him, partly because the returning uncle from America, Australia, South Africa or what not was, in those days, a stock character who wore deplorable yellow boots and smoked cigars in church. From the heights of pre-war British priggery, I was ready to condescend in order to satisfy my curiosity; but it was up to Uncle Nick to Make Good with me, as, presumably, he had done in the wilds of savage America. He had chosen to submit himself to my scrutiny. Very well; I would investigate and in due course give my verdict. You can imagine that, at twenty-one years of age, I had no doubt whatsoever that my verdict would be infallible.

For perhaps the first three minutes of our acquaintanceship my expectations were fulfilled. As the train pulled up, a large loose figure stumbled from a first-class carriage and stood undecidedly within ten feet of where I was waiting. The man wore light grey clothes, of a cut unmistakably devised in what we regarded as the back-of-beyond—a sack-back coat, no waistcoat and floppy trousers. His hat-brim was noticeably wide, and lacked the even rigidity of London fashion. He wore a belt, and the toes of his shoes were stunted and knobby. A fearful conviction seized me that this was my Uncle Nick; that in his company I was doomed to trail about Oxford under the sardonic eyes of my acquaintances; that I should never hear the last of it, and that the whole affair was the limit. I pulled myself together, stepped up to the stranger, and enquired with the frigidity of shyness:

" Er—are you Mr Dering? "

I hardly know what I expected him to do—probably to start yodelling or to punch me in the chest or to spit productively and shout " Put it there, son." Certainly I did not expect that he would swing slowly round, smile with one side of his mouth and look at me thoughtfully, until I dropped my eyes in embarrassment. When at last he spoke, it was in a low rather lazy voice, to which the American burr gave an attractive richness.

" Boy! " he said.   " You are like y' father to look at.   Let's thank God for that, as a start."

By the time we were through the subway—that enduring feature of the Oxford railway station—I had forgotten that I was to pass final judgment on my Uncle Nick, in the nervous hope that he would consent to pass tolerable judgment on me.

At first he talked little, apparently content to move through the streets and quads with his long easy strides, listening to my clipped and uninformative comments, and occasionally prodding me with a brief request for further detail.   It was, therefore, not so much what he said as the manner of his silence, which convinced me he was a far from usual person.   He gave the impression of complete self-mastery and—this I took to be strange—of a slightly amused interest in the sights of Oxford. Two men in commoners' gowns; a don in bands, mortar board and M.A. gown, on his way from the Schools; a tram-car; a group of decorative undergraduates in jumpers and scarves of Hall's latest pastel colourings; a more than normally solemn common-room scout in conversation with the porter at a college gate; the main entrance to the Bodleian, tucked away in the corner of an obscure and gloomy quadrangle—these in turn provoked the one-sided smile which creased his clean-shaven face with wrinkles.

He seemed a tireless tourist.   The sun was very hot; but we forged steadily from sight to sight, did the Cathedral in detail, completed no fewer than three times the tour of the Meadows, visited every available college garden between Merton Street and the Parks, walked all round them, and descended on Magdalen by way of the old Racquet Court and Long Wall.   I found myself talking almost volubly about Oxford and its ways, while my uncle fell more or less silent, merely giving me a side-long glance from time to time.   But he showed no sign of boredom and I continued to chatter.   At last, after more than three hours of wandering, we stood at the gateway leading from Magdalen Garden into Addison's Walk. My uncle threw up his head and shook himself.

" My golly, Nick, this is a darned lovely place, but no part of the world as I know it. What's it all for? Where is it going? And where are all you boys going, when you're through with lotus-eating? "

I forget what I replied. It was something inarticulate and a little confused, for I was at a loss to meet this unusual criticism of a place whose ultimate purpose it never occurred to us to criticise, however carefully mocking we might be of its administration and of one another. But he hardly listened, as he stood gazing through the trees toward the meadows of Mesopotamia, lost in some queer reverie of his own. Then suddenly:

" I want a drink. Which is the best bar? And where do we eat later? I have to go back to London this evening and have a few things to say."

My recommendation of the at that time best-reputed hotel had, I hoped, the air of being based on experience. In fact it was not; for in those days the bar and hotel-lounge life of the undergraduate on narrow means was almost non-existent. But there was something about my uncle which made me reluctant to appear inefficient, and my instinctive amiability prevented me from concealing ignorance under a cloak of superiority. Which, as matters turned out, was fortunate.

He lit a cigar with his whisky, stuck out his long legs so that the lamentable shoes were more than normally in evidence, and quite suddenly began to talk.

" Listen, boy. I'm going to say a lot of things to you out-right, which may shock or even offend you. It won't hurt you to be shocked—that's what this country seems to me to need; but I'd be sorry to give offence and want you to believe here and now that I don't mean a word beyond what I say.

" To begin with I'm more or less of a stranger, even though I am your father's brother. And that's the first thing. I am

a stranger to you, but you are far less one to me.   Your father
and I were closer than most brothers, and anything or anyone
who is part of him means something rather special to me.

" You probably know that your mother and I never got on.
I won't say that when she married your father she came between
him and me, because that implies intruding and, after all, as his
wife she was already the centre of his picture.   But she registered
a sort of permanent disapproval of me and, naturally enough,
that gradually made the poor fellow self-conscious and pushed
him into the defensive so far as I was concerned.

" Well, I stuck around a bit and did my best to keep up the
old relationship.   I did everything I knew to conciliate your
mother.   You'd laugh if I were to tell you of some of the absurd
circumspections I used to work out ahead before seeing her, and
painfully carry out.   Of course they merely made matters
worse, for they embarrassed your poor father and did not affect
your mother one atom; but I was young then, and believed
likes and dislikes necessarily hinged on externals.   It never
occurred to me that I might represent something much bigger
and more to be resented than my unimportant self; nor did I
realise that, when a woman shows a distaste for the habits or
humour or hobbies of one of her husband's intimates, she is
really out against the very stuff he's made of, and for one reason
only—that she sees in him some sort of threat to her own
domestic supremacy.   And for that reason she means to get
him out."

I interrupted :

" But surely it was merely a sort of natural jealousy—
jealousy of your having known father so well before she did ? "

" No, no.   A woman can be jealous of another woman—for
obvious reasons.   Or she can be jealous of a man's job or
interests, if she is not sufficiently involved in them to feel able
at will to control them.   But the idea that she can be personally
jealous of one of her husband's male intimates is just untrue.   A
lot of people want it to be thought true—and not only women.

But that doesn't alter the fact that it is bunk. In my case I stood in her eyes for a particular sort of worldliness—not the obvious mixture of flesh and devil, but a subtler compound of irreverence towards stuffed shirts and their codes, and of restless curiosity about all sorts of funny places and people.

" And yet I don't know " he went on, with a gesture almost of apology. " I'm not putting it right. I sound as though I thought your mother a mere respecter of persons, and timid and insular. Heaven knows, she was none of those. But she had —and I've no doubt still has—certain tremendous principles, to which she was determined those about her should conform. They are grand principles; but I have always jibbed at the idea even of perfection being imposed on one person by another or on a thousand people by a hundred; and I think she knew, when she began to use her influence on your father, that I should not be on her side.

" Anyway, it soon became evident that I only made my brother's life more difficult by trying to keep up our old com- panionship; and that my utmost care to avoid any suggestion of interference between him and his wife was useless. So I decided to clear out, and clear out I did. I'd had a good train- ing as an engineer, heard of an opening in the States, took myself off and—which is really rather extraordinary—have stayed that side of the Atlantic ever since. Yes—this is my first visit to England in nearly fifteen years, and it's a queer feeling to be back again—queer and not too comfortable. I guess I've lost the knack of it. Or maybe there are too many memories which I had thought dead. . . ."

After a moment's silence he cocked an eye at me.

" Sorry to talk so much. I expect I am boring you. But it doesn't matter. And I hope, when I'm finished, you will see that it is meant as a compliment, and is not without point either."

I said nothing. There wasn't anything to say. As a matter of fact I wasn't bored a bit, though I confess I didn't see the relevance of a good deal of my uncle's talk. But the real check on speech was that I felt considerable indignation on my mother's behalf.   I had resented her discipline often enough; but it was hardly suitable for someone who had not seen any of us for twenty years to stroll in and pick holes in our family.   And yet this stranger impressed me.   I was conscious still of that air of definition, of that easy self-mastery which had struck me within ten minutes of having set eyes on him.   This man knew where he was; and to know that seemed remarkable even to the confident fledgling-me of all those years ago.   To-day, of course, I realise it to be miraculous.   So I kept silence and nursed my irritation against a later crisis.

Uncle Nick had not, apparently, expected any comment; for, having refilled his glass (to the waiter's injured astonishment he had insisted on keeping the bottle at his elbow), he proceeded with his story.

" Then one day I got a cable—saying my brother was dead. I tell you, Nick, that was the nastiest knock I've yet had.   There may be more to come, but I hope not.   Not only would I never see him again, but I could not even get over in time to pay my last respects to the best friend—more than that—to the only real friend I ever had.   I tell you, I sat there in my office-chair holding the cable in my hand, feeling there wasn't anything at all—any more.   I must have sat there an hour.   They tell me they came in and spoke and I just took no notice, but sat staring at the piece of paper like a man doped.   Even when I pulled myself out of the stupor, the sense of the futility of everything remained.   I sat down and wrote to your mother, and for the first time felt I could talk to her without any restraint. I threw up my job, cleared out of New York and went to Mexico. It was an end, and so it had to be a beginning.

" Ah, well—that was long ago; and by the world's standards things have gone all right for me.   I worked harder in Mexico than I ever worked before, and was lucky to find profit in doing so.   I struck oil in both senses.   But then one day I thought of you people over here, and realised that my brother's children were growing up, and wondered what the hell I was doing, piling up money at the other side of the world and never even making acquaintance with my own nephews. So I came over."

" And here you are " I said, rather fatuously, feeling it was time I said something, which of course it was not.

He looked at me with quick suspicion.

" What does that mean—here I am ? "

I felt a complete fool, but had the sense not to start stammering excuses.

" I'm sorry " I said humbly. " It was just silly. Please go on."

He grunted, settled himself in his chair again and resumed:

" It wasn't very sensible, because as a matter of fact I'm not—yet. I haven't got so far. I said that I came over. That was two weeks ago. I took a few days to get my London bearings, then gave it up as a bad job. London's a wonderful place, but not for the reasons Londoners seem to think. A queerer jumble of mistaken vanities I never saw. And the hotels! However—my next move was to get in touch with your mother. I wrote to her and asked if I might pay her a visit at home. She replied that she would be in London two days hence and would meet me at the Army and Navy Stores— in the members' waiting room—at half after noon. This sounded unpromising to me, and what in heaven's name were the ' members ' of the Army and Navy Stores ? I'd understood the place was just a department store like any other. Why ' members '? Still—I went along, dug out the waiting-room and there your mother was. I recognised her at once; and not only her, but also the old feeling of embarrassment from all those years ago, even (despite her friendly greeting and the extreme commonplace of our opening words) the sense of being politely but firmly disapproved of. I said she was friendly; but it was a friendliness so matter of fact that it disconcerted me. You see, I had counted on my sudden reappearance to give me a sort of advantage over her. There must surely be an element of surprise, perhaps even of emotion, in a meeting so unexpected, so reminding of the past. And by using that surprise or emotion, I reckoned on taking the lead—if you know what I mean, and for once, having her follow me. But it didn't work out like that. Your mother's self-control is astonishing—really astonishing. She shook hands with me and smiled agreeably.

" ' How do you do, Nicholas? It is a long while since we met. You look well, which I am glad to see. Are you staying long in London? '

" As she spoke, all my old sensation of being unwanted returned to me. I had been shut out once and must stay out. But I made an effort.

" ' I should have known you anywhere, Harriet ' I said. ' And it's real good to see you again. I want all your news and to hear about the boys. As for staying—I can do that indefinitely, if I'm any help to you all. Or ' I added ' I can go away again.'

" She made no direct reply and her expression did not change.

" She consulted a small black note-book she was holding in one hand.

" ' I have not quite finished my shopping ' she said. ' If you will wait for me here, we will go and get some luncheon upstairs. I shall not be many minutes. The department I want is close by.'

" And without giving me a chance to agree or disagree, she turned calmly and walked away.

" Well, I tell you, Nick, that during the ten minutes I waited in that damned waiting-room I developed a pretty healthy fury. Over the other side a man is given a chance to prove his worth and his motives; and whatever the faults of the folk I've been working and living with all these years, to snub anyone in advance or to be deliberately unwelcoming is not among them. I always gave your mother credit for having what seemed to her good reasons in the past for keeping me at arm's length. I think she got me wrong; but I could see what was in her mind, and she had a right to order her own circle as she wished. But now everything was different. I wasn't asking to be taken on by any of you. I wanted to see my nearest relatives and to be of any use to them within my power. And this was the kind of reception I got! Believe me, by the time your mother reappeared I was nicely worked up, and ready to give as good as I got.

" But she bested me even there." He threw back his head and laughed suddenly: " I didn't ' get' anything, so had no chance to give. We had one of the stickiest lunches I ever remember, squeezed at a small table in the middle of a crowd of shopping ladies, all with the light of matinée in their eyes. Your mother remained perfectly calm, and talked as though I were someone who used to be a neighbour in a place where she no longer lived. It was no good being angry. No good at all. Nor was it any good trying to make the conversation personal. I can hardly believe it, now that I look back at that god-awful meal, but we never once mentioned your father's name. Fact. Not that I wanted to—once I'd got the tone of the occasion. But it's queer, isn't it?

" I found out where Geoffrey was and where you were. I said I should like to see you both. She looked at me, serene as ever, and said she was sure the boys would like that very much. When we parted a little after two, I wished I were back in Mexico City. And almost went back, Nick. I did really. But then I thought of your father again, and that Geoffrey and you were his sons, and that I mustn't behave like a silly girl and sulk because I hadn't been made a fuss of. So two days after my meeting with your mother I called Geoffrey at his office to make a date with him. He sounded a bit feudal, but said he would call at my hotel about six.

" By the way " my uncle glanced over at me and gave his voice the quality of parenthesis. " Is a lot of this stale news to you? Have you heard all about my encounters with your family? "

I shook my head.

" Not a word " I said, feeling rather ashamed of having to admit it.

He looked pleased.

" All the better.   I guessed you hadn't, but one never knows. Well—Geoffrey came; and you'll allow me to say that he's a better specimen of the young Englishman as depicted in American legend than I conceived possible.   When I think how often I've disputed with Americans, when they make fun—or worse— of a certain type of Britisher, telling them the type is a stage-invention and doesn't exist, it makes me smile.   For there one was, right in front of me.   And was he a prize specimen?   I didn't get cross, because it was so comic; but for la-di-da— my God! "

There was something so genuine in my uncle's disgust, that, almost without realising it, I chuckled.   I could see Geoffrey standing there in his correct business suit and his high-up-and-down collar, wearing that look of strangled superiority which he put on whenever, between disapproval and embarrassment, he confronted an unwelcome situation.   Geoffrey was always the choked sort of Englishman—a type which must not be confused with the stuffed sort, or with the beetroot heartiness so apt to leave its mouth open between jokes.

Uncle Nick sat up rather suddenly in his chair.   I think his long residence among Americans must have infected him with something of their extreme sensitiveness to ridicule, for he actually thought I was laughing at *him* (as of course I was, but not in that way).

" What's the joke? "

The last time he had challenged my reaction to his tale, I had nervously subsided; this time, however, (encouraged, perhaps, by the realisation that he also had his timidities) I felt no dismay, but an even greater desire to laugh.

" It's funny—the picture of you and Geoffrey " I said.   " I know so exactly how he was.   But don't be too hard on him.

It's mostly shyness, which unluckily takes him that way.   And what happened?"

"What happened?   What could happen?   Damn all— that's what happened.   We exchanged 'Hullos' and a little small-talk, had a drink and parted.   He was too much for me, that guy, and obviously I wasn't enough for him."

"No, no!" I corrected.   "You were too much also.   Much too much.   I expect poor Geoffrey was terrified."

"Bunk!" retorted my uncle.   "Fright doesn't set a man sneering.   I was *wrong*, that's what I was; not 'the sort of thing one does', or knows, or is.   The only thing he was afraid of, was being seen with me.   Well he needn't worry."

There was a pause.   My courage, instead of ebbing away, now became a sort of recklessness.   We were nearing the crisis of the story so far as it concerned me, and I felt a sudden impulse to provoke it.

"After two failures I wonder you persevered" I said.   "Our family cannot have promised very well."

There was, I admit, a tinge of sarcasm in this remark, but oddly enough he did not appear to notice it.

"I am an obstinate person" he replied.   "When I start a thing, I like to finish it.   As you say, prospects were poor; but I did not let that affect me, except in one way.   Hitherto I had tried to adapt myself to the prejudice of others—been conciliatory, you know, and very careful not to seem more outlandish than I could help.   For my third attempt I decided to go to the other extreme—and in consequence treat you rougher than either of the others.   I know enough about college-boys to realise that they can be even more self-conscious than school-boys, and more thoroughly slaves to good form because more nearly grown up.   I said to myself 'Here's this Oxford boy in the middle of his class-mates and likely to be scared to death of anything a bit unusual.   I'll go seek him out in Oxford and take care I shall be noticed.'   So I worked it that you should meet my train at a busy hour of the day, and have a good long afternoon walking me round the city, in and out of collegiate buildings and across campuses, and me dressed as a sort of museum-piece among comic Yankees. ' That'll be a test ' I thought. And I was right, wasn't I? "

He didn't look at me, but leant forward to pour another drink. Even in the midst of my embarrassment, which had now flooded back and submerged courage more deeply than ever before, I was grateful for what I now recognise to have been a piece of very characteristic tact. But my main preoccupation was to collect my wits in the face of this quite unexpected challenge. Desperately I tried to remember whether I had betrayed confusion or shame during the afternoon, or had suggested going to ground in my rooms, or in any way showed signs of wishing to escape. I doubted having done any of these things, because, as I recalled our time together, I had not, after withstanding the first shock of my uncle's appearance, wanted to do them. Still, one never knows; so I searched memory still more anxiously.

Probably it was only a few seconds that I sat in flustered silence, looking, I have no doubt, pinkly idiotic; for suddenly I heard my uncle speaking again with the easy normality of one hardly conscious of interruption.

" It was a test all right, Nick, and you passed it splendidly. I can tell you I was on the look-out for the slightest sign, first of instinctive recoil, then that your apparent friendly courtesy was merely assumed. No lad could keep up a fake civility for nearly four hours of a hot afternoon spent in the most tiring kind of sight-seeing; and I reckoned that if you were acting at first you would sooner or later give yourself away. Well, you didn't; so I concluded you weren't acting. Were you? "

" Oh no " I mumbled, feeling the most utter fool. " I wasn't acting."

" That's fine " he returned, quietly. " I'm glad I have found my brother at last." And added after a pause: " Shall we go and get something to eat? "

∽   ∽   ∽

Over dinner he became practical:

" Listen to me, Nick. I'm not out to play fairy godfather to anyone. But I want to do something to commemorate your father, and to help to create a cosmopolitan mind is as good a memorial as I know. You are capable of being made cosmopolitan. This afternoon has proved that much. What you are like otherwise, I neither know nor care. I hope you have sense enough not to let weakness or self-indulgence get you into a real mess; but that is your own affair and you take the risk. You are twenty-one years old and have been at this university nearly three years. You tell me you think of staying another year, and then trying an exam for some official job or other with, as second string, a business career. I'll make you another proposal: You will leave Oxford at the end of this term and in the autumn go to Europe. You will learn to speak German and French. About eighteen months hence we will meet again, and you will convince me that you have learnt, not only those two languages, but also something about the life of other countries. You should then be capable of standing on your own feet. Between now and then expense is my affair. What happens beyond that depends on how you have made use of your time. I promise you I won't let you down, if you play fair by me. What about it? "

∽ ∽ ∽

There was a good deal about it, one way and another. My mother was little pleased at her brother-in-law's invasion of family territory. The college authorities disliked an eleventh hour alteration in their plans and mine. Geoffrey was actually disagreeable, hinting that I had played up to Uncle Nick on purpose and no doubt considered myself damned clever. There were several weeks of unpleasantness, and though I had no compunction in telling Geoffrey to go to hell, I was unhappy in the face of my mother's opposition. It was perfectly true that she had done everything for me, and my uncle—so far—

nothing.   It was perfectly true that I might be risking my whole
livelihood by throwing up Oxford for a year and a half on the
loose with nothing further in prospect than a promise of support
from a man we none of us really knew.   But in my heart of
hearts I realised that Uncle Nick's suggestion was one I meant to
accept; and as there is a streak of obstinacy in my otherwise
pliable nature, I stuck to my decision.   At last, and quite
suddenly, my mother swung round and gave her consent.   I
believe—being herself a person of very firm determination—
she appreciated stubbornness even in a cause she could not
approve; and that this appreciation, combined with her great
fondness for a son, was deliberately allowed to outweigh her
dislike and suspicion of my new way of life.   Rather charac-
teristically she insisted on seeing Uncle Nick herself, and made
another appointment with him in—of all places—the waiting-
room at the Army and Navy Stores.   This made me laugh,
until I had qualms as to how he might re-act; but fortunately
he also thought it funny, and I gathered from both sides afterward that the interview, though strictly business-like, passed off
without incident.

Thus it was that toward the end of November I clambered
down on to the platform of the Friedrichstrasse Station in
Berlin, prepared to shed my insularity.   Thus it was also that—
because, thanks to my instinctive willingness to believe that
unfamiliar things are not necessarily inferior to familiar ones, I
had shown no sign of mockery or dislike for my uncle's challeng-
ing Americanism—the whole course of my life was changed.

III: RUTH

I HAD been in Berlin a couple of months before anything happened relevant to this story. Then, on a mild evening in early February, I embarked on my first significant love-affair.

That evening at the Theater des Westens they were playing *Ein Walzertraum.* There was nothing very special about that, for they played it every evening. The operetta had taken the town, and many experts in musical comedy declared that Oscar Strauss had beaten Lehar at his own game. Week after week the little tabular charts of theatre arrangements in the morning papers had read from left to right, from Monday to Sunday night, seven separate times: *Ein Walzertraum.* So in the mere playing of it at the Theater des Westens that evening there was nothing very special.

But that I should be sitting in the window of the old Café des Westens, with two thirds of a bock in front of me, staring into the dusk across the crowded uneasy square and waiting for Ruth—that was special. Damned special, in fact.

I was taking her to see the show; and although lads of twenty-one may nowadays smile at such childishness, I felt all hollow inside with triumph and terror. This was long ago, remember. We were not so proficient in staging our gallantries as the young men of to-day seem to be. I say ' seem ' advisedly, because it is possible that even to-day, for all their road-houses, and backless *piqué* waistcoats, they are at bottom just such goofs as ever lads were. But at least they do not look it. Whereas I did. Goof I felt and goof I must have looked—sitting there in the Café des Westens, with a suit too thick for the weather, and a collar that didn't meet properly and kept pinching a tiny fold of skin over my Adam's apple, and a horrid shirt with buttoned wrist-bands instead of cuff and links, because I had dropped one of my pair of links between the floor-boards of my room and had not had time to get it out.

All these things seemed to matter terribly, although (as I realise now) Ruth would not have noticed them or cared if she had. A girl is mainly interested in the way a young man is turned out for the purpose of comparing him with the young men of other girls. He either does her credit or he lets her down, and her rivals flinch or triumph accordingly. If they triumph, the luckless youth gets what is coming to him; if they flinch, he may get it or he may not. At a musical comedy in Berlin West there would hardly be girls whose rivals Ruth considered herself to be. Ordinary German girls were not part of her competition, any more than she was part of theirs. So I need not have worried. But I did. I worried like hell.

∽   ∽   ∽

I have already indicated the two influences which combined to challenge my maternal training in character and morals, and ultimately to overcome it. One was Uncle Nick; and you have seen with what effect he took a hand in my career. The other was a waltz tune, and that tune was the theme-melody of *Ein Walzertraum*. Because I heard this tune in company with Ruth Hatton, the sentimental excitement which it caused me centred on her and was temporarily identified with her. The extent to which I fell in love with Ruth, how the affair prospered, and what in the end became of it, you are now going to learn. When the story is over, I think you will agree that it is not an exaggeration to attribute some part of my maturing and an important modification in my attitude toward young women, to one waltz tune and to the romantic spell which it cast over me. You may find that the narrative reads with a certain meticulous stateliness—even with pomposity. That is because I cannot recall it save in the mood of youthful solemnity which ruled me at the time. I took myself, my successes and my failures very seriously; and as what happened involved plenty of all three, the seriousness persists.

∽   ∽   ∽

Ruth was the daughter of a resident English journalist—
Berlin correspondent of *The Monitor* I think he was—and lived
with her father in a flat just off the Nollendorfplatz. She was
two or three years older than I; and these years, added to the
instinctively greater poise of femininity and her easy familiarity
with the life of a foreign city, made her alarming and remote.
She studied music behind the revolting façade of the college in
Hardenbergstrasse, and it was at one of their " evenings " that
I first met her. That had been early in my stay in Berlin, when
German conversation was a grave responsibility and the chance
of an hour of English talk had the thrill of a reprieve. Probably
the mere fact that being introduced to Ruth meant talking
English was the foundation of the pedestal on which, after two
or three more meetings, I established her.

She was a tall girl, with masses of dark red hair, rather high
cheek bones and one of those drooping mouths which have
regularly been my undoing. (Yes, Sally, regularly. It was
your mouth—the loveliest of all the mouths in the world—which
first got me. You may think it was your intelligent conversation or the way the hair curls over your ears, or even that smart
little hat. But you are wrong. They were all splendid when
I got to them; but the mouth came first.) As I remember
them, Ruth's figure and carriage were not impeccable. She
was big-boned, and walked with the lunging freedom acclaimed
by certain nitwits as the glory of the ' open-air girl '. But I
was only twenty-one and English trained, so thought face and
colouring the vital points of beauty, whereas they are of course
only two among many. Her voice was a little bleak; her
way of speech abrupt. She would knit her thick eyebrows while
talking, and for a while seem so armoured in self-sufficiency,
so indifferent to everything but some secret concerns of her own,
that a young man much less diffident than I would have found
her disconcerting. But then, quite suddenly, the eyebrows
would part into two delicate curves, the amber eyes would
soften and the whole face light up with one of the gayest smiles

I have ever seen.   The girl would be transformed, and not only
in appearance.   Her manner changed utterly.   No longer
aloof, she would show eager interest in what you were saying,
doing, thinking.   Maybe the transfiguration was itself a little
disconcerting; but it was also marvellous.   At least I found
it so.

   After the first meeting I had to consider how to engineer a
second.   Saturdays and Sundays were the only possible days;
the rest of the week I was immured behind the walls and crowded
time-table of the Institut Nissrandt at Dahlem.   But for a
piece of good luck, I doubt if I could have managed it at all,
in any case not within reasonable time.   As things turned out,
I saw Ruth only a fortnight later.   I was in Berlin one Sunday
with two of my fellow-students at the Institute and, in the large
café at the corner of Friedrichstrasse and the Linden, fortune
placed us at a table next to one occupied by a couple of youngish
men who were talking English.   There is nothing like a chance
encounter abroad to break British reserve, and before long we
were all in conversation, eventually leaving the café in company.
One of our new friends was in the Berlin office of an English
bank; the other was employed by some exporting firm.   " Let's
go and see old Hatton " proposed the first; and before we quite
knew what was happening we were all on a west-bound tram.
I think we three Dahlemites had the grace to make a show of
reluctance when it became evident that we were about to invade
the flat of a perfect stranger; but our companions waved protest
aside.   " Everyone goes to Hatton's on Sunday.   He likes it."

   I suppose there were thirty people, men and women, standing,
sitting and sprawling in the large front room of the hospitable
Hatton's home; and as our contingent of five crossed the
threshold (the two leaders very hearty and sure of themselves,
the others diffident and not particularly sure of anything), a
large untidy man, with a bottle of Rhine wine in one hand and
half-burned cigar in the other, came rosily forward, beamed
' hullo ' at the new-comers whom he knew, with his cigar

gestured a vague welcome to those he did not, and swayed onward. We had, it appeared, the freedom of the flat.

But not, so far as I could judge, the freedom of anything else. Our guides vanished into the crowd in search of friends, and we were left, a rather absurd little group of shy intruders, wondering what was expected of us. Somehow I got separated from my fellow-sufferers (I think they must have drifted toward a book-case, to cover their embarrassment by a show of literary absorption) and in the very moment that I realised I was standing alone, I saw Ruth. She was only a few feet away, though there were two people at least between us, and was talking to— or rather being talked at by—a voluble Hebrew in an astonishing striped suit. Her eyebrows were in a fierce bunch, and even from where I stood I was conscious of her mood of angry seclusion. The excitement of seeing her at all was, therefore, gravely tempered with alarm. Bad enough to be standing uninvited in a strange room surrounded by folk I did not know, and if not looking an ass certainly feeling one, without having to contemplate meeting an obviously difficult young woman in an obviously difficult humour.

Alarm turned to something like panic; for panic is always next door to vigorous self-assertion in the tormented heart of the amorous youth. I swung away from the dangerous encounter and, forgetting how very near to the wall I had remained, found myself almost nose to nose with myself in a hanging mirror. This was terrible. I had merely exchanged a bad predicament for one even worse; worry in wonderland had become worry through the looking-glass. Instinctively I swerved to one side. But the crowd had closed in to left and right, and the only chance of escape from a now dreaded encounter lay in pretended interest in something below the mirror's level. This was a shelf, on which stood a few small vases, an ash-tray and miscellaneous ornaments. One of these last caught my eye, and I felt that sudden spurt of interest which a glimpse of the unusual in a throng of the usual nearly always provokes. It was what is called a vinaigrette—a little bottle-shaped container for aromatic salts—and over its gleaming surface of black enamel ran an intricate design inlaid in gold. I picked it up—I believe I had quite forgotten the social embarrassment which had put me where I was—and turned the thing over and over in my hand, marvelling at its perfect proportions, at its delicacy of pattern and workmanship. It was queerly out of place—this distinguished fragment of the past—in the bourgeois huggermugger of Hatton's flat, sharing a painted shelf with a litter of commonplace oddments, surrounded by lumpish furniture in the worst Wohnzimmer style of pre-war Prussia. Interwoven with the design, which like a golden web covered both sides of the vinaigrette, were two initials. They were not easy to decipher and, half-turned toward the centre of the room, I peered at them.

"It's pretty, isn't it?" said Ruth's voice. "My only heirloom."

She was standing at my shoulder, and her glance was wide and serene.

"You are Mr Dering, aren't you?" she went on. "I remember meeting you at the college not long ago."

I explained confusedly my uninvited presence in what now appeared to be her home.

"I didn't even know you lived here" I concluded, with a naïveté which might easily have been mistaken either for presumption or clumsy incivility.

She was pleased to regard it as neither.

"Oh yes, I live here" she said slowly, "very much so."

There was a moment's pause; and then, with a sudden briskness as though she had thrown off some secret preoccupation:

"I'll get hold of daddy in a few moments. Some of these people will be going. Meantime, how did you discover my pretty vinaigrette?"

"Well, I—I—I suppose I just saw it—on the shelf."

She took it from me and let it slide to and fro on the palm of one hand.

" It was my mother's. And her mother's. And so on. The initials are those of some great-great or other. French, of course. And you can still smell the salts. Try——"

Lifting the hinge cap, she held the bottle for me to smell. Through the tiny grille which closed the bottle's neck came a faint aromatic scent—a ghost of a scent, whose frail persistence was like a message from the dead. Blended with it, enfolding and strengthening it, was the fragrance of the hand which held the vinaigrette, the warm vital fragrance of Ruth Hatton. The two combined in a peculiar pungent sweetness which even to-day I can recall.

They are both ghosts now—the eighteenth-century essence of the vinaigrette, the fragrance of the Ruth of all those years ago. Nevertheless my first sojourn in Germany, and the first actual phase of my sentimental education, began with this distillation of a dual scent. They were to end with the echo of a tune.

ᕤ   ᕤ   ᕤ

Ruth's father was a queer fellow. Presumably his years in Germany had influenced both his appearance and his manners. He wore his scanty hair bristle-short in the Prussian manner, and gold pince-nez, stuck fiercely on his short and shapeless nose, echoed the aggressiveness of his moustache. He talked gruffly and in jerks, stumped along the street wearing a small feather at the back of a rather inadequate Tyrolese hat, and evidently aspired with half his inclinations to that brusquerie and arrogance which the German is apt to mistake for virility. But the other half of Hatton damaged irretrievably his fire-eating ambitions. Ingrained in him was the untidy geniality of bohemian Fleet Street. His clothes were always dusty, and had no shape beyond that of the massive body inside them. He liked to live in a crowd ; to scatter cigar ash everywhere he

went; to drink and enjoy himself first, and only second to do
his work. So he was perpetually in a rush, scribbling for the
post or shouting into the telephone, living his life in a frowsy
bustle such as no genuine Prussian with a pride in orderly
efficiency would tolerate for a moment.

His relations with his daughter were at once intimate and
aloof—as queer a mixture as his daily existence. Occasionally,
in true north German fashion, he would bark at her; and that
she should wait on him at meals, or if he mislaid his cigar-case,
hat or newspaper, was regarded by both of them as a matter
of course. But they were evidently deep in one another's
confidence over happenings in their respective lives, and it was
in the manner of this intimacy that Hatton's Englishry came out.

On the first Sunday evening that I took supper with him and
his daughter, the three of us were alone, and I had a good
opportunity of getting the sense of the ménage. The whole
work of preparing the table and serving the meal was done by
Ruth and a stolid Saxon maid with a bright pink face and tow-
coloured hair. My natural impulse, on seeing the pair of them
pulling a table from against the wall, putting up its flaps and
finding in the drawers of the huge sideboard cutlery, cloth and
glasses, was to offer assistance. But they both looked a little
shocked (there may have been a gleam of amusement in Ruth's
amber eyes) and Hatton from his arm-chair growled to me to sit
down and fill my glass. So I subsided; and while fitting a
'yes' or a 'no' into the gaps left by my host's spasmodic
conversation, pondered my surroundings, and wondered a
little uneasily how long it would be before the Rhine wine and
a stifling atmosphere set my head spinning.

The Hattons had meals in the same large room as was used
for parties. Being Sunday there had been a party that afternoon,
and the air was heavy with smoke and not without memories
of alcohol and miscellaneous perspiration. No one had opened
a window; the huge tiled stove blared on its way. Inexperienced in the ways of wine, I was nevertheless aware of the

delayed menace of mild-seeming hock, and would have resisted Hatton's pre-supper hospitality had I dared to do so. As it was, I sipped with infinite caution; yet still had qualms, as the heat and smells of the room pressed ever more heavily upon my senses.

Preparations for supper and Hatton's gutteral talk continued, maybe, for a quarter of an hour. Then suddenly the English element in this hybrid household came to the surface.

" Up you get, Daddy! " said Ruth from across the room. " Go and wash and give Mr Dering a chance to do the same. The soup will be in directly and we must clear the atmosphere. It's foul."

Obediently the big man lumbered to his feet, ground out his cigar against the stove, and with a gruff " Come on! " led the way out of the room. When we returned, the window—still wide open—had done at least a part of its work, and a large tureen of coarse white pottery stood lidless and steaming on the table. Supper began.

Conversation over the meal was ordinary enough. My hosts asked the usual questions as to a stranger's activity; and Hatton, where opportunity offered, enlarged on the peculiarities and qualities of the Berliner with a gusty violence which became queerly attractive. He had abandoned wine in favour of a vast tankard of beer into which—often in the middle of a sentence, and as often in the middle of a mouthful of food, he would stick two-thirds of his face. When he emerged, his fierce but somewhat intermittent moustache would be dripping and frothy, but thanks to an agile lower lip little enough was wasted.

At intervals father and daughter exchanged remarks, to which, as discretion required, I was politely inattentive. But I could not help noticing how well they seemed to understand one another; how quickly allusive and yet how informative they contrived to be. This was particularly evident in the course of a conversation about my own trivial concerns.

" What do you do for exercise? " Ruth had enquired.

I explained that we skated, walked, went bicycle rides, and once a week at least played football.

" Oh yes " she said at once.   " Against the Cadets."

I suppose I looked surprised, for she went on:

" I remembered as you were speaking, one of the students at the college had a brother at the Kadetten Anstalt and he told me that they played against the English boys.   How do you get on with them? "

" Well, so far I've had no chance to get on at all.   We arrive at the field, play and go away again.   But then I've only been there a month or so."

" They don't invite you to go in, ever, I suppose? " asked Hatton.

" They never have " I said.   " Not me, anyway."

" Great sticklers, the officers in charge " laughed Hatton. " They behave as though the place were an arsenal.   You remember Crawshay, Ruth?   Lord, what a rumpus.   One of our bright boys "—he explained to me—" sent out by the paper to buck us old ones up.   He got himself through the court-yard and into the main lobby beyond and, when challenged, said airily he had come to interview the Kommandant.   They not only threw him out quick enough, but raised hell with the office."

" Crawshay was a fool " she said shortly.   Then added more gently: " But I am sure Mr Dering is not that."

Later in the evening, Ruth and I found ourselves alone.   " It seems funny " she said suddenly, " to meet German boys week after week at football and not to get friendly with them."

The fact had never before occurred to me; but now, bemused as I was with hock and amorous inclination, it loomed emphatic-ally.   It was more than funny; it was absurd.   It argued—on the part of inmates of the Institute—either lack of enterprise or narrow insularity, both of which were intolerable to anyone of my newly-developed cosmopolitan pretension.   Further (my mind leapt easily from fallacy to fallacy) what better method

C 2

could be devised of seeing Ruth often and naturally than the formation of a circle of Berlin acquaintance? Obviously two or three friends among the Cadets would in a very short time mean the entrée to all manner of social gatherings here and there about the city. So I nodded my head with much solemnity and declared that something should be done.

Not long afterward I prepared to take my leave. She came to the flat door with me, and stood rather close while I collected my belongings. I said something about saying goodnight to Mr Hatton.

" Oh, daddy's working. I'll give him your message. Anyway you'll be coming again soon? "

" May I? You know I'd love to."

" Just whenever you like. We are always in on Sundays."

I took my courage in both hands.

" Would you ever—I mean, are you ever free—one evening —a show or something? "

" That's very sweet of you " she said easily, and her eyes were smiling. " I'd enjoy a show one evening. But do they let you come into town any night? "

" One can always get leave, if one is going to talk and hear German."

" Oh dear! That would be an odd party. Could we keep it up? "

" No. And we shouldn't attempt to."

She shook her head disapprovingly.

" That would perjure both of us. What a pity you haven't a nice German family with whom to take an early Abendessen. After all, who knows what you mightn't meet after leaving them? "

Amazing girl! Her mind seemed to be working exactly as my own had done half an hour earlier.

" I'll get a family all right " I said firmly; bade her goodnight; and departed, a little breathless at my own successful daring. She stood at the open door as I went downstairs and,

when the turn of the staircase was about to hide her from my
view, waved her hand.

          ꙍ   ꙍ   ꙍ

I will not weary you with the stages by which I became, first
an acquaintance, and then a friend of Kurt von Eberling. They
were easy enough and fairly speedy, thanks to luck and (though
I say it who shouldn't) a moment of decisive ingenuity on my
own part. The important thing is that I did make friends with
him, and at a peculiarly fortunate moment, for he was shortly
due a week's leave at home and his home was in Berlin. In
consequence, not more than three or four weeks after my conversation with Ruth Hatton on this very subject, I was able to
tell her that I had indeed a friend among the Cadets, that he
had invited me to spend half a day with him and his family;
that at half past seven or so I would be free and would she do
a show and supper afterwards? She did not even pretend
hesitation. We would meet at the Café des Westens at seven-
thirty and go to the Waltz Dream.

And that is why I was sitting—seemingly on a café-chair,
actually on the edge of a precipice of excitement, anxiety and
triumph—staring into the dusk across the busy square, nervously
counting my money in my head to be sure I had enough,
fiddling with my tie and the sit of my collar—and waiting for
Ruth.

IV: DIGRESSION ON TUNES

I ONCE heard a very clever woman say that you can tell any
woman's age to a year or two by noting the tunes at which
her eyes go misty. The remark is profoundly true, and liable—
with slight adaptation—to be as true of men as of women.
Not of all men, of course. There are many who never

mist at all but, by their own desire or because they cannot help it, maintain perpetually the bright stuffed look of a boiled cod. Nevertheless there are others—the masculine sentimentalists (' romantics ' if you prefer to be arrogant; ' sensualists ' if you dare to be candid); and they can give themselves away over a tune as easily as can any woman. But not (here is the difference) so precisely. A woman's romantic memories are apt to date from the time of her excited emergence into the adult world—from the time, that is to say, of her late 'teens and early twenties. After this period, she has either achieved the equilibrium she wished for or, having failed to do so, applies her natural genius to the prevention of self-betrayal. To a tune-conscious male, on the other hand, eye-mistiness is more likely to be a serial-affair than a once-for-all. He grades his ecstasies less steeply, and in consequence is always ready for another peak-moment in his emotional life. But even he has got to start some time, and in nine cases out of ten he does so at much the same age as a woman. So, no matter how often and how rapturously he may subsequently ' mist ', he never forgets the first experience of all nor quite recaptures its pristine flavour. Let us, therefore, venture on one good round generalisation, and then apply it and the rest of this digression to my own story.

The tunes of one's early twenties are the best tunes in the world. They were then, and they remain so ever afterward. The young of today find adequate cause for mistiness in the nasal croonings of such pseudo-American cockneys as adorn the dance-bands of their neighbourhood; no doubt even hot jazz can set their eye-lids drooping. They think it is the music which has this quality of enchantment, and for the next twenty or thirty years they will continue to insist that this or that particular song or dance is among the dozen loveliest there have ever been. But actually it is nothing to do with the music. It is the fact that, when they heard it, they were twenty-one.

As I was, when in Berlin I listened to *Ein Walzertraum* ; and though there have been many other tunes in my life and I can guarantee to go misty over any one of them, I still confess (and shall always confess) to a special tenderness for the first of all.

V: BACK TO RUTH

AND now, I fear, you will be expecting a frenzied narrative of my theatre-party. While comic opera, now frivolous now melancholy, held the stage, the passion of Tristan and Isolde must (you will conclude) have thundered in the stalls. I am sorry, but it did not. Certainly I was thrilled to find myself where I was; to have her sitting beside me, our elbows competing for an arm-rest, our knees occasionally touching. Certainly, as the richly sugared harmonies of this most luscious of all operettas, sent voluptuous echoes through the huge and crowded house, I felt that Strauss had written his music for me, and that the yearnings and transports of Niki, and of the two girls who loved him, were admirably suited to me and to Ruth if only she could be made to realise it. But there was nothing of Tristan and Isolde in this, and, to do me justice, I never thought there was. I did not of course tell myself that I was twenty-one and had met my first " tune ". But neither did I regard Ruth as the passion of my life. Which, as matters turned out, was just as well.

The particular type of amourette in which I now considered myself as formally involved, is a difficult and thankless one to describe. It was not ' calf love '—that semi-pubescent urge so delightful to novel-readers who like books about love but dislike ' all that nasty sex business.' Indeed, in its fumbling way, it was definitely sexual. I thought myself in love with Ruth because she was feminine; because, when her eyes and her voice said different things (as they often did), the very discord was exciting; because her fingers were girl's fingers— long and flexible; because her skin in the crook of the elbow was white and faintly-veined in blue; because her hair was iridescent with brown and golden red; because her lower lip drooped full and moist and crimson; because (perhaps most of all) I had dared to ask her out for the evening and she had accepted. But by being 'in love' I meant little beyond a vague emotional delight in her proximity. I wanted to kiss her; but the idea of going to bed with her never occurred to me. Presumably, had the chance been offered to me on a plate, I should have taken it; but I neither expected nor desired it; had no conscious scheme (and certainly no capacity) for contriving it, and should have been painfully uncertain what to do when I got there. So, first and last, this amourette was a tiresome, half-and-half affair, too fleshly to please the scrupulously nice, too crudely innocent to interest grown men and women. I can only apologise to both classes, and pursue my trivial theme.

The third act drew to its end. Quite alone, standing at the top of the flight of steps which rose from the back of the stage, Franzi played her farewell rendering of the operetta's theme-tune. She had lived her few days of happiness, had won her game, then deliberately lost it, and must now set forth on her lonely road once more. The voice of the solitary violin grew fainter and more wistful.

Einmal noch leben
Einmal in Mai

The last note hung in the air, then floated into silence. The curtains swung down. The play was finished. For a few moments the glamour held; and I sat, lost in a delicious melancholy, while the now lighted theatre bumped and scraped itself back into ordinary life.

Ruth jogged my knee:

" Wake up, stupid! The game's over."

Confusedly apologetic, I followed her up the now emptying gangway. We took a taxi and drove to Rheingold.

This large, lavish, but on the whole inexpensive restaurant must have been one of the earliest specimens of a type of establishment since become common.

It had the décor and mannerisms of a real restaurant-de-luxe—thick carpets, shaded lights, an orchestra, crowds of waiters, much parade of chafing dishes, warmed brandy-glasses and similar ostentatia. But its prices were modest, its public a great deal more modest than they pretended, and its menu more exciting to read than to taste. Nowadays, with our grandiose Tea-Houses, our Super-de-Luxe Hotels, our mammoth cinemas with Palm Courts, thé-dansants, Pompeian lounges and all the rest of it, we recognise marble and gilding and mirrors for what they are—sheets of quarter-inch veneer on plaster, vegetable gold leaf, and acres of opportunity for the young of both sexes to persuade themselves they are looking even better and more alluring than usual. And all for three and six a head, or less if you come earlier. But in those days we were not so blasé; and I, at any rate, came to Rheingold with a comfortable feeling that it was grand enough for the occasion, but not too grand for my resources.

Ruth was inclined to be conversational in the taxi, choosing her supper in advance, telling me she had once bought a hat in a shop we had just passed, that So-and-So's were splendid for gloves, that etcetera and etcetera. I suppose I made satisfactory noises at satisfactory times, for she chattered on quite happily, and neither blamed me for inattention nor made ironical apology for disturbing my reverie. But I'm afraid that I was not paying very much attention. The influence of the Waltz Dream was still very strong. I felt that Ruth and I had been transported on to a plane of our own; that the moment demanded a romantic and contemplative serenity; that all this brisk actuality was out of tune, if not with the whole Infinite, at any rate with our particular slice of it. But, as I say, I seem to have concealed my pre-occupation, for we reached a suitable alcove and ordered supper before any significant contact was made between her mind and mine. Even then its preliminaries were gentle enough.

" Well " I said. " Did you enjoy the show ? "

" A lovely show!   And such a pretty tune! "

Even to my inexperience, ' pretty ' sounded wrong.

" I thought it a *marvellous* tune! " I said warmly.   " They were all marvellous tunes.   And the whole thing has a plot. And, thank God, they didn't stack the stage with chorus-girls at the end! "

Ruth laughed and patted my hand.

" Oh, my dear, you are perfect.   So fierce about everything."

Suddenly confused by my own fervour and afraid that she was making fun of me, I beat an embarrassed retreat.

" Sorry " I said.   " But so long as you enjoyed it. . . ."

She gave me a quick look; and that exciting mouth pouted, sumptuous as a ripe fig.

" Of course I enjoyed it.   It was sweet of you to take me."

" Sweet of *me* ! " I mumbled.   And dived into my soup.

For a few moments we were busy with the meal.   Then a foolish urge to say something, no matter what, landed me within sight of a scolding.

" Do you often go to England? "

" About every two years.   Daddy goes, of course, just for a day or two, fairly frequently; but I prefer staying here.   I don't think I care for England much."

" Have you lots of relations and so on? "

She gave me a curious glance.

" What's the idea?   Am I filling up a form or something? "

She spoke laughingly, but I had a faint sense of something amiss.

" No, no, of course not! " I replied fatuously " I mean, I'm sorry.   I didn't want to be inquisitive. . . ."

" That's all right.   And after all why shouldn't you make conversation?   That's a young man's job on this sort of party, isn't it? "

Dismayed at the queer turn things had taken, and at the same time wounded by the tone of her last remark, I let alarm and irritation tempt me into a too-quick retort.

" On the contrary, it is more usually the young woman's; so this time I apologise for trespassing."

And I paid sudden attention to my plate of fish. Ruth was silent and when, a few moments later, I ventured to steal a glance, I saw that the eyebrows had drawn into a horrid knot and that a flush on each cheek showed ominously. The dignity with which I had returned to my supper melted into panic. Was this a quarrel? And what in the world about? My wonderful evening threatened to end in misery because—evidently—I had been an idiot. What sort of an idiot did not matter. The vital thing was to get back into her good graces. Acting on some primeval instinct, I finished my second glass of wine, bravely laid my right hand on her left, and, allowing the emotional enchantment of an hour ago to capture me once more, said in a low, eager voice:

" Ruth, you look lovely tonight."

And so she did; for the urgency of her recent indignation had heightened her colour, her eyes were bright, and little flames seemed to flicker in the shadows of her hair.

The flush of her cheeks and neck turned, as by a miracle, to a quite different rosiness. In what the difference lay I could not say. But there it was; and I observed it with astonished admiration and (admittedly) with not a little relief. For my remarks and my gesture had seemed dangerously rash, and liable to have unpleasant consequences. In fact, of course, they were the only sensible things to do and say.

Her hand moved gently under mine on the table cloth.

" Do I? " she said simply. " I'm glad." And added, with a mischievous twinkle " So long as you enjoy it. . . ."

At which we both laughed, touched glasses, and drank a little toast.

She looked at me mischievously.

" Funny the young man in the show being Niki. I think I shall call you Niki. And then perhaps, when all else fails and I am touring Europe with a girls' orchestra, you will slip

out of your Schloss and come down to the little town and give
us all a party."

" Must I give you *all* a party ? "

" Well, we'll *start* together. And perhaps the others will
leave early. Or I *could* send them to bed. After all I shall be
the boss." She wriggled with sudden amusement. " Oh,
how lovely you'll look in a tight tunic and high shiny boots. . . ."

" And a cap with a pom-pom sticking up in front " I added.

" Yes—and lots of corded braid looped all over your
chest. . . ."

" And a natty moustache with a parting in the middle. . . ."

She pretended serious consideration.

" I'm not sure about the moustache. I think not at first.
Then you can grow one between the band's first and second
visits—and we'll compare results. What nonsense we are
talking, Niki, and what fun we are having! But I want to hear
about your visit today. What are the von Eberlings like?
Where do they live? What did you do? All about it, in
fact."

I described the Charlottenburg flat in which I had taken
Mittagessen. It was a first floor flat in the Schlüter Strasse, at
that time as solid and Prussian and generally dreary and upright
as could well be imagined. I described the Frau Oberstin
and her plump and flaxen daughter; the twin portraits of old
Fritz and of Bismarck which hung on either side the tremendous
overmantel in the living-room. I described the conversation,
both at the meal and after—the details of the Kaiser's where-
abouts, the slightly puzzled hatred of the new Reichstag (why
were these absurd Social Democrats allowed to win so many
seats?), the civil avoidance of any discussion of Anglo-German
relations.

I told how Kurt and I had gone out in the afternoon: how
we had amused ourselves; how queer it was to feel in sympathy
and at ease with this boy alone, yet, when his family was there,
how charged with mutual silences the atmosphere had seemed.

" And I suppose he talked about the Anstalt and his work there? "

" Oh yes.   They are kept very hard at it.   And the discipline is terrific.   He has got his week's leave because some exam. or other is just coming on."

" So he is working at home? "

" All the morning, I gathered.   Eleventh hour cramming, you know."

" Will you be going there again? "

" Rather! " I said eagerly.   " And I want to talk to you about that.   Kurt asked me if I'd go for the whole of the next week-end.   Saturday midday onward.   I'm sure I can get leave, and I'll be two whole days in town and . . . well, can't we . . . you and I . . . fix something or other? "

This time her hand closed tightly over mine.

" Oh, Niki, what fun!   Let's go out to Grünewald on Sunday morning, if it's fine, and see all the crowds.   They'll want you on Saturday—the von Eberlings I mean—won't they? "

The hint of wistfulness was almost too much for my common sense.   I just checked myself from undertaking to be free all Saturday and Sunday as well—hardly a suitable proceeding from one week-ending elsewhere—and agreed mournfully.

" Yes, I suppose they will expect me to be there some time."

We sat a moment in melancholy silence, until Ruth pulled herself together.

" Never mind " she said cheerfully.   " Sunday will be divine.   And, Niki, will you be a dear and do something for me—or rather for daddy? "

" Will I not! " I replied, with all suitable fervour.

" Well, listen.   Daddy has got to send his paper some stuff about German military education—you know, ideals and methods and all that—and it's not very easy for a journalist to go enquiring for information.   They are fearfully suspicious of foreign newspaper men here—afraid of undesirable prying, I suppose, which is natural enough. Of course daddy wouldn't do a thing they didn't like; but he *is* a newspaper man and they'd freeze up at once if he started asking questions. I know that he's particularly anxious to have correct information about the Lichterfelde Anstalt. It's a very important place. Now, you could get him what he wants from your friend, couldn't you?"

I did not reply quite instantaneously—not, I think, for any reason save that my mind was tired with its emotional experiences and a little vague after the hock we had been drinking. But evidently my momentary silence was taken for hesitation.

" Couldn't you, Niki?" she repeated, and there was a touch of sharpness in her voice.

I confess that, although I noticed the sharpness, I was merely distressed by it, thinking that in some way I had offended her, and that the progress I had made that evening was in danger of being lost. I tried hastily to make amends:

" I'm sure I could. What exactly do you want me to find out?"

She was all sparkle and friendliness again: and as she leant towards me, her face alight with grateful pleasure, I saw the smooth column of her neck, as it ran down beyond the set of the shoulders to the shadowy division of her breasts. I felt a moment's dizziness, and a new quality crept into my infatuation for this vital, glowing girl.

Simultaneously my eye chanced on a big clock, fixed on the wall of the restaurant. It was ten minutes after midnight. My suburban trains did not run after one o'clock, and I was actually supposed to be back at the Institute by twelve-thirty. That, at any rate, was impossible; but get back some time I must. The real world, with its hateful conglomeration of practical necessity and next morning and work and duty, had killed the magic of a new and dangerous revelation. I jerked myself upright in my chair and turned to summon the waiter.

" Ruth " I said. " Look at the time! I must be going. Oh, and I don't want to go. . . ."

She sat, while the bill was brought and paid, with her two hands resting side by side on the table-edge in front of her, her head a little bowed, her knees together.   The droop of her whole body was a poignant echo of my last words.   Then:

" Lovely party " she whispered.   " Lovely, lovely party."

I helped her on with her cloak, retrieved my own paraphernalia, and followed her in miserable silence from the restaurant. All the lights seemed to have gone cold and dead.   The evening —the great evening which had been planned so carefully and looked for with such anxious longing—was over.   There was nothing now, except daylight and sweating at German literature and other beastly young Englishmen and Americans.

Yes there was though!   There was next Sunday.   And she had asked me to find out things for her from Kurt.   What things?   She had never told me, never answered my question. We were hurrying towards the Potsdam station, and I took her arm, holding it above the elbow with gentle fingers.

" Ruth.   About this stuff for your father.   What exactly . . ."

" I know " she interrupted.   " I was just thinking.   He can tell you better than I.   Or he can tell me and I can tell you. Wait . . . let me work it out.   Could we possibly meet for just a few minutes on Saturday?   Then I can explain . . . and, perhaps, by Sunday you will have been able . . .? "

I thought hard.   " A few minutes on Saturday."   Another and an earlier glimpse of her.   And for a real, serious reason. To get instructions.   All businesslike and important and quite innocent of philandering.

" Will this do?   I might get away from Dahlem half an hour earlier and be at the Café Am Knie—you know, the big one on the corner of the Berliner Strasse—just after twelve. We can have a few minutes, and I'll still get to the von Eberlings by 12.30 or so."

" Splendid!   And wasn't it a good idea of mine to work another tiny party? "

We were at the Potsdamer Platz, and the huge arc-lights

glared on roadways still noisy with trams and cars, on pavements still thronged with hurrying or sauntering crowds. The clock on the ugly yellow station opposite said half-past twelve. Was it only twenty minutes since I called for my Rheingold bill? It had seemed hours. My wonder-evening was dying a lingering death.

I stopped dead, tightened my grasp on Ruth's arm and turned her towards me.

" I must run " I said. " You are an angel to have come and——"

She kissed me full on the mouth, and I realised that her hands were on my shoulders.

" Goodnight, my dear," she said. " It will not be long to next Sunday."

Then she kissed me again and walked quickly away, slipping between the traffic toward Potsdamer Strasse and home. I reached the station with twenty minutes to wait for the last train. When at last it started, it rumbled along to desultory waltz time.

The night porter at the Institute looked sourly as he let me in about half-past one. Whether he thought I was drunk, or merely disapproved of such late hours, I neither knew nor cared. I smiled blandly and waved goodnight as I crept toward the stairs. The warm caress of Ruth's lips still felt moist on mine; my head sang with the melodies of the night.

ᔆ   ᔆ   ᔆ

There was a little difficulty about the week-end. Herr Nissrandt (who, although by origin a Swede, had become more Prussian than the Prussians) was never happier than when pursuing discipline for its own sake. He had me on the carpet, the morning after my outing, to reprimand me for being late home. He catechised me about my movements in Berlin, and it required the agility of a rather jaded mind to produce a narrative at once convincing and coherent. Fortunately he was very susceptible to details of good-class military society; and by repeating (and I fear grossly elaborating) the conversation of the von Eberling family, I succeeded in diverting his attention from my personal shortcomings to those of my country. He delivered an angry lecture on the policy of Britain toward Germany—a policy which seemed to combine obstinacy, treachery, stupidity and frivolous ingenuity in a manner confusing but inexcusable—and ended up by saying that a fuller knowledge of opinion and character in the right sort of German circles might eventually convince me of the vices and follies of my government. I had never regarded the Cabinet and bureaucracy of the day as my property, nor did I particularly want them. But I was willing to fall in with Herr Nissrandt's view of their status, because it offered an unexpected chance of asking permission for the coming week-end.

"I shall have the opportunity of meeting Colonel von Eberling himself" I explained in conclusion. "I am particularly anxious to do that."

Herr Nissrandt blew his nose noisily, fixed me with his fierce little eyes and nodded ungraciously.

"Very well" he said "but you must be here by nine o'clock on Monday morning. Not a second later or I shall stop your Berlin leave for three weeks."

I bowed submissively and went humbly from the room. But when I had closed the door, I danced up to my room like a five-year old. "Monday morning." I had assumed all along that leave would end Sunday night, and I knew the von Eberlings expected me to leave them after Sunday supper. A gift of nearly twelve hours! And the old brute thought he was being severe!

Nearly twelve hours. What could I do with them? Throughout the classes for the day, though my eyes were busy with the German reading and German writing, though my mouth was filled with phonetic noises and linguistic constructions both complex and sonorous, my mind was busy with those twelve miraculous hours. What could I—and Ruth—do with them?

Alas! When one got down to it, we could not do very much. Sunday was the day when she and her father kept open house, so that all the afternoon and probably till after supper she would be surrounded by people. But I wanted an evening with her. Grünewald on Sunday morning was all very well; but you do not get the best out of being in love with a girl, just trailing about among pine trees and watching Germans at play. As though they were the pieces of a jig-saw puzzle, I arranged and rearranged the various periods of my precious two days. The whole of Wednesday passed and by Thursday morning I had evolved a possible plan.

After the midday meal we were free to go walking in and about Dahlem. Giving the others the slip, I made my way to a semi-distant post-office and rang up the Hattons' flat. Luck was with me. Ruth was at home. I explained what had happened. Was she free Saturday afternoon *and* evening? From six o'clock only; before that she was busy. Would she be in the flat for another half an hour now? Of course, if I wanted her to be. Then I would ring her again as soon as I had spoken to the von Eberlings. Frau von Eberling was sorry, but Kurt had gone out. With much tongue-twisting formality I explained that it was to her I really wished to speak: that I had most inopportunely been invited by some English friends to sup with them on Saturday, which was their only evening; that if she were so very kind as to permit me to pro-long my visit to her till Monday morning early, I should not lose any of the pleasure and advantage of being with her family and could at the same time arrange to meet my friends as re-quested. The good lady was more than amiable. Indeed she definitely preferred the new arrangement to the old, for her husband (who wanted to see Kurt's English friend and had planned to do so on the Saturday night) had been bidden else-where at the last moment. But on the Sunday evening he

would be at home. How fortunately things had fallen
out!

Fortunately, indeed, I thought. The very stars in their
courses were fighting for me. But probably Sisera had the
same impression in the early stages of his adventure, and before
his tête-à-tête with Jael.

I revised my appointment with Ruth. Same café, but six-
fifteen instead of noon. Then dinner. Then whatever we
felt like. Marvellous! I was so gay that sending her a kiss
over the telephone made me giggle. She asked what I was
making that funny noise for. I told her. But the joke didn't
go well, because she hadn't heard the kiss. The affair developed into one of those tiresome explanations, polite puzzle-
ments, more explanations, which go on too long, never arrive
anywhere, and had better not have been started. Our conversation ended in something of a scurry. But what did that
matter? Saturday was only two days ahead—Saturday from
six-fifteen to heaven knew when.

ം   ം   ം

The Café Fürstenberg was a large place, with a curious series
of rising terraces—in winter shut in by plate-glass windows, in
warmer weather as nearly in the open air as the average Berlin
café aspires to be. It was the hour of the aperitif and the place
was very full when, after Mittagessen and an afternoon with my
hosts, I arrived five minutes ahead of my appointment with
Ruth. I had to mount to the third or fourth of the terraces
before I could find an empty table; then took my seat, and surveyed the crowded scene as it sloped away toward the street.
The clients were largely students from the Technical College
and the Art School, both of which were near at hand. But
there were numbers of podgy Berliners of the regulation kind
and, here and there, pairs or groups of officers or cadets, their
uniforms bright against the sombre clothing of the civilian
crowd.

Almost to the minute of six-fifteen I saw Ruth emerge from the Underground Station and cross the street towards the café. The day had been sunny and warm—as though March were a commercial traveller in summer weather and showing advance samples of what May could do; but the evening was fresh and she wore a coat with a high fur collar and, as counter-concession to the day's brightness, a smallish white hat pulled low over her eyes.   From the pavement she swept the crowded terrace with an expert eye, noticed my signalling newspaper, waved a hand in quick greeting and began to pick her way between the tables. She had mounted the second of the rising steps when, as she passed a couple of young men seated by the gangway, one of them rose and saluted her.   She stopped, smiled rather more readily than I cared to acknowledge, and held out her hand. The young man bent over her fingers, presented her to his companion (now also on his feet, poised to click heels and bow from the waist) and evidently invited her to take the vacant chair at their table.   She hesitated, threw a glance in my direction, said something to the man, who nodded equably; then pursued her upward way and in a few moments was at my side.   Almost as our hands touched, she began to speak breathlessly:

" Niki dear, I'm fearfully sorry, but will you be an angel and forgive me just five minutes?   I must go and speak to that man there.   Really only five minutes. . . ."

And before I could answer she was slipping away from me, in and out of the crowd, back to her friend.   The two men rose to greet her; then the three of them sat down, and I could only see two cropped heads and a smart little white hat, which drew together, then separated, then swayed this way and that, as is the way of hats and heads whose owners are happy in conversation over a café table.

As the time went by, I began to feel that Ruth's five minutes were outsize specimens and that, not only had I been put out of countenance, but was being badly treated.   I plunged into

sulky resentment and buried myself in my newspaper, only to
emerge at the sound of Ruth's voice and the touch of her hand
on my arm.

" Oh Niki " she said.   " I *am* so sorry!   Now you are cross
with me, aren't you?   And I don't wonder.   But I'll tell you
all about it, if you'll order me a drink."

Very stand-offish, I turned to summon the waiter.

" What sort of a drink? " I said, without looking at her.

" Sherry, please, Niki."   Her voice was dangerously submissive, but I took no heed of omens.

While we waited, I glared at my own shoes and wondered
uneasily whether it was more impressive to be serene or to
hector.   Should a resentful male take the aloof, no-concern-of-
mine attitude toward a woman's vagaries, or jump in straight
away with a now-then-what's-the-meaning-of-all-this?   Being
too mortified to contrive the former and very uncertain how to
make the latter convincing, I compromised.   As the sherry was
placed on the table, I managed to glance in Ruth's direction and
remarked drily:—

" How many minutes make five? "

Paralytic, of course.   Anything would have been better
than rather feeble sarcasm.   As I immediately realised; for
Ruth flushed with annoyance and at once seized the initiative.

" Please, Niki " she said, " don't be horrid.   I've told you
I'm sorry, and if you're going to be beastly to me I shall go
away.   That man is a friend of daddy's and mine, very musical
and interested in the annual concerts at the School.   I had to
see him some time, and this was an obvious opportunity.   In
any case I was only quarter of an hour.   You're being both rude
and silly."

In face of this obvious attack, my combative spirit collapsed:
and as usual, when I speak from flustered instinct and do not
try to be ingenious, I said the right thing.

" I hated losing even quarter of an hour of you " I muttered
miserably.   " That was all."

From that moment it was peace.

∾ ∾ ∾

Over dinner we chattered of a hundred things.

" By the way " I said. " Kurt showed me a lot of his note-books this afternoon. Lecture-courses and so on. Is that the kind of thing Mr Hatton is interested in ? "

" Gracious! I had nearly forgotten the official reason for our being here." She laughed gaily, and the hint of our mutual conspiracy enchanted me. " Lecture-courses? Yes, that's the sort of thing. Particularly the group with some funny initials to them. . . . Oh dear, don't say I've forgotten! Daddy told me specially. . . . ' Gu ' I think it was. Yes, that's it. . . . ' Gu.' Goo! Can you goo at all, Niki ? "

Instantly I was back in Kurt von Eberling's rather spartan bedroom, with a table strewn with books and papers, and the wide candid eyes of my friend smiling at my curiosity from under his broad forehead and short fair hair. Once again I was turning the note-books this way and that, noting the various subjects, admiring Kurt's neat handwriting and laughingly disclaiming my ambition to share his complex studies. At the bottom of the pile was a book of a different colour; and I had just picked this up and noticed on the cover a large black cipher of two letters, when Kurt, who had turned away for the moment, came behind me and saw it.

" Please " he cried, and almost snatched the book from me.

My first idea was that it was a private diary or something similarly intimate.

" I'm sorry " I said. " It was among the others. You shouldn't leave your love-poems about."

" No, no! " he replied quickly. " Not love-poems. I was mad to leave it there. . . ." Then, as though he had changed his mind, he looked carefully self-conscious and bridled, as young men like to do when charged with gallantry. " Not love-*poems* " he repeated, carefully emphasising the last word.

" You must excuse me for snatching the book.   I was startled to see it in your hand."

He walked quickly to a large cupboard near the door, thrust the book inside and slammed the cupboard to.   The incident was closed, although for a short while after I puzzled over the obvious contradictions of his final words.   He had been about to deny that the book was any sort of private journal, and certainly, when now I recalled its appearance, it had not looked like one.   Then he had decided to make use of my suggested interpretation, and seem suitably embarrassed.   But the embarrassment had been too clearly assumed.   No, the book was something different; but what it was I had no idea.   Anyway it was clearly not my business.   And with that I had let the whole thing slip from my mind.

Until, in this restaurant some hours later, Ruth spoke of the lecture-courses marked ' Gu'.   For that had been the cipher on the cover of the mysterious book, the book which Kurt was so anxious I should not see.

When I tell you that I forthwith confided to Ruth everything that had happened in Kurt von Eberling's room, you will judge me even more of a fool than you guessed.   Granted, granted, *and* granted.   But remember what kind of a fool—a fool of twenty-one; an inexperienced fool; a fool convinced that he was in love with this glowing female creature, whom consequently he regarded as the most sacred of confidants.

Anyway, confide in Ruth I did; and she showed precisely the interest and understanding which I expected of her.

" Niki, how *thrilling !*   Of course you couldn't do anything but change the subject.   And now we've done our job for daddy and can get back to ourselves.   I don't feel awfully like a show or wandering from café to café, do you? "

I looked at her sitting there, all tenderness and rosy flesh. She was leaning forward, her golden eyes shining into mine. I remembered how the other night she had leaned forward, but lacked the nerve to look elsewhere while she held my glance

thus questioningly.   Nevertheless I meant her to go on leaning
forward.   Again instinct came to my rescue:

"Stop like that, Ruth!   You are divine, fore-shortened."

She laughed up at me; then, with an embarrassment upon
which I had counted, dropped her eyes to the table cloth.
Mine slid down towards the shadows.   I realised, with a sudden
excitement which shook me like a moment's fever, that the whole
evening lay before us.

"Would you be very bored, if we went home?" she asked
gently.

"Of course I wouldn't.   But will Mr Hatton want me?"

"He'd be delighted—if he were there.   But he's away
tonight.   Gone to Hanover on some business or other."

"And you're alone?   Oh Ruth, how marvellous!"

She laughed.

"Flattering to poor daddy!   'Will Mr Hatton want me?'
You're a fraud, Niki—a wicked fraud, though terribly trans-
parent—and rather a dear."   I suppose I showed some sign of
confused apology; for she laid one hand on my arm, leant still
nearer and said softly: "If you won't be bored, I won't.
Shall we go?"

ᔕ   ᔕ   ᔕ

In those days, so far as youths of my kind were concerned,
the science of the petting party was in its infancy.   Cars, freedom
from chaperonage, an inexplicable supply of pocket-money, and
American methods generally have provided young people with
so many protracted opportunities of being alone with one
another, that they can dispense with curiosity and give their
attention to technique.   But we were less mobile, and stayed
more in one place; were considerably under adult control;
and waited, often in vain, for chances to explore the contours
and mentality of our feminine friends.   In consequence, our
sexual dalliance was as primitive and dowdy as our domestic

lawn-tennis.   The latter meant changing into sand-shoes and
happily lolloping the ball over the net with the two girls from
the vicarage and the doctor's son.   The former meant holding
hands, then kissing, then perhaps cuddling up, then kissing
again.   Monotonous?   Certainly over any considerable period
of time.   But such periods were so rare as to be uncatered for.
The menu, like that of a quick-lunch counter, was designed for
persons with little time to spare.

When, as on the present occasion, time was plentiful, the
usual procedure was almost worse than none.   Ruth and I sat
side by side on the Hattons' sofa.   We held hands.   At intervals
I kissed her—sometimes on her lovely mouth, sometimes on
the ear within reach, sometimes in the curve of her neck.
Occasionally I kissed her eyebrows—those once alarming,
now ravishing, eyebrows, whose very surrender seemed to seal
my victory.   All of which was fine; and if we had been sitting
out a dance or had stolen away from a picnic for twenty minutes'
solitude in the woods, I should have reappeared in public with
the satisfying sense of having exploited my chances to the full.
But here, in this silent curtained flat and with over three hours
in front of me, I felt stultification coming even before it came.
For a few minutes longer I persisted in the trivial philandering
which with each repetition became more tedious.   I had a
confused idea that Ruth would be insulted if I stopped stroking
her hair or softly moving a finger up and down her arm.   She
lay against me, with her head low on my chest, one leg tucked
under her and the other stretched out along the sofa.   Five
minutes ago the weight of her, the bronze hair just below my
lips, the white band of her neck and her body flowing away in
graceful relaxation, had been precious as answers to a prayer.
Now they were suddenly an embarrassment.   My repertoire of
standard caresses was exhausted.   What, I began to ask myself,
would happen next?

I suppose my sudden sense of futility and nervous hesitation
in some way reduced the tempo of my fondling, or, maybe,

dulled the beating of my pulses. In any event Ruth, with that extra sense which makes a woman instantly aware of any weakening in her lover's concentration, gave a little shake, sat upright and, brushing the hair out of her eyes, looked at me quizzically.

" Poor Niki " she said lightly. " Are you very squashed? You shall have a rest. I'll get some coffee and play the piano to you."

While she was out of the room, I took stock of my position. It was not yet nine o'clock. There was ample time for any amount of daring gallantry; but what might not happen, if daring were taken for impertinence and gallantry for insult? I shuddered to imagine myself coldly shown the door, and felt that to stay out my time in Berlin, knowing that Ruth's father and probably Ruth's friends had been told of my grossness and presumption, would be impossible. True, she had been neither coy nor clumsy in accepting my kisses; true, she had lain fondly in my arms. Perhaps she regarded that sort of thing as the usual preliminary to greater enterprise. If so, and I failed to attempt it, should I not be for ever contemptible? After all, one can be shown the door for too little as well as for too much. It was all very difficult; and when she came back from the kitchen with coffee on a tray and a bottle of Kirschwasser, I was no nearer a decision on policy than before.

We drank our coffee, sipped our drink and chatted devastating commonplace. The time crept on. At half past nine she went to the piano and, after some preliminary skirmishing, plunged into our Walzertraum. She played not only the theme waltz, but five or six of the other melodies also. The gift of playing by ear has always filled me with astonished envy; but this performance of Ruth's set me almost beside myself. Those enchanting tunes, heard in her company and therefore—as it were—signed with her name, sounded as rich and as drenchingly sweet as though we were back in the theatre but (by a miracle) alone. I filled myself another glass of liqueur, drank it with

restless speed, got up from my seat, walked here and there
about the room. Still she played:

> *" Ich hab' einen Mann*
> *einen eigenen Mann*
> *den feschesten Ka—va—lier . . ."*
>
> *   *   *
>
> *" . . . Es waren berük-ken-de Weisen*
> *bald jubelnd, bald sehnsuchtsbang*
> *der süsseste Wiener Walzer*
> *der innigste Liebesang . . ."*
>
> *   *   *
>
> *" O, Du lieber, o' Du g' scheiter*
> *O' Du . . . .*
> *Siehst Du, das ist g' scheiter,*
> *O, Du ganz gehauter Fratz!*
> *Küss' mich, küss' mich weiter*
> *mein geliebter Herzens-schatz."*

I was standing behind her as the last melody came to an end.
Presumably the same extra sense which had warned her of my
sudden lassitude now told her that the fire was blazing. She
tilted her head backwards, placed her arms round my neck and
drew me down to her, saying in rather a strangled voice:

" Kiss me, Niki!   Kuss mich doch weiter! "

I bent eagerly; and as our lips met, my hands slipped over
her shoulders and, hardly knowing what they did, closed over
her breasts and there remained.   One hand, quite unwittingly,
had found its way down inside her dress.   She pressed her
mouth hard against mine, then pushed me an inch or two away
and, between still parted lips, murmured:

" Don't move.   I like your hand there."

I was getting beyond the control either of caution or civility.
But before I could venture further, she spoke, still in a half-
whisper:

" Listen, darling.   If you will do one thing to please me, I
will do everything to please you.   I want that note-book of
young Eberling's.   I want it terribly.   Get it for me, Niki,
and come quickly back and be thanked.   Will you, dear sweet
Niki? *Please!* "

The astonishment, the delicious pleasure, the doubts and the excitement which jostled one another in my mind as the sense of Ruth's last words slowly took possession of me, cannot be conveyed in written retrospect. They came and went in a flash of time. Fragments of memory and reasoning and wild anticipation were inextricably mixed together. I realised that over our coffee I had said the von Eberling flat was empty, the family having decided on the opera because both the master of the house and the English visitor were engaged elsewhere. I remembered how the subject of the note-book had been dismissed at dinner, as though for ever. But when I fumbled after a coherence in the apparent contradiction between Ruth then and Ruth now, the firm but yielding miracle of her breast within my hand set my head reeling, and all power of argument, every inclination to common sense, were consumed in the flame of a boy's longing for the body of a girl.

Releasing her gently, I stood for a moment looking down at her upturned face. The eyes were half-closed; the mouth still drooped in passionate invitation. Without a word I hurried into my coat and hat, and left the flat.

I took a taxi to the corner of Kant Strasse and Schlüter Strasse, and from there walked quickly to the apartment-house where my friend lived. It was nearly ten-fifteen, when, having let myself in and switched on a light, I stood in the hall-way listening to the silence of the deserted flat. And as I listened, there came over me the same queer feeling of being shut off from everything save myself, which two hours ago in that other flat had isolated Ruth and me from all the world. Then it had enclosed the two of us in an impenetrable lovers' privacy; now it shut me in with my own errand and brought a gradual understanding of the part I proposed to play.

It was not an agreeable part. I had come here, to the home of people who had made me welcome and of whom one was my friend, in order to steal something. That was one aspect of my undertaking. There was another equally distasteful. I was a foreigner, who proposed to hand over to another foreigner a note-book which I knew its owner—my friend—did not wish even me to see. What was this note-book? Why did Ruth want it? A sensation of fear began to steal over me. I went to my own room, sat on the bed and tried to think more clearly. But visions of Ruth haunted me. Her skin was satin-smooth against my hand: now I could feel it against my cheek. The book was only next door. The cupboard was not locked. I could be back with her in quarter of an hour, and then . . .

My hand was already on the door-knob, when once again my other self awoke.

What was this thing I had actually contemplated doing? A theft—and a peculiarly beastly one. I must escape from the von Eberlings' flat, must escape instantly.

I had covered nearly the whole length of the Kurfürstendam before I began to consider my next move. There were crowds in the August Viktoria Platz; a concert in the Gedächtnis Kirche had just finished, and people were streaming across the Square and along all the neighbouring streets. I welcomed the idea of a crowd. I had known two solitudes this evening, and neither was tolerable in memory. So I joined a desultory throng at the entrance to a large café, went in with them, and was lucky to find a small table in a remote corner where, alone and yet in company, I could decide what to do.

Of course I had by now more than a glimmer of the truth. I understood that an attempt had been made to use me; that I had first been deliberately excited by a girl's beauty, and then sent on an errand both shameful and dangerous. And yet somehow I did not really mind. At any rate I did not blame Ruth, even if I thought to blame anyone. She had been so sweet, and the memory of having touched her still set my pulses racing. I felt myself more in love with her than ever, and the problem of what to do next was partially solved in advance by the thought of the companionship and of the few minutes of delicious pleasure she had already given me. Obviously I could not just remain away, until she realised I was not coming back. For the sake of what had passed between us, I owed her a frank refusal to do what she desired.

I must not even make excuses—I must not say that the von Eberlings were at home after all, or that I could not find the book, or this or that. If she believed me, she would expect me to try again; and I felt that to allow her to prolong her wiles (I knowing all the time that they were wiles) would be to degrade her intolerably. If she did not believe me, she would despise me, not only for failing her but for lying about my failure.

No, she had to be told. But how? Was I to go back there and then, and make my priggish speech? For it would sound priggish—that I knew. Then, suppose she flew out at me? I had a horrid prevision of the scene—Ruth turning suddenly from languorous welcome to savage contempt; I, awkwardly bundled in my overcoat, playing the upright Englishman, and wondering how to get out of the room and flat with any semblance of dignity. The prospect appalled me, and I compromised. With a slight feeling of shame I decided to telephone.

" I'm sorry, Ruth. I couldn't do it. Please try to understand, I just couldn't. Kurt trusts me and I am staying in his house. But you won't want me back now, so I am telling you this way."

She was unexpectedly submissive. " Very well. I think I understand. Good night, Niki, and thank you for dinner. I suppose I'll see you again some time? "

" I hope so. Good night."

I did not at that moment really think I should see her again, nor in view of what had happened did I particularly wish to. As I walked back to my table, I told myself that an episode was closed.

∽   ∽   ∽

Next morning, however, heroics and desire had both given

way to apologetic melancholy—apologetic on Ruth's account, melancholy on my own. I wondered whether I had managed things quite so well after all. I had jumped to the conclusion that, in her accessibility the night before, she had been playing Delilah. I now saw that she might equally well have been genuinely aflame; but, having promised her father to try me out as an auxiliary, checked our joint slide into lovers' oblivion and, before it was too late for her to remember or for me to obey, sent me on my disreputable mission. I was the more ready to be convinced of this new interpretation of what had occurred, because of the otherwise dismal prospect of the future. I had not realised, until threatened with its disappearance, to what an extent this involvement with Ruth (and all that it meant of ingenious planning and warm anticipation) had given savour to life. Now there would be nothing to look forward to; no opportunity of pitting my wits against Nissrandt and circumstances; no delicious secret to cherish and enjoy. *And*, of course, no more meetings with Ruth, unless of a kind worse than no meeting at all.

All the same was the situation much improved?—even supposing I were to adopt the new reading of the situation, even supposing I persuaded myself that she, no less than I, had been cheated of a passionate fulfilment? Manifestly I could not make the first move; almost as manifestly she would not. I cursed myself for a coward, using the telephone for what ought to have been a vital verbal encounter. And yet it might have turned out too vital for anything.

In a mood of ' perhaps ' and ' maybe ' and ' should I ' and ' did she ', I passed a miserable Sunday with the hospitable von Eberlings. I accompanied them to their Lutheran Church and wilted under the protracted thunders of the most fashionable Pfarrer of Berlin West. I passed the afternoon out and about with Kurt—gay, unsuspecting Kurt—petrified at the thought of meeting Ruth or her father, relieved yet disappointed at not doing so. Abendessen brought its own exigent problems, for the Colonel was there, and in considerable force.   I thought I knew my Nissrandt well enough to be sure he would ask for the Colonel more or less verbatim; and though there was now no particular point in conciliating the old swine, there was even less in annoying him.   So I gave all that I had of nervous attention to my emphatic (and admittedly impressive) host, with the result that by ten o'clock the dual strain of avoiding political and linguistic gaffes had tired me out.   Nevertheless, early next day and well before the stipulated hour, I was back at Dahlem, almost eager for cross-examination by the Principal. It never came.   He had either forgotten all about me and my military friends, or he guessed I was ready for him and deliberately burked the issue.   So right to the last my famous week-end was one of frustration.

∽   ∽   ∽

Drearily enough the weeks went by.   I had foreseen flatness and monotony, and there was plenty of both.   Indirectly they were of benefit, for I made vast progress with my German and even the bearish old Principal ventured some words of compliment.   But prospects of future culture were poor consolation for present boredom; and as gradually, in order to escape from the present, I began to relive again and again that enchanted evening before the catastrophe, my wish to see Ruth again became a longing, and longing almost a frenzy.   I was very unhappy, with the unhappiness of youth for the first time at grips with something bigger than itself.

∽   ∽   ∽

What queer details one remembers, thinking back to a past period of stress—details which, however slight their relevance, come to represent a whole tangle of feelings and hopes and worries.   During the weeks which followed the collapse of my affair with Ruth, I was in genuine emotional torment.   No matter that the affair had been callow and elementary.   In proportion to my experience and conception of what love-tragedy could be, it was terrific. And yet virtually the only concrete feature of the entire phase which I can clearly recall, is that every time I went into the city I seemed to see, in popular print and picture shops, coloured reproductions of two particular pictures. One was called *Vertige*, and showed a gentleman in full evening dress with a fine pair of moustaches leaning over a sofa and kissing a lady on the mouth. She was of the 'Gibson Girl' variety (it was the heyday of that now unattractive fashion) with hair piled high, a sumptuous décolletage, and quite six inches of black silk stocking thrusting from under her flounced skirt, as she lay with her head pressed into the back of the sofa by the ardour of her lover's kiss. The other picture was more dashing. It also had a French title and was called *La Loi de l'Honneur*. It showed the interior of an expensive bedroom, in the midst of which was a beflounced but thoroughly disordered double bed. Crouching in the bed, with the sheets clutched tactfully but revealingly in her hands, was a naked girl. In the open doorway stood a man wearing a travelling ulster and holding a smoking pistol in his hand. On the far side of the bed from the door (but on the side nearest to the spectator) a second man—naked as the girl I regret to say, but helped by the bed-flounce to preserve the decencies—sprawled on the carpet, a bullet through his heart.

It is now many years since I saw either *Vertige* or *La Loi de l'Honneur*, but I believe I could describe even their colouring, so vivid is my remembrance of them. Certainly I can still recapture something of the stimulus they gave—a stimulus adapted to its moment and admirably adequate.

It is fairly obvious, in view of my reaction to those two engravings, that my longing for Ruth was by now mainly physical. I suppose that the fiasco of the note-books had stripped the affair of its garment of romantic sentiment, and left exposed what had really been its impulse all the time. But even now the exposure wasn't so complete as to make me conscious of any more definite ambition than before. I had lost the only real excitement of my life, and what remained was drudgery and boredom. I wanted excitement back, and for some reason the effect these pictures had on me was to bring the possibility of its renewal a little nearer. That was all.

∽   ∽   ∽

And then one day I could bear it no longer, and wrote her a letter. I begged her to let me see her again; and I am afraid I used a number of well-known clichés to convince her how miserable I was and how badly I needed her. For ten tortured days I watched in vain for a reply, but on the eleventh there came a little note—a marvellous, gentle, friendly little note—to say she had been from home, would be glad to renew our friendship, and if I were free the following Sunday we could have an evening together. Would I, she ended, come to the apartment about seven o'clock?

Would I! That the invitation meant one of the Hatton family suppers mattered not an atom. I should see Ruth and talk to her, and watch the sulky beauty of her mouth, and know that I was forgiven for having once failed to do her bidding.

∽   ∽   ∽

My Sunday evening passed very agreeably, with an undercurrent of emotional satisfaction which swept me out of my listlessness into a new phase of hopeful anticipation. There was one other guest besides myself—an upstanding, rather pale young German called von Maltzahn, whose face seemed vaguely familiar to me.

Hatton was in great talking form, his eye-glasses more crooked than ever and his large head shining with declamatory sweat. Over supper he had a tremendous argument with von Maltzahn about the fundamental character of the new English government. Von Maltzahn, with that detailed knowledge of English politics common to many intelligent foreigners, argued that Asquith's real policy was that of Grey and Haldane; that the pacifist party though ostensibly well-represented in the Cabinet, would in effect be side-tracked, and that England was Germany's enemy. Hatton waved his arms in disagreement, until his mouth was empty enough to be of practical use. Then for a short period, while he filled it up again, he harangued his guest in rapid, food-ridden German, stabbing the air with his knife to emphasise his points. He declared that foreign adventures—imperial or otherwise—were finished with. England had internal problems and to spare, and only wanted to leave others alone and to be let alone.

The war of words swayed back and forth. I took practically no share in it, partly because I was a typical young Briton who, never having been taught to regard international politics as of any significance to him personally, knew next to nothing about them, partly because I preferred looking at Ruth. This was the more easily done in that, as organiser of the meal, she was continually moving about and giving opportunities for help in plate-carrying, salad-hunting, drink-pouring and what-not—opportunities I was urgent to take.

She had greeted me with a frank cordiality, the technique of which I could not but admire.

" Isn't this nice! It's ages since we saw you. And how is everything? The German must now be word-perfect."

Hatton had wrung my hand and patted me on the shoulder and even chaffed me for neglecting them. Then I had been presented to von Maltzahn, and settled to the pre-supper bottle of rather sweet hock and one of Hatton's cigars, while Ruth and the rosy Saxon began their operations between parlour and kitchen. It was all so normal and traditional, that I felt the uneasy breathlessness with which I had arrived give place to one of another kind. Had I imagined the drama of my last evening in this flat? Was Hatton merely telling the obvious truth, when he called my prolonged absence 'neglect'? No matter now. Here I was again and here she was; the only

D 2

essential problem was to know whether a fresh start really meant a fresh start—whether, that is to say, I was back at the vinaigrette and had to work through theatre parties and small talk to renewed love-making—or whether we could go on from where we left off.

After supper was over and the débris removed, we sat and talked. Von Maltzahn and Ruth were discussing some musical event in the near future, and she suddenly turned to me and said:

"Niki, you *must* go to the College concert. Wednesday week. It's going to be really good."

As she spoke, I remembered where I had seen von Maltzahn before. It was he who had greeted her on the lower terrace of the Fürstenberg on that historic evening many weeks ago, and by taking some minutes of her time had provoked me to imprudent sarcasm. Of course; and she had said he was involved in the concerts given at the College of Music. Well, he evidently was; I felt a minor and unexpected relief, as though some forgotten discomfort had been removed. I assured Ruth I should like nothing better than to come to her concert (I was now more or less a senior member of Nissrandt's Institute and better able to dispose of my time), and went on chatting, while the secret places of my mind were busy with plans for seeing her alone, before or after the gathering or if possible both.

I need not have troubled. She did it all for me. At about ten-thirty von Maltzahn rose to go. I naturally got up also, and began those vague skirmishings and mutterings which, in terms of English social polish, are preliminary to taking leave. But Ruth plucked at my sleeve, murmured "wait", and followed her father and the departing German (they were still disputing about something) into the little hall. I heard her say: "Walk a little of the way with him, Daddy. It will do you good and you can argue better in the fresh air"; then the shutting of the outer door. The next moment she was standing in front of me, with a half-pout on her lovely lips and her hands demurely clasped in front of her.

" I thought you had quite forsaken me, Niki " she said plaintively. " It's such a long while . . ."

It was on the tip of my tongue to protest; to remind her of what I had said in my letter; generally to start overmuch explanation. But for once I had the sense to see an opportunity just before it had passed. I took her by the shoulders, pulled her against me and kissed her roundly and well.

She was panting and laughing when she came to the surface.

" Gracious me! The Briton roused with a vengeance. But I rather liked it, all the same. Now, before daddy comes back, two things—first about the concert night. Will you call for me between six and seven, carry my fiddle for me, and perhaps take me out to have some food? I must be in the hall before eight, but there'd be time . . . that is, if *you* have time, there would be . . ."

It was agreed there would, and Ruth continued:

" The other thing is a little service you could do me. Don't look alarmed, it's nothing burglarious—like—the other—I've learnt my lesson all right."

She dropped her eyes and began fiddling with the button of my coat. We were still standing facing one another, just inside the door of the living-room, and I remember a feeling of slight impatience with a conversation so uncomfortably staged. Also I wanted to kiss her again; but I could not very well interrupt her to do so, and now that she was visibly in difficulties with a confession it was hopeless.

" Niki " she said uncertainly. " I was crazy to send you out to get that book—you know, that night—and I've been so miserable. It put you in a horrible position, and I can't imagine what you have been thinking of me. Am I forgiven? "

I put one hand under each of her arms and pushed her slightly from me.

" Look at me, Ruth. That's better. Now kiss me again and you are forgiven any mortal thing."

" Oh, Niki " she murmured. " You are a dear."

" And now what am I to do ? " I asked.

" Just find out from your friend the name of his instructor at the Anstalt; the man who was preparing him for the exam. It must be either Captain H. or Lieutenant von K. There is no secret about the names of the staff; but their functions are complicated and daddy wants to be accurate. Will you do that for me, Niki? I made such a mess of my first attempt to help daddy and he was so cross with me. He said it was a monstrous thing to ask of you. I suppose it was. But I didn't understand. I thought that was what he wanted me to do. There's nothing monstrous in asking you to find out an officer's name, is there Niki? "

She had been talking with her head against my shoulder, but now raised her eyes. They looked suspiciously moist, and a surge of romantic pity broke over me. Poor child! Even the father she had tried to help had rounded on her, merely because she had misunderstood what he said. Goodness knows, the man was obscure enough himself, what with shouting and gesticulating and talking with his mouth full! I felt indignant with Hatton, who should be compelled to realise his good fortune in having such a daughter.

So I laughed cheerfully at Ruth's woebegone face, kissed her once more, and assured her that I would find out what she wanted the very next time I saw Kurt von Eberling.

～　　　～　　　～

We played the Cadets on the following Saturday afternoon, and I walked over as usual to chat with Kurt before the game began. Now that the moment had come to ask my question, I felt a little embarrassed. What had seemed a trifling enquiry, with Ruth at my side and the sweetness of our joint conspiracy heavy on the air, now struck me as awkward and even impertinent. It was no business of mine; and, anyway, why should I want to know? But I had promised Ruth to help her, wanted most desperately to please her, and was determined to go through with it.

" Do you mind " I began " if I ask you something about the organisation of the Anstalt? "

" I don't think so " said Kurt cheerfully.   " What is it? "

" Well, do you have regular tutors as we do at Oxford—one who takes charge of you and is responsible for your work generally? "

" Well, I suppose you might say we do have a special tutor— in a sense.   But of course there is such a lot of practical work as well as theory, and that is run on usual army lines.   So we don't belong so exclusively to any one instructor as I imagine a student does at your universities."

" But, for example, take your case.   Who prepared you for that exam—gave you texts to read and told you what to prepare? "

The casual friendliness faded from Kurt's face, and I saw in his eyes a look of wary alarm.

" What do you mean?   Who—by name?   And why do you want to know? "

I could only hope I did not look as uncomfortable as I felt. Kurt's change of expression disconcerted me badly, and I began to wish I had never started a questioning which was so obviously to be badly received.   But I had to go on, and the thought of Ruth jogged me into a sort of reckless jauntiness.

" Oh, just curiosity—and the wish to settle an argument.   A man I know was debating the names in the published list of your officers, pretending he knew all about them.   You see I feel sort of involved in your exam, through staying with you while you were working for it; and I'd like to catch the fellow out in a mistake."

He stared at me a moment, and I could almost read what was passing through his mind.   He was thinking back to my visit, to our conversation in his room, to the note-book. . . . There was now suspicion in his eyes and, behind that, fear.

" Who is the man ? " he asked, rather breathlessly.

Airier than ever, as my embarrassment increased, I did not stop to think.

" Oh, a journalist."

Kurt thrust his face close to mine.

" A newspaper man? His name, Dering! Tell me his name! "

I now realised only too well what a babbling fool I had been. To give Hatton's name would be at once betrayal and false accusation, for the poor man had had no direct share in my clumsy curiosity. But to refuse the name would make my own behaviour sinister, and perhaps dangerous—alike to Ruth and her father and myself. I was seized with panic.

" I—I'm sorry—I—don't want to know anything . . ." I stammered.

At this moment the whistle blew for the game to begin.

" You wanted to know what you asked " he snapped, and turned away to find his place on the field.

At half-time there was a brief interval. I had sunk during the first part of the game into terrified depression and was standing alone, gloomy and wretched, when I heard Kurt's voice in my ear.

" Listen, Dering " he said, speaking low but angrily, " for the sake of our friendship I shall try to forget what has just happened. I must hope that you did not understand what you were doing. I ask you, on your side, to realise that we are forbidden to talk to strangers about the Anstalt—even German strangers; and that I shall be ruined, completely done for, if I am thought to have been indiscreet. Another thing. I must demand that you never tell a soul about that note-book you saw in my room. You do not understand, you English, what Prussia is like in such matters. If I thought you had mentioned it to anyone, I should kill myself. I should have to. Promise me, Dering—swear to me! Otherwise I shall report the matter of this journalist."

Between fright and fury he was almost beside himself. I could only stand there, cursing my own folly and wracked with sympathy for my friend. With an effort I pulled myself together.

" Oh, Kurt! Of course I promise. I am so dreadfully sorry . . ."

Then the whistle went once more and the game resumed.

On the way back to the Institute I was in great unhappiness and perplexity. I had been spared a downright lie, because by sheer chance I had not been asked whether indeed I had spoken of the note-book to anyone else. But I knew, had it been necessary, that I must have lied; and the knowledge shamed me worse than ever. Further, was it certain Kurt would not report the whole incident? If he did, the authorities would find out quickly enough who the journalist was, and then anything might happen. Finally, what was I to do about Ruth? I could never explain to her the beastliness of my experience with Kurt. One has to be present to appreciate the cruel atmosphere of such a conversation as ours. She would merely learn that once again I had let her down. And that would be the end.

In the evening I wrote to her. It was a short note, but took a long time to write. I said I had tried my best, but that Kurt von Eberling was not permitted by the rules of the Anstalt to answer any specific questions and had indeed been annoyed with me for asking one. I begged her not to be angry with me, but that I couldn't pester my friend when he so obviously wished me not to. The letter finished:

" *I am dying to see you, and just live for next Wednesday. Don't be so cross that I mayn't come. Please, Ruth, let me come !* "

I heard nothing till Tuesday evening, when she sent me a telegram:

" *Expecting you tomorrow night as arranged.*"

෨   ෨   ෨

Intense relief at having escaped censure, and the fact that there were only twenty-four hours between the arrival of the telegram and my appointment to fetch Ruth from her flat, combined to prevent my envisaging, as I might otherwise have done, the curious incidentals to my amourette. I was quite conscious that something needed explaining, both about Ruth's persistent interest in the Kadettenanstalt and about the part I had been twice invited to play in it. But I deliberately closed my mind to speculation and to retrospect. She was still in my life; and I had suffered so greatly during the time when she had dropped out of it, that I was taking no risks of spoiling a delicious present for the sake of making sense of the past.

And there was a further and a more practical reason for shirking—at least temporarily—the reading of riddles. Between Tuesday night and Wednesday night I simply had not time. I had not time, because I took a sudden and (as it seemed to me) masterful decision. My time at Nissrandt's was running out. Indeed I had already planned—before the renewal of my relations with Ruth—to go south and try my Institute German on casual Bavarians. My letters home had been conveniently vague as to dates, for which I was now thankful. I could stay over in Berlin with no need for any explanation save a reference to plans temporarily changed. On the spur of the moment, therefore, I decided to say good-bye to the Institute forthwith, and move myself and my belongings into the city. There I would spend two weeks or more, actually ' on the ground ' and my own master.

I packed desperately. Farewells and tips and a hundred little jobs kept me hard at it. But what matter? I was all set for a ' big moment '.

On the early afternoon of Wednesday I quitted the Institut Nissrandt finally and for always. As much to annoy my ex-preceptor as for any other reason, I had ordered a car to drive all the way into Berlin; and the Swedish ogre had glared at me when I announced my intention, and even said one of his favourite pieces about the luxury-loving English and *echt deutsche Sparsamkeit*. This was a triumph and amply justified my extravagance.

I chose a small hotel off the Friedrichstrasse, paid my chauffeur with a lordly air, dumped my luggage, and went out into the town. The time passed quickly enough. In more than one shop-window I noticed *Vertige* and *La Loi de l'Honneur*, and threw them a condescending nod. Such things were two-a-penny to a man of the world.

At six-fifteen I called for Ruth, took her to a café and then to eat. She was very sweet, though a little subdued; and I decided forthwith to make my apology for having failed with Kurt, and so dispose of the subject for always. Of the possibility that my indiscretion might have involved her father, I did not dare to speak.

" I really couldn't press Kurt " I concluded a little disingenuously. " You do see that? He was so obviously unwilling. I don't seem much use to you, do I? "

She gave a sad little smile and with a gesture brushed the incident away.

" Never mind, Niki. It was nice of you to try."

She began fiddling with the knives and forks, and, when next she spoke, kept her eyes on the table. Her voice was low with a hint of breathlessness.

" I have asked you to do more than I should. Every time I see you I seem to want something. You will think I am just one of those girls who—who are—nice to a man for what they can get out of him. But I'm not, Niki. It fell out so unluckily. Really I'm not. I—I want to show you I'm not, to do my share—if you still feel that way. . . ."

This was almost too much for my restaurant manners. But I managed to limit myself to pressing a knee hard against hers under the table. She continued:

" After the concert I shall have to stay around a little while. The committee will be sort of taking stock. Suppose you come round behind, pick up my fiddle—I'll have it ready for you in the passage—and slip back to the flat with it. Then you can—can—well, get things ready, and I'll join you in half an hour. There's no one there. Daddy—Daddy's gone away, and Anna is staying at her home for a few days. You won't mind going back there before me? I'll be very quick. Then perhaps I will play to you—you know, *our* tune—just like Franzi did to her Niki. . . ."

Her voice faded to a whisper. Still without looking at me, she pushed her coffee-cup toward me as though for replenishment. Under the rim of the saucer lay a key.

∽   ∽   ∽

I closed the front door quietly behind me and stood under the passage light with Ruth's violin case in my hand, listening to the delicious silence which meant an empty flat. I felt a strange exaltation, with no desire to marvel at what had happened nor indeed any particular curiosity as to what was to happen. The hour was perfect of itself, and in due time would know the measure of its own perfection.

" Get things ready " she had said.

I found a bottle of wine in the sideboard cupboard, hunted glasses in the pantry. In the larder there were half a Dutch cheese and some pumpernickel in grease paper. All this I arranged on a table in the sitting-room, pulled the sofa forward, drew the curtains carefully together. As it was a warm night, I left the windows wide behind the curtains, took off my coat, and lay back on the couch in my shirt-sleeves. There was no traffic in the street. Only the footsteps of an occasional passer-by broke the near silence, and for a moment drowned the distant clamour of crowds and cars and horses, which came faintly from the Potsdamerplatz two or three blocks away.

And then suddenly the latch of the front door clicked sharply; there were steps in the hall; and before I had time even to

wonder what could have happened, Ruth walked into the room
with two or three young people at her heels. She stopped short
on seeing me and stared, first with astonishment, then with
evident anger.

" Well, really! . . ." she said.

There advanced from behind her the now familiar and un-
palatable figure of von Maltzahn.

" What's happened? " he asked her. " What is this fellow
doing here? "

She looked at me with a sneer I shall not easily forget.

" He seems to be very much at home " she replied. " I only
asked him to take my violin back after the concert and lent him
a key so that he could leave it safely in the flat. Apparently
he took this to be an invitation to rob the larder and stage
an orgy."

Suddenly she changed her tone. In place of elaborate
sarcasm came the coldness of rage.

" Now that you are here, Mr Cock Sparrow Dering, and
just before you go, I would like my friends to know what you
have done." She turned to the group behind her and went on
in German—slowly and with cruel emphasis. " This innocent
young man offered to get information for my father—information of a kind more suited to a grown spy than to an ex-school-
boy. He couldn't get it, and told me a sob-story about not
wishing to embarrass his German friend—the very friend he
had offered to trick. It occurred to me at once that he might
have gone farther and told the friend that we—father and I—
had put him up to it. So I warned father to get out of town for
a while. And now look at our honourable Englishman!
Pretty, isn't it? "

Then to von Maltzahn:

" Go on, Liebchen, deal with him! "

The term of endearment, as well as the sight of von Maltzahn's
pale elongated face and his clenching fists, roused me from
the paralysis caused by Ruth's treachery. I now understood

enough of von Maltzahn's position to take a chance. Facing him squarely:

" So you are in this too? " I said. " For God's sake and your own, spare us heroics. You can't start a scrap here without getting yourself mixed up in the whole affair if it comes out. As it might, you know . . ."

He hesitated and I turned to pick up my coat; but with a snort he forestalled me. Next minute he pulled back the curtain and hurled the coat into the street.

" Go after it, Schweinhund! "

I passed through them without looking at anyone, out of the door and down the stairs. The coat hung forlornly on the railing which bordered the tiny front-garden. As I disentangled it from the iron spikes and from the laurel bush growing against them, there was a burst of laughter from the lighted windows above. Then a few chords were struck on the piano, and immediately afterward came the wail of a violin. It was the theme song from *Ein Walzertraum*.

I struggled into my coat and hurried away. The refrain had been reached, and the violin must have come close to the open window, for the sound grew suddenly clearer and I distinctly heard a girl laugh.

As I turned the corner of the street, the luscious, heart-breaking tune was quivering to its end:

> " *Einmal noch leben*
> *Ein—mal in Mai* .. "

      ᔆ   ᔆ   ᔆ

After all, therefore, I went to Bavaria, and even sooner than I had intended. The train journey and the three weeks which followed it no longer rank with my avowed memories. They were a bad time. My instinct was to hide; my chief dread an encounter with anyone I knew or with anyone likely to know of me.

I was still bitterly ashamed of my half-betrayal of Ruth and

her father, and now deeply shocked by her treatment of my quite
genuine adoration.   She had played me up from the very first,
to serve some purpose of Hatton's and (presumably) of von
Maltzahn's also.   What their purpose was I did not at the time
trouble to think.   It was enough to realise that von Maltzahn
was her lover, and that he and she had laughed together over
the stages of my emotional progress.   Later, however, when the
pain dulled and I came to know more about German affairs,
I guessed that Hatton was collecting information for British
use and that von Maltzahn was of the party opposed to Prussian
domination, and ready to collaborate even with foreigners in
its destruction.   Ruth had, of course, invented the suggestion
of my having put the authorities on their track.   I could be
grateful for that; it had given me the idea how to deal with von
Maltzahn.   But they would not have laughed so gayly at my
final discomfiture, if they had known how near to the truth her
reckless words had come.

You understand now why I was always a little shy about
Bavaria.   I saw some lovely places, and knew them for lovely.
But I never felt that I could re-visit those mediæval and baroque
towns without a return of the old shrinking and of the old
dread lest, round a corner, I run into someone familiar with my
shaming.

The final irony came years later.   In the course of a talk
with Uncle Nick in the Café Viel in Paris (a very important talk,
as you will see when you come to it) he suddenly threw up his
hand and cried:

" Sakes alive!   I almost forgot.   Among some old papers the
other day I found a letter from that guy Nissrandt near Berlin—
you remember, the German teacher."   (I remembered.)   " It
was a kinda report on your progress; favourable on the whole.
But at the end he said a thing I couldn't rightly figure out at
the time.   Here we are."   He pulled a letter from his pocket and
handed it to me.

" I am glad " (I read) " that your nephew is interested in musical performances. He is on the whole inclined to prefer high-class work and you might allow him some latitude as regards expenses in this direction. Money spent on such things as *Salome* or *Walzertraum* is, in my opinion, worse than wasted."

" Worse than wasted " wasn't bad, was it?

VI: DENISE

BETWEEN Germany and France was a month's interlude at home. It was pleasant to see the family again, to look up one or two friends and to taste the suave amenities of an English June. But already I was conscious of reserves vis-à-vis my native land and its people, and Geoffrey—with his silly jokes about sausage-eating Germans who prefer beer-swilling to football—made me really cross, though I could hardly have explained why. Underneath, of course, I lived and re-lived the mortifying history of my love-affair, now feeling Ruth's smooth skin tremble once more beneath my hands, now hearing again the click of the outer latch, the irruption of mocking strangers, and her cold cruel voice saying " Well! Really. . . .'

In one respect my feeling about the whole episode had changed. The wound to my pride was still unhealed, but I no longer dwelt wretchedly on my individual folly. Indeed I was beginning to think that, apart from my discreditable performance on the football field, I had behaved—if not with intelligence, at any rate with reasonable sanity. How could I possibly have foreseen that Ruth was waiting on revenge? There was no outright answer to this question, and I found some consolation in repeating it. In consequence, I ended by convincing myself that I had not been cozened at all, but definitely ill-used; and the substitution of this mood for one of apologetic shame was important, because it sent me to France on my guard against waywardness of temper, but not against cony-catchers.

∽   ∽   ∽

I will not bore you with an account of my two months of heat and hard work with M. le Professeur Lacombe at Fontainebleau. I got there early in July, and the weather was already very warm. August was sweltering; but I was by then more or less acclimatised, and with the help of an occasional thunderstorm got through without discomfort. Lacombe was a charming fellow (a very different proposition from old Nissrandt) and a good teacher. But he saw no reason for letting off a pupil more lightly on account of hot weather, so I had to get right down to work and stop there.

During my last week under his tutelage, the programme was relaxed, and I had opportunity to explore the far fringes of the forest over by Barbizon and the Bassin de la Mare. But for most of my time I had leisure to do little beyond swim in the river, and occasionally wander about those parts of the forest which abut on the Château grounds. By good luck the famous fête of the Grandes Eaux came off in the Bassin de Neptune just before I left; and from that admirable experience of the gracious elegance of France in a mood of formal gaiety was born an enduring love of her profound civilisation. The crowd on the terraced edge of the huge sunk garden was not, perhaps, so dense as it is nowadays; but it was dense enough and eager enough to give a certain insecurity to one in the front row. I got through the ballets without mishap, and even the sudden leap into play of fountain after illuminated fountain did not dislodge my carefully propped security. But the burst of horn-blowing, followed by the whistling shriek of the great rockets, was too much for an excited family immediately behind me; and when a small boy plunged between my legs and a massive mamma showed signs of climbing up my back, I lost my balance and toppled neatly over the edge into the twigs and gnarled branches of the trees which are trained to run along the terrace-wall. The accident enchanted those who saw it (and they, as the fireworks were now continuous and bright, were fairly numerous), with the result that to delight in French civilisation was now added pleasure in French good-humour and courtesy. The family responsible for my collapse hauled me to my place again, brushed me down, all talked and laughed at once, and finally accepted me so thoroughly as one of them-selves that I spent the rest of the evening in their company— doing the fair in detail, and finally sitting over a café-table with papa and a grown-up son until after two o'clock in the morning.

Three days later I left Fontainebleau for the valley of the Loire. During nine weeks the devoted Lacombe had taken me slowly and severely through the various preliminaries of linguistic flight; it was now time to try my wings in the open. Thanks to his good offices, a suitable home had been found—with pleasant surroundings and a promise of considerable garrulity. The latter was of importance. The spoken French of the Touraine being notoriously the best of its kind, the more of it I could hear and assimilate the better.

I warn you, Sally, that I incline to be rather wordy about the little town of Ronsenac-le-Château, in which I spent the delicious autumn of 1913. We spoke more than once of going there— you and I—but never managed it; so in a way a sight of the place is due to you. Also my expectation of conversational plenty was more than fulfilled; and I dare say Ronsenac and verbosity have become so nearly synonymous in my memory, that I could not speak tersely of it even if I tried.

The place lies some seventeen kilometres from Tours, in a pocket of the tableland above the Loire. On every side of it lie rolling agricultural uplands, laced with infrequent roads, dotted with scattered farms. The town itself ('town' one must call it for the sake of its age and one-time dignity, though by the standards of nowadays it is only a large village) has the peculiar local animation which even the most remote provincial settlements in France possess. At dead times of day it was just a straggle of discordant buildings of all periods, slung haphazard along half a dozen narrow streets which converged on an irregular space of trodden earth—studded with chestnut trees, flanked by a fine fragment of an unfinished church, and known to authority (though not to the inhabitants) as the "Place de la République". But on a fine evening, and for more or less the whole of Sunday, the *bourg* had its areas of crowded activity. I remember particularly a straight stretch of road by the side of the shallow untidy stream which ran through the lower fringe of the town. On either side were pollarded plane-trees; and up and down this unpretentious avenue the citizens of Ronsenac would promenade and chatter, saluting one another with grave civility, with genial emphasis, or (as between the young of both sexes) with embarrassed gallantry and either primness or giggles. It was a great place for cock-chafers—this riverside walk—and I cannot now recall the place or its people without hearing again the hum and crackle of those curious insects as they whirred and blundered from tree to tree.

There are other noises beside that of the cock-chafers which to me must always remain part of Ronsenac. There is the slap-slap of wet linen, on pale frayed washing-boards, which used to come (it seemed at all hours of the day or night) from the spot just above the bridge, where the stream had been dammed and widened to make a convenient tank with stone-flagged edges. There are the cries of players at *boule*, and the thud and crack of the woods as they struck the planking or one another—noises peculiar to the evening and to Sunday, and native to the area of the principal café at the corner of the Place. There are the dull rumble of the steam-tramway and the anxious puffing of its debilitated engine, rounding the corner of the rising road from Tours and trundling across the few hundred yards of level track to the tiny terminus. There are

the cries of the children playing endless games in and out of
the pillars of the high mediæval shed, which long ago served as
market for the *bourg*. There is the rattle of the long farm
wagons, plodding their way from the uplands to the Route
Nationale beside the river.

But the sounds of Ronsenac—and all but one of its sights—
were, as I fully realise, ordinary enough, and common to hundreds
of similar villages in every part of France. My excuse for
dwelling on them is that they came to have special significance
for me, as necessary accompaniment to the period of my re-
ceptive youth, than which (for its greater part) none was more
peaceful and rewarding.

I suppose it is because the only unusual ' sight ' of the town,
and the only ingredient of my sojourn there which was neither
peaceful nor rewarding, were intimately linked together, that I
have prolonged so far as possible the normalities of reminiscence.
But it is time to pass to things less commonplace, of which the
first and most important is the diadem of Ronsenac—the only
feature of the place which earns for it mention in the guide-
books, and even tempts some of the more leisured tourists to
risk a détour on their journey through Touraine.

The northern slope of the otherwise rather characterless
hollow in which the town lies is unexpectedly broken by a
single spur of rocky hill. Crowning that hill stands the ancient
Château of the Ducs de Ronsenac—a building older than
Langeais, than Chenonceaux or than Azay, and for that reason
more the fortress. Slim grey towers—cylindrical, peak-
roofed, lit here and there with windows so narrow that they are
little more than loopholes—rise like a group of poplars from
the rocky headland on which they have been built.

They are irregularly linked by high battlemented walls,
which run into the overgrown rocks to either side and clamp
the castle to the hill, leaving a level entry from the northern
plateau. No doubt in the old days this northern approach—the
most vulnerable of all—had been fiercely walled and bastioned.

But with the coming of more peaceful times, all defences had been removed and the mediæval gate-house now stood isolated and meaningless, with farm buildings scattered about it, and vegetables growing where formerly there had been a moat-like ditch. At the time of which I write, the Château of Ronsenac had the distinction of being still a private residence, shuttered save on rare and brief occasions and inaccessible to the general public even on fête days. For the greater part of the year it slumbered forlornly in charge of a resident caretaker, who (it appeared) did a little farming on the side.

Measured in feet, the distance from the parapet of the terrace facing the valley to the roofs of the houses below was not very great; but owing to the rapid fall of the ground at this point (it seemed the steeper in contrast to the kindlier slopes to left and right) and to the skilful disposition of the ducal masonry, Ronsenac retained a properly feudal air, as of a settlement at once protected and enslaved.

This atmosphere of ancien régime caught at my youthful imagination. I used to be very ' grand style ' in my historical preferences, and the dependence of Ronsenac, starved and dreary though it was, chimed with my nostalgia for other, more flamboyant days. I felt that there was something admirable in the fact that this deserted castle was still a noble residence and not, like its more complacent and accessible fellows, a mere museum of antiquities. In consequence, once I was established in the little town and had settled to a regular time-table of reading, writing and walking abroad, hardly a day passed without my climbing the zigzag path of uneven setts that from the *bourg* led up the hill toward the château. By striking off from this path I found places of vantage on the neighbouring slopes, from which I could study the clump of lichenous towers, attempt reconstruction of the scheme of fortification as originally planned, and discover how far the aggressive purpose of the mother fortress had subsequently been modified.

Overlooking the terrace and the town of Ronsenac the

building was partly mediæval, partly of sixteenth-century date, with a double line of windows of the flattened ogive type, a spiral corner stair in the Italian manner crowned by a flèche, and other—though unimportant—specimens of that Renaissance ornament which the French so tirelessly admire. This small patch of non-defensive building seemed the only alleviation of a pile otherwise bellicose. On the inland side of the castle was little of interest. Indeed the only amusement available was to peer beneath the gate-way at the worn mounting-block; at the portcullis slat; at the holes where once the drawbridge chains ran up and down, before the moat was filled with earth and vowed to cabbages.

It was not long, prowling about the purlieus of the castle, before I began to take regular notice of a thin thread of smoke rising from some chimney behind the pallisade of towers. This smoke could only have been provoked by him who, for want of a better garrison, held the château for the Duc de Ronsenac. Gradually I began all manner of absurd speculations as to the appearance, duties and identity of the castle's *gardien*. One thing about him I knew, could not help knowing. His name was Hanan. One day when I was passing the main gate on my way back to the town, a man with a cart—anxious to deliver some goods and unable to make anyone hear—began to bawl at the top of his voice for " Monsieur Hanan ". Whether the shouts did their job I never knew, for I was round the corner and some way down the hill before they stopped; but the name I had heard and the name I remembered.

The more I indulged in this game of ' conjure the caretaker ', the more fascinating it became. Also the more secret. Nothing would have been easier than to enquire about him in the town; probably he was one of the café habitués and visible twenty times a week. But I did not want my mystery solved, still less to realise there was no mystery. So I kept silent and elaborated my private fantasies.

Hanan became one improbability after another. First he

was a dogged old retainer who, crouching in the heart of the ancient building, stood as bulwark between Ronsenac family tradition and the scheduling, ticketing enthusiasm of the Beaux Arts Ministry.

Then he shrank to the stock comic of satirical fiction, became short, stout, felt-slippered, peppery but incompetent. Then swelled dangerously and became a kind of ogre, a half-human monster living a troglodytic life in the castle vaults. Then came complete transformation. He was not a caretaker at all, but the Duc de Ronsenac himself, bankrupt of all but pride and dwelling in secret squalor among the ruins of his dignity. Then, alas, he was no Duke. He was a trespasser on ducal property, a hunted man, a criminal in flight from justice. And so I passed from one absurdity to another, each more extravagant than the last and more delightful. All the time I kept my counsel, asking no questions, affecting indifference both to the château and its history.

It is comical, in view of what happened, that I wasted so much thought and ingenuity on Hanan himself and never devised my fairy tales so as to provide him with a family. But I never did. It was reserved for a chance remark at meal-time to give my shadowy *gardien* a domestic setting and so to put an end to my serial make-believe.

∽   ∽   ∽

It is time you were introduced to the house in which I lived during my three months in Ronsenac, and to its owners. Not far from the tramway terminus and almost on the outskirts of the *bourg*, the Villa Coralie stood high above the road. It was among the more personable houses of the town, though desperately ugly with its panels of red brick enclosed in stucco frames, its disproportionate windows, its poor but pretentious iron-work. The hill rose gently behind it, and an untidy garden sloped upward to a boundary half-fence half-hedge, beyond which vague fields of beet and stubble rose indefinitely.

The owners of this house were two widows—mother and daughter. Whether either of them was called 'Coralie' I never discovered. I prefer to believe that the villa was christened by a speculative builder, for as applied to either of my hostesses the name would have been a misnomer so gross as to be intolerable. But although the delicacy of a stage fairy was denied alike to Madame G. and to her already mature daughter Madame R., both were very kind to me and, from a technical point of view, exactly what I needed. They were of the class of reduced gentility, which is ideal company for the student of language. They spoke beautiful French and a great deal of it; they were the very essence of commonplace, so that their abundant conversation teemed with phrases of everyday utility; they had all the domestic skill and industry of the French bourgeoise; they made no attempt to trespass on such leisure as their paying guest allowed himself. It arose, therefore, that meals were occasions of an intense conversational activity. My hostesses could talk incessantly about nothing in particular, and yet use the wealth of idiom, inflection and gesture that to a foreigner offers such unrivalled training. Also they would correct my mistakes (as it were at full gallop and between dashes) so that our talk suffered no irksome instructional jars, but rushed headlong on its way, a torrent of comments, questions, exclamations, small jokes, grammatical adjustments, mutual compliments, second helpings and coy bridlings of flattered housewifery, sweeping me to a very fair knowledge of colloquial French and the agreeable widows to a pleasant exhaustion, compound of shortness of breath and fullness of stomach.

No less striking than their talent for conversation was their instinctive courtesy. Only rarely (apart from the give and take of domestic detail) did they exchange remarks in which I—an outsider and a foreigner—could not be expected to take part. But one day at déjeuner Madame R. observed in a rapid undertone to her mother that Hanan had been buying hay from Perronet. Something in her tone—a tone both flustered and conspiratorial—gave this very ordinary observation an importance beyond face value. It seemed to indicate an event of some sort at the chateau. Actually it did nothing of the kind, Madame R.'s change of tone being merely a reflection of the general disapproval felt locally toward the castle's caretaker. But I did not know of this disapproval at the time, and was in any event eager to seize the opportunity of probing my private mystery. Elaborately casual, I enquired whether there were horses in the castle stables. Only when the Duke came into residence. So the Duke did visit Ronsenac? Yes, but rarely. Sometimes he brought a party for a short period of *villégiature*. I must understand that he had another château in Normandy, that he wintered in the city or at Cannes, that Touraine was very hot in summer and the shooting about Ronsenac of the roughest. Then (with something of an effort) who looked after the castle in his absences? But the Hanans, of course! Oh, the Hanans—the family of Hanan? The elder widow pursed her lips. There was Monsieur Hanan; there was his wife; there was also (after a pause) his daughter. I wanted to ask of what age was the daughter; but just as I was about to speak, the younger widow made so obvious a feint with a dish of admirable green figs that I realised the subject of Mademoiselle Hanan to be a delicate one. I asked no more questions, but felt that there was even better reason than I had thought to study the caretakers of Ronsenac.

∽   ∽   ∽

I have spoken of the café at the corner of the Place. Just as the latter—for all the faded name-plates affixed years ago by departmental officialdom—was known locally as ' à côté de l'Église ', so the former was everywhere ' chez Dorbon ', although large letters across the front of the building proclaimed it the Grand Café de Touraine. I had formed the habit of taking my periodical drinks chez Dorbon, and soon got on terms of friendly familiarity with the easy-going patron. It was under the awning of this pleasant café, about half past five one beautiful evening toward the end of September, that my interest in the family of Hanan was transformed in a single moment of time from the academic to the practical. I was sitting on an iron chair, the *père* Dorbon was on another iron chair, and between us was a small iron table. We were, I remember, discussing the forthcoming local elections, about which, as you can imagine, I knew nothing at all. Suddenly round the corner of the Rue de l'Église came a slim, almost a sinuous, figure—hatless, basket on arm, with ankles of a nervous elegance plunged into a clumsy pair of sabots. As the girl walked quickly across my line of vision, I noted a long oval face, dark hair and bright black eyes. I noted also that in movement she had that slant from shoulder to knee that tells of an admirable body, lithely swung. Dorbon watched my glance and snorted softly. I cocked an eye at him. " It is the little Hanan " he observed. " She has the devil in herself, that one." The girl was now at the far corner of the Place. The huge figure of a peasant lad loomed in front of her. They spoke a moment; then the girl tossed her head, and with an angry swish of skirt and shawl slipped away and out of sight. The *père* Dorbon chuckled. " She is not for the likes of Jacques " he remarked. " She has her fancies, our pretty Denise, but not of such simplicity."

M. Dorbon's insinuation that Denise Hanan, though exclusive, was not unapproachable, was rapidly confirmed and in rather a startling manner. Two days after my first conscious sight of her, I chanced to take an evening walk in the fields above the town. The great heat of July and August had settled to a long drought and to temperatures unusually high for late September. The day had been rainless and really hot; and over the torrid tableland with its alternating areas of stubble, cut-clover and turnips, hung a light cloud of dust. The colour of the whole landscape was a pale drab. The rare hedgerows were drab with dust; the cart-tracks, their ruts moulded into rigid contortions by the drought, were pale as a scree. Not a leaf stirred, so airless was the day. To my right the towers of the château sulked beneath an exhausted sky; in front of me was one of the abrupt pit-like valleys which break from time to time the uplands of the Loire. I reached the lip of the valley— it was rather a large dell than a valley proper, for the distance from edge to edge could not have been above a hundred yards— and saw that a rough track led downward to a copse that filled the stony bottom of the glen. Absent-minded and rather tired with the lack of air, I picked my way downward among the stones and came to the little wood. It seemed at first a place of impressive gloom. But after a few steps I grew accustomed to the dimmer light, and saw that it was little more than a large thicket—a tangle of bramble, thorn and fern, from which elm, oak and a few sycamores grew densely upward.

Because my head was full of the grave problems of language involved in a short story that I was trying to write in French, I walked toward the centre of the copse, conscious of nothing beyond the stony path beneath my feet. Until with a queer start I became aware of a man's hat, lying askew on the dense branches of a thorn. It was a hat of some pretension—of the type affected by the sporting Frenchman—and was certainly accustomed to hang on a decorous peg, rather than lie at hazard on a prickly shrub. This unusual discovery dispelled my absence of mind. I raised my eyes and saw the man to whom, no doubt, the hat belonged. He lay upon a patch of grass that centred the little wood; and he was not alone. For Denise (to judge from the fragmentary glimpse which was all I had of her) was there also.

I was by now sufficiently aware of things to respond to social implications even less obvious than this. Clearly I was better out of the copse and away. I withdrew with scrupulous stealth, and walked home, turning the problem of Denise Hanan in my mind.

ꜱ   ꜱ   ꜱ

I continued to turn that problem in my mind; and I am afraid that, as I turned it, what had been an interesting but detached question of psychology, became an even more interesting and very personal question of possibility. Candidly, Sally, my involuntary intrusion on the privacy of the young lady and her sporting friend had shaken me up and, as they say, put ideas into my head. It was obvious that Denise, though no wayside blossom to be picked by any passer-by, was not, once contact had been made, inhospitable. I realised that another two months of Ronsenac—of Taine and Balzac and the classical dramatists; of the amiable widows with their chatter and their pot-au-feu and their astonishing mastery of sauces; of Dorbon and his political enthusiasms—would be none the worse for a dash of love-making, provided a suitable companion were within reasonable reach. Denise was suitable enough; it was for me to do the rest.

For more than a week I puzzled vainly how to contrive the initial acquaintance. In the end (as so often happens) luck pure and simple solved the problem for me; and luck's agent was, ironically enough, a Roman priest.

A youngish man, large and muscular, with cheeks shaved black and that blend of animal and spiritual which in a Latin priest betrays a peasant origin, the Abbé Delort had for some time shown a readiness for friendship with the English visitor to Ronsenac. I suppose he had a hope of my conversion to his Church; for from time to time he favoured me with his company, and his ambition could hardly for long have been the learning of English. Admittedly he made a tentative suggestion of the kind; but when I resolutely declined to speak English at all, the Abbé's amiability suffered no check. Now and again we walked the lime-avenue together in the evening light; now and again we met chez Dorbon and played the *jeu de quilles*. On one occasion, when there was a great Church fête in Tours, he invited me to spend the day in the city, driving me there in the ancient Peugeot he used for parish work. His

explanations and considerable local knowledge had made the
expedition both interesting and valuable. I came, therefore,
to regard him as an agreeable companion; to look forward to
his rather ceremonious conversation, and to the attractive but
transient smile, which could suddenly lighten his gravity and
disappear again.

One afternoon, on my way to the café from the house in
which I lodged, I fell in with him and stopped naturally to pass
the time of day.

" I wonder if I might ask you to do me a favour? " he said
with diffidence. " I have a commission to execute up at the
château; if you have nothing better to do and would come with
me, I should be grateful and you might be interested."

As you can imagine, I expressed extreme readiness, but failed
to see why I deserved gratitude. He explained that the Hanans
were difficult people, misliked in the town, and into the bargain
obstinate freemasons, who kept pointedly aloof from clerical
intercourse.

" As it happens " he continued " I shall for once be welcome.
A sister of Madame Hanan—who lived in Belgium and was, I
rejoice to say, a true daughter of the Church—has recently
died and entrusted to her own priest a somewhat valuable brooch,
praying him to convey it by safe means to her sister in Ronsenac.
It is my task to deliver it. Priests have strange duties " (the
smile flashed and faded) " even in these reasonable days. For
candidly I am afraid that if I show myself at the gate alone—
even on so secular an errand as this—I shall fail to make anyone
hear, or if I do, I shall suffer some stupid insult. Yes "—as I
glanced at him in astonishment—" it is as bad as that. But
my appearance in company with the famous Englishman . . ."

I laughed.

" Please, M. l'Abbé. Call me the village freak and be done
with it! "

" But, M. Dérainge, I assure you. . . . You have no idea of
the distinction Ronsenac derives from your sojourn. You

should have heard the good Dorbon boasting a week ago to a group of friends in Tours of the fact that our little town had been selected as the best place in the whole of France for an Englishman of the highest breeding to learn our language."

His little black eyes twinkled. He took me by the elbow and urged me gently up the street.

" So you see that curiosity will of itself tempt the famille Hanan, when they see you on their doorstep."

As we climbed the hill and drew near to the château gate, I felt a growing excitement. It was partly the eagerness of a sightseer promised a chance of forcing an obstinate privacy. But partly also—maybe more than partly—it was the prospect of an encounter with Denise. That she would not be visible I refused to believe; my luck could hardly desert me now.

Nor did it. The Abbé pulled the big bell and stalked, with me in his wake, through the tunnelled entrance into the vague untidy space before the château. The clang of the bell had hardly stopped, when Denise appeared round the corner of the building and came towards us to enquire our pleasure.

The Abbé briefly explained his business, bowed with impersonal courtesy and made to pass on. But my own purposes required more drastic action. The moment for enterprise had come. With a courage at which I can still marvel, I raised my hat and asked point-blank whether, while M. l'Abbé transacted his business with Madame, Mademoiselle would have the kindness to show a stranger of keen archæological enthusiasm such portions of the noble castle of Ronsenac as could without impropriety be visited. The Abbé, a good man, found the suggestion excellent, and added his request to mine. If Mademoiselle would oblige the English gentleman . . .

The girl hesitated; then saw, I think, a light other than archæological in my appraising eye. With a quick shrug and a faint mischievous smile, she threw back her head. The proposal was irregular; but of course if Monsieur wished . . .

I took correct leave of the Abbé. " I cannot thank you

enough " I said, " this is an opportunity I had despaired of winning." Then turned and followed in the wake of my charming guide, whose slim ankles and jaunty petticoats were already vanishing beneath a shadowy arch.

During that half hour's inspection of the antique tedium of Ronsenac (it was a sad, barren place inside, that lovely castle, and had been rudely cut about to suit the ideas of comfort and convenience current in the eighteen-nineties) I made good going. I soon found that Mademoiselle Denise responded more readily to personal than to historical comment.   By the time we parted at the courtyard-gate, she had consented to spend an afternoon and evening with me in Tours and, for discretion's sake, to meet me on the bridge that runs across the Loire towards the cathedral.

∽   ∽   ∽

I now felt myself launched with credit on a genuine adventure. Nor did the events of our day's outing lessen my complacency. Denise was excellent company.   She appreciated the quality of meals supplied, the *loge* at the Alcazar, the ices and the drinks with which our excursion was enlivened.   Also she was even more attractive to look at than I had suspected, and possessed what is now called ' sex-appeal ' in such natural plenty, that being with her was a strenuous experience.   She chattered freely of her life in the château; of the Duke; of the Duke's agent, who lived a few miles away but came over frequently (I had a feeling that I knew his taste in hats); of the stuffy limitations of the people of Ronsenac; of her own longings for just such glimpses of a larger life as I—in my generous courtesy—was giving her. In short she played her part to perfection; and by the time I got home—what with her physical loveliness, her mental agility and her discreet but potent flattery—I was happily convinced that a beautiful girl was ready to fall head over heels in love with me.

Before   parting,   we   discussed   future   arrangements.   It appeared that to meet in or about Ronsenac would be unwise, but for social rather than family reasons. Madame Hanan, I gathered, was not the obstacle.

" Maman has no prejudices " declared the young lady, with a candour that to infatuated ears rang charmingly, " but those cats below in the town are on the watch for trouble. Already they have tried to make papa's position impossible."

" How—impossible? "

" With the Duke " she replied. " There are several who would like the château in their charge."

" And the Duke would listen to gossip? "

She shrugged her shoulders.

" He is a proud man, and would waste no time over the rights and wrongs of humble folk."

" When does he come again? " I ventured to enquire.

With impudent agility she evaded my question:

" Who knows? Any time it is possible. But M. Nicholas need not be interested. Has he not seen the castle—such as it is? "

ᔕ   ᔕ   ᔕ

For three or four weeks my life at Ronsenac went pleasantly on its way. Reading, writing and talking were enlivened by frequent meetings with Denise, much nonsensical talk and a growing freedom of caress. Then one day the Touraine branch of the League of Republican Youth, or some equally comic organisation for patriotic junketing, announced by poster and hand-bill the holding of a great costume-ball in Tours. The event would take place ten days hence, on the evening of a local anniversary of unforgettable importance, every detail of which has left my memory. At my next rendezvous with Denise, I convinced her without difficulty that the chance was too good to miss. We too would make a day and half a night of it.

I proceeded to all manner of elaborate arrangements. I

hired a costume of the Murger order—wide trousers, short tight coat, slouch hat.   I felt that, as a Romantic of the best period, I could with credit play the Romantic of a more prosaic age.   I bought the dance tickets.   I hired a car to bring us home to Ronsenac at whatsoever hour of the night or early day the League of Republican Youth might pall on us or we on them.   I was determined that this expedition should be a triumph of organisation and masculinity, should prove a worthy climax to these weeks of philandering.

It may be imagined that, as the days passed, I wore myself away with nervous anticipation.   At times everything promised so well that I became quite poetical.   I told myself that two young hearts now fluttered in unison against the time of their love's consummation.   In other words, I should only have to hint at the right moment and we would slip away to some hotel and there (once again poetical) lay eager hands upon an hour of pleasure.   But at other times I was despondent.   From sheer nervousness I should commit some gaffe, so that she turned on me in anger, made a public fool of me, and swung away with the disgusted flounce of petticoats that—as I knew—she could so cruelly contrive.

The day of the fete was the perfection of a mild December. The drought had broken about the middle of November, and there had been rain nearly every day.   But the great anniversary chanced on one of those brief interludes of pale cloudless skies and gentle air, which sometimes precede a plunge into winter. The steam-tramway ran an extra coach, and even with its help could hardly contain the crowd of Republicans—some very Youthful, some just Youthful, some not Youthful at all—who at every stop struggled for admission.   In the city itself the streets were thronged, and the cafés (which had ventured on a partial re-opening of their terraces) hardly showed a vacant seat.   Denise and I had the temerity to argue that, on such a day as this, the bistros of the old town would tend to be deserted in favour of the Rue Nationale, the Place du Palais Justice and the adjacent Boulevards. But although we did at last find a corner in a small café off the Place Pluméreau, it was evident that, if slumdom had turned elegant, elegance had gone slummy. Or perhaps the temporary clients of the old town were as much concerned to avoid chance encounters as we were. Anyway they were very numerous and very gay.

By the time we left the café, it was quite dark; and in a new mood of cheerful bravado we set out to the fair. We wandered among the booths; sampled the roundabouts; bet on the guinea pigs, who were spun on a disc and, when the movement stopped, bolted into one or another of the ten numbered doorways which surrounded them. Then had another drink. Then settled to an excellent dinner. By this time Denise was affectionate and flushed and generally more enchanting than ever. With the rakish and slightly alcoholic dignity of one to whom no daring could come amiss, I escorted her to the small hotel where (most respectably) we had secured two rooms in which to change for the ball. Leaving her there, I went to the near-by garage and saw that the car was ready; ordered it to be at the hotel in half an hour, and, returning, tackled my fancy dress. By nine o'clock we were but one item in a crowded hall of dancers. My adventure had entered on its last and most dramatic stage.

∽　　　∽　　　∽

By midnight, what with heat and noise and the continual provocation of Denise in my arms, I felt that the League of Republican Youth had served its purpose. I had already from time to time murmured into my partner's ear. She had laughed, or from under lowered lids flashed one of her devastating glances, or pretended pouting disapproval. At last—and quite firmly—I told her it was time to go. She submitted prettily, and we were soon at the entrance to the dance hall, pleasantly conscious of the cold night air. I put an arm around her. We would slip back to our little hotel—for an hour, for two hours. The car should wait for us by the bridge. No one would see us.

But she shook her head, and stood there biting her lip and with eyes cast down.   Then suddenly:

"Let us go back at once" she whispered.   "Back to the château.   A hotel room would be horrible.   Up at the château . . ."

And she clung to my arm, her head pressed against my shoulder in what seemed a delicious confusion of modesty and wantonness.

It was no time for making difficulties.   Her ordinary clothes and mine must stay where they were.   I could fetch them later in the day, or the next day even.   We climbed into the darkness of our car; and in a state of suspended excitation travelled the long pale road to Ronsenac.

I stopped the car before it reached the *bourg*.   Denise knew a field way to the castle, and to clatter through the sleeping village at such an hour would be obvious folly.   The elderly chauffeur relished his tip, and promised to call at the hotel and leave a message about our things.   He was a fatherly old soul, but not too old for mischief.   "Bon appétit, mes enfants" he said with a broad wink.   Then backed his car, and started on his return journey.

Hand in hand, Denise and I stole through grass and over muddy tracks.   Although it was a moonlit night, the darkness was quite sufficient to make progress hazardous.   I thought of Rodolphe and his fellow Bohemians of the eighteen-thirties. They were no doubt very splendid fellows; but I questioned their efficiency at country walks.   Their style of costume would have proved at once hampering and insufficient.   Their shoes would have been lamentably thin; their wide trousers a lure to every thorn.   By the time we reached the château, I was dishevelled and a little out of breath.   Also my feet hurt. But the glory of adventure shone ahead, and in pursuit of it no romantic of my age must falter.   Also, thank heaven, at least it was not raining.

At the castle gate Denise cautioned me to walk softly.   We
E 2

crept across the outer yard, and turned the corner to the caretaker's quarters. The door opened quietly. The kitchen was
hot, thick with cooking smells and very dark; but she guided
me skilfully past every obstacle and up a spiral stair, with treads
worn hollow by generations of climbers less cautious and more
heavily shod. At the top was a short corridor, with the moonlight shining faintly on a strip of drugget laid on bare boards.
We reached an open door, into which Denise with a backward
glance beckoned me to follow her. The room was pitch black.
I heard the door close very gently behind me and Denise'
fingers on my arm.

" Stand still a moment. I will make a light."

A match spurted, burnt blue and pungently, and then flared.
I saw Denise' profile, and her fingers busy with the wick of a
small table lamp. Then a dim but steady flame showed me
the room.

It was high but not very large. There was a double bed, a
washstand, a wardrobe with a mirror-door, a square of carpet
on a polished floor. Over a chair lay some tumbled clothes,
and odds and ends of toilet trivialities were scattered on furniture
and mantelpiece. I had just realised the tremendous truth
that I was in Denise' own room and that she had brought me
there, when she flung her arms round my neck, pressed her body
hard against mine and drew me down to her eager lips.

The next half hour neither permits nor merits description.
The same as every other half hour of its kind, it was yet utterly
different, because it belonged to me and to Denise and not
those two lovers or to those or those. When it was over and
we lay in lassitude, she fell quietly asleep. For a few moments
I struggled with fatigue, the more thoroughly to relish the
doings of the day. But all to no purpose. In the faint light
of the lamp the ceiling billowed unsteadily; shadows crept
upward from the corners of the room. Just as they met over
my head in a dark canopy, I slipped into oblivion.

ᔐ   ᔐ   ᔐ

When I awoke, it was with an uncanny completeness. With a sort of silent click, I became as wholly aware of what was going on as, a moment before, I had been unaware. The light in the room had moved also; whereas the little lamp on the table had burned steadily, the light now shining flickered and swung. I was lying on my side, the bed-clothes hunched high about my ears and my face turned away from the centre of the bed toward the wall of the room. The wardrobe was exactly in my line of vision, and in the tall mirror of its door I saw a strange sight. Denise was sitting up in her place, her hair hanging loose, her slim body a dusky olive in the uncertain light. Facing her from beyond the end of the bed was a short stout woman, with hair in a tight knob at the back of an aggressive head. She wore a dark blouse and apron, and carried a flaring candle in her hand. As I watched, I saw her frame silent words to the girl who drooped so pale and yet so attentive by my side. What was said I could not divine, but Denise nodded gently, and it seemed that the forbidding figure at the bed-end turned and looked in my direction.

What was afoot? To the obvious explanation that two defaulting children had been caught red-handed by an outraged mother, there was the strong objection of Denise' serenity. No daughter, whose mother had surprised her naked in bed with a strange youth, would normally retain such evident unconcern. There remained—as alternative solution—the alarming thought that I was the victim of a plot; and on this point I was not long left in doubt. I saw the old woman move; and the next moment (she covered those intervening yards at record speed) the clothes were twitched roughly from my grasp and I was harshly shaken by the shoulder. With elaborate pretence (I doubt I over-acted it) I struggled to wakefulness, twisted myself on one elbow, and surveyed the scene with sleepy bewilderment. As I did so, I can swear that Denise smiled—a little secret smile, that fluttered the corners of those lovely lips and made them venomous. Then the old woman spoke. Her torrent of words broke over my now terrified head. Disgrace—seduction—violation of a sacred hearth—honest and trusting folk betrayed by a licentious Englishman—so it went on, until in a calmer moment I might have wondered whether Madame Hanan were not the best teacher of French rhetoric in all Touraine. But humorous reflection was the last indulgence for which I felt inclined. I was caught like a rat in a trap. What in the name of Heaven was to happen now? To the old woman's tirade I made no reply. My knowledge of French seemed to have oozed away with my power of efficient thought, and anyway I was hardly in a position to argue, even in English. I just sat and stared at her. A pretty pair we must have made—Denise and I—propped there side by side, both silent, both mother-naked, the girl so wickedly at ease, the youth struck dumb by fright.

At last I found courage and sufficient French to ask the old woman what she proposed to do next. Unwisely she broke into fierce threats of vengeance. She would fetch her husband, her sons; they would teach foreign pigs to soil the whiteness of French innocence. This mistaken violence did more to restore my composure than any other treatment could have done. I knew that she had no sons; I knew also that my mistress' skin was considerably clearer than her innocence. The situation was only too intelligible. A hook had been baited with a wanton girl, and I had greedily swallowed both bait and hook. But the distressing fact remained that I was in my captor's hands. What could I do? The answer was, presumably, in terms of cash.

With a fair assumption of self-possession, I enquired whether the old lady objected to my getting out of bed.

" I am naked " I said " but what is nakedness to the mother of mademoiselle? "

This angered them; and the hag yammered at me, while Denise, snatching at a wrap, slipped out of bed and crouched with bitter looks in the far corner of the room. Then the old woman turned with cold abruptness from insult to business. The outraged modesty of family life must be compensated for its suffering.   On the other hand she could make excuses for the hot-headedness of youth.   She had no desire to tarnish the traditional courtesy of France by a demand brutal or unreasonable.   What did I say to two thousand francs?   To two thousand francs I said something indelicate.   What, then, did I suggest?   I estimated at one hundred francs the pleasure-value of mademoiselle's complaisance.   One hundred!   The old witch waved the candle in her horrified surprise.   Did I imagine that I could blaspheme against the gods of French domesticity, and then placate them for a paltry hundred francs? One thousand was the very least that could persuade her not to make public the wrong that she had suffered.   And once the story was out, monsieur—for all that he was a dirty Englishman and thought the world his playground—might find himself in trouble of which the end could not be foreseen.

I rose my offer to two hundred; then to five.   But she was adamant.   Try how I would, I could not beat her down below one thousand francs.   She was in a strong position and knew it; I was in no position at all and knew it equally.   One thousand francs was an inconvenient sum to pay (in those days, remember, the franc was only a little lower than its now vanished par), and I had a feeling that the entry would not look too well on the expenses account which Uncle Nick would certainly expect and have a right to see.   But the results of non-payment would be more inconvenient still.   The prospect of a public scandal was frankly intolerable.   Suppose the Duke were dragged in? He might care little enough for the Hanans or even for the sanctity of the French home; but he would almost certainly resent his private castle being used as a love-market for foreigners.   In his angry wake would come a subservient gendarmerie and a suitably outraged population.   And then there were my English relatives, who would be shocked and grieved to their most secret core by the very possibility of one of the family being mixed up in such a disgraceful escapade. And last, but by no means least, there was Uncle Nick. If he were likely to jib at an extravagance, he would do more than jib at public exposure of his protégé. He would stand defenceless against my mother's quite natural wrath; and his fury with me would be, in part resentment at being himself let down, in part contempt for my own greenhorn gullibility. It would mean the end of Uncle Nick, so far as I was concerned; and I had the honesty in this moment of crisis to admit to myself that I should deserve everything I got. I had played the vain, sensual fool, and nò amount of gloss could make my excursion into gallantry anything but a profligate incompetence.

So I accepted the inevitable and, looking no doubt as much the beaten puppy as I felt, mumbled agreement to the demand of Madame Hanan. She should have her money. But she must let me dress and leave the castle, before she could be paid. She laughed roughly. Did I take her for a fool? Certainly not, I replied with careful courtesy; but Madame must not be unreasonable. If she were to search my clothes, she would find that I had perhaps fifty francs left over from the jaunt of the previous day. Would she permit me to dress myself? Then we could discuss ways and means. After a whispered consultation with Denise, the old creature declared she would lock me into the room for ten minutes. During that time I must devise some method of getting the money into her hands without myself leaving them. " And " she added, as she shepherded her daughter into the corridor, " I will have my own plan also, in case that of monsieur is not practicable."

The lock snapped and a bolt was shot on the outside. I began to dress hastily, my wits in desperate activity. At all costs I must shut the mouth of this revolting old woman. But how in the world could I get money from the Villa Coralie, without either fetching it myself or throwing my friendly widows into a dangerous flutter of curiosity? Could I write them a note? But who would deliver it, and not set them asking

all manner of questions? Could I appeal to the Abbé? I
should have to make a clean breast of the whole affair to him
and throw myself on his mercy. Not a pleasant prospect, but
any other would be worse. As I finished putting on that
damned fancy dress—feeling, I think, more of an utter fool
than ever before or since—I had more or less made up my
mind that the Abbé was the only hope. Denise could go and
fetch him with any one of a dozen excuses. Sunk in terrified
misery, I wandered aimlessly across the room and, hardly
knowing what I was doing, pulled aside the window curtain.
Behind the curtain the panes were closely shuttered, but I
managed to let down the bar and open one fold. I peered out
into the night, and for the first time there crept into my mind
the idea of escape. I suppose I had been too crushed even to
consider the possibility of flight; besides which, supposing I
had considered it, what conceivable chance should I have of
getting away from an upper room in the huge mass of Ronsenac
castle? But now, as I say, the idea came upon me; for what I
saw from the window showed that luck might not altogether
have deserted me.

The moon was still visible above the hill and, as I pressed
my face against the glass, I could see clearly—and quite close
to my eyes—the delicate filigree of a flèche in keen black
silhouette against the silvery dark. How I blessed those days
I had spent here and there on the hill-side, those scrutinies of the
castle from every angle of approach! Thanks to them (and
to the miracle of moonlight) I now knew exactly where I was
and—better still—that there was at least a possibility of escape.

For there was only one flèche at Ronsenac. It capped the
spiral outside-staircase which adjoined the short stretch of
renaissance building, and I had always studied it with affectionate
care as being the only frivolous member of a grim family of
mediæval towers. I knew every detail of it, as also of the
balustraded stair which it adorned.

If you imagine the famous outside-stair at Blois reproduced

with less elaboration and in miniature, you will have a fair idea of the staircase of Ronsenac. You will also realise that to an active youth such a spiral, with its intricate open-work, its crockets and its carved balustrading, would offer a negotiable, if difficult descent. Here, at any rate—difficult though it might be—lay the only way to freedom.

I began cautiously to clamber over the window-sill, and soon as heartily thanked the costume of the bearded thirties as, shortly before, I had cursed it. The low heelless shoes, the neat short coat, the trousers which, for all their bagginess, were tight at the ankles, were a much better uniform for roof-climbing than modern dress. There was an awkward moment as I felt feverishly for foot-hold among the crockets of the flèche. It was necessary to trust my weight for one moment to these doubtful friends, while I swung myself from the window-sill and clutched the slim spire in my arms. And indeed only the fact that desperation gave me speed saved me from falling. The first crocket snapped beneath my feet, which slid down a rough space of roof but caught just long enough on the knob below to give my hands time to take firm hold upon the flèche. Thereafter was little difficulty. Over the curving balustrade I lowered myself cautiously; once on the stone staircase I ran with silent speed into the court below, straddled the wall that topped the castle-cliff, and began to scramble down the rocks and grass to safety. Once again my hours of scrutiny stood me in good stead. Many a time I had amused myself by plotting out routes by which scaling parties might make combined assault upon the castle. These surveys were my saving now. Certainly the cliff was anything but sheer, nor was its total height tremendous; but there were steep places, the tufts of grass were slippery, and in the darkness (the moon had plunged behind the hill and dawn was still two or three hours away) an ignorant fugitive would surely have fallen dangerously. But as it was—and apart from one bad slip, which strained an ankle, and slightly bruised an arm—I got safely to the bottom. I turned my back on the Château of Ronsenac and limped for home.

~   ~   ~

And then what? Hustle then, Sally, and hard thinking and plenty of both. I was back in my room at the Villa Coralie by about four o'clock. By half past five I had packed everything I possessed; changed my clothes; tied up Rodolphe, razor, toothbrush and a couple of handkerchiefs in a paper parcel, and decided on what seemed the only possible course of action. I must get out of Ronsenac, and at once. I was not afraid of further direct trouble from the Hanans, who, when they lost control of me, lost control of their only evidence. But I could not envisage staying longer in a place where I had been so thoroughly fooled. Every glimpse of the castle would have set me squirming. And there was always a danger of gossip which, if it led to nothing but suppressed smiles and occasionally a gross word shouted in the street, would soon make existence insupportable. Besides I might meet Denise face to face, and she was not one to control herself out of consideration for my feelings. No; from every point of view I had to leave Ronsenac with the least possible delay. But there was my luggage, and there were the widows. Tours was a long way off; the tramway did not run before seven o'clock, by which time the owners of the Villa would be up and about. I could think of no excuse with even a reasonable chance of acceptance, for a sudden determination to leave by the seven o'clock tram, complete with trunk and rug and box of books. And I could not create too sudden a suspicion of crisis in the minds of the widows. They were quite capable of writing in shocked dismay to Professor Lacombe; and he though a wise old man, knew my home address and might, with the best intention in the world, send out the alarm that I had disappeared.

All the time I was packing I thought the problem up and down.

Finally, I chose what seemed, not a good solution, but the best of a bad lot. I would—after all—go to the Abbé, and ask him to help me.

It was a quarter to six when I knocked him up. He was already dressed and showed little surprise when he found me on his threshold. I had heard tell of the amazing quality of composure possessed by priests of the Catholic Church, who must be prepared to hear all manner of terrible and unexpected things and show only such disapproval as their duty bids them. I had banked on finding this quality in the Abbé Delort, and I was not disappointed. I told him the whole story—not in great detail, but accurately. I said nothing to exonerate myself, nor wasted time on denunciation of the Hanans.

" You will see, M. l'Abbé " I concluded " that I must leave Ronsenac at once. I have come to ask you to drive me to Tours *now*; then on my behalf to settle with the ladies G. and R. and finally to see to the despatch of my luggage. I have no claim on you to justify these troublesome demands, except that there is no one else who can help me and that it is better for Ronsenac, as well as for me, that this wretched affair be as quickly forgotten as possible."

He sat quite motionless during my story, his always swarthy face blacker than ever for being unshaven, his eyes fixed steadily on me. When I had finished, he got up and reached for his heavy coat.

" I will get the car " he said " and pick you up at the second bend down the road. If you walk quickly across the fields behind this house, we shall arrive there about the same time."

∽   ∽   ∽

In the corner of the station-café at Tours, we swallowed hot coffee and felt the cold of that early drive slowly ooze out of us. On the way in we had hardly spoken. I had reckoned in my head how much I owed at the Villa Coralie, and how much I should have owed had I stayed out the remaining fortnight of my time.   To these sums I now added an additional amount as a Christmas present to my deserted widows, and a generous estimate of the personal expense in which I had involved the Abbé.

Handing him the total, I explained its composition.

" And I would like, as a very small return for the great service you have done me, to ask you to accept these further two hundred francs for any purpose of the Church which you have at heart."

He gathered up the money with a word or two of thanks.

" I must be getting back " he said.   " I will devise some suitable explanation of your non-return last night from Tours. The trunk and other things had better not be sent by tramway. They would attract notice.   I will bring them this evening about six o'clock and leave them here in the station cloak-room. The ticket, in an envelope, with your name on it, I will give to the gérant of this café who is a friend of mine.   If you come about seven, he will be on duty behind the bar.   And now I must bid you—I should like to say ' au revoir ' but in the circumstances . . ."

" M. l'Abbé " I said, grasping his hand, " I shall not try to say how grateful I am.   Merely—thank you.   The last thing I have deserved is to find such a friend."

He smiled his fleeting smile.

" After all, M. Dérainge, it was I who took you into the château, who—to all intents—led you into temptation.   It is natural that I should help you to get out.   Besides, as I have said before, priests have strange duties.   Goodbye, M. Dérainge, and thank you for your offering to Holy Church.   Perhaps in time you will come to have some pleasant memories of Ronsenac."

His powerful figure, with soutane flapping below the skirts of an ungainly overcoat, crossed the broad road in front of the station to where the shabby old car slumped against the curb.

When, late that night, (for the Abbé was as good as his word and delivered my luggage according to plan) I limped up and down the platform of S. Pierre des Corps waiting for the express that should take me south to Angoulême, I realised that my good fortune at Ronsenac had been as undeserved as my ill-fortune in Berlin. At every stage of the *affaire Denise* I had acted with vanity or recklessness. I had thought to condescend to her, to play the man of experience choosing a pretty toy. Toward Ruth on the other hand, I had felt an adoring humility, which may have looked foolish but was at least genuine. I had looked up to Ruth, who from her pedestal had stooped and smiled at me; then bidden me climb and stand at her side; then tempted me; then (and in public) smacked my face. Denise also had tempted me, using her body for purposes of gain. But at least she had given what she offered; and I had only to recall her bright treacherous eyes and the generous skill of her love-making to admit that, though I had fallen among thieves and nearly lost much of my money and all my self-importance, I had had knowledge from her and delight. Of the two—Ruth, the respectable, who cheated even in cheating; Denise, the harlot, who played a dirty game but at any rate played it—I preferred Denise.

So much so, that by next day I told myself she should at least have had her little present. I had myself fixed the amount, but (in effect) welshed on her. From Angoulême, therefore, I posted her a mandat for one hundred francs.

VII: SKIRMISHING

I REACHED England just before Christmas, having worked out the unexpired portion of my French sojourn here and there between Limoges and the Pyrenees. In January I was to report to Uncle Nick, who had returned to Mexico shortly after my departure to Berlin and was now not only due back in England, but actually—and by invitation—coming to stop at our house. The influence of the Army and Navy Stores on his relationship with my mother had certainly been remarkable.

Christmas was great fun. Geoffrey had moved over from editorial activity to advertising; and the problem of making one's publications alluring in the smallest possible space seemed agreeably to have affected his own deportment. I suppose that the job of writing letters of rejection tends to embattle one against a world of pestilent authorship, whereas the "come hither" mentality of the copy-writer has just the opposite effect. In any event he was much more pliable and forthcoming than I remember him; and we laughed and gorged and paper-hatted our way through the traditional jollifications of an English Christmas without any of the tetchiness which had previously thwarted our intimacy.

My mother was more stimulating than I had ever known her. She had always a gift for tart humour, and on this occasion made admirable play with it. As often as not it took the form of making fun of me, which in the past I had frequently and uneasily disliked, but now not at all. I remembered thinking that she, no less than Geoffrey had somehow become "easier". Not till afterwards did I appreciate that the alteration was more in me than in either of them. I was growing up; and although I still retained the youthful conviction that my own personality was the unchanging pivot of its little world, and that the success or failure of its impacts with other people depended on their behaviour and not at all on mine, I had undoubtedly mellowed a little, and to the advantage of everyone concerned.

And I noticed another thing also. Among the girls we met at parties or dances, there were several who seemed less intimidating and more approachable than they used to be. I had known most of them before—a few since childhood—but even those I knew best struck me as subtly different. In this matter I had an inkling that the change was not all on their side. But my glimmer of perception was solely from my own angle of vision. It never occurred to me that I could seem different to them. I was merely aware that I appraised them more thoroughly than in the past, and why I did so. After all, my traffic with Ruth and with Denise, ill-starred though it had been, had taught me things about feminine physique and its possibilities of which earlier I had had only theoretical knowledge. So quite consciously I tended to assess my young women acquaintances by standards more structural than formerly. Indeed, to put it crudely, I looked them over in detail, took the initiative in conversation and, when dancing, held them with firmness and competence. They seemed to like it.

But there was a line beyond which was " going too far ", and evidently on one occasion I over-stepped it. Sitting out a late-extra at a big dance in the Corn Exchange I kissed my partner in what I must presume was the wrong way. She was a tempting thing; her dress did her full justice, and earlier in the evening she had exploited two waltzes to excellent effect. But I forgot that kissing a ' nice girl ' at an English subscription dance was not the same thing as kissing under the auspices of the League of Republican Youth in Tours. She thought herself insulted, and smacked my face.

The incident demonstrated with admirable clarity what appears an ineradicable tendency of Anglo-Saxon maidenhood— to go all out for allurement, but to resent the consequences.

Nowadays one is invited to relish all manner of calculated immodesties, and great offence is taken if one is not duly grateful. (Indeed, the adornments of any bathing beach can only be explained on the assumption that men have an inexhaustible appetite for semi-nudity and boiled silverside; whereas, as a matter of fact, they are content with quite moderate helpings of both.) On the other hand, if one really *is* grateful and proceeds accordingly, the next scene may be a police court, so virtuously indignant are many amateur strippers at being taken for professionals.

Some time during January Uncle Nick arrived. My mother and he were on the best of terms. Certainly they sparred with one another; but it was sparring for sparring's sake and not the manœuvring of two instinctive hostilities. One day he took me to town with him, and at lunch introduced me to a German business acquaintance. This man spoke very little English, Uncle Nick next to no German, and I supposed my duty was to act as intermediary between them over the lunch table. This elementary test of my capacity (which Uncle Nick had presumably thought out very carefully) amused me a little.

Amusement was premature. After lunch the host rose briskly:

" And now, young man " he said. " You can begin to be useful. Herr Beck is very interested in the history of London and wishes to view in detail the museum in Lancaster House. I am busy this afternoon, so thought of you as an efficient guide. Herr Beck kindly suggests you dine with him this evening, and I shall not see you again till you get home—maybe not till tomorrow morning."

He shook hands warmly with his German guest, patted me lightly on the shoulder and departed.

That was an afternoon! The Germans are naturally a pertinacious and enquiring people, but Herr Beck was a phenomenon even among Germans. We started blithely enough, walking along the Mall and exchanging small talk about the Admiralty Arch and the Brandenburger Tor, the contrast between Carlton House Terrace and the buildings in the Wilhelmstrasse. I even toyed with the idea of telling my companion what old Lady Cork said when they put up the Duke of York's column; but I was none too sure of my phraseology, and not sure in the least how the story would go. Then came the London Museum, and the real work of the day. It was terrific. As I began to tire, my more distant memories of German became inextricably tangled with recent memories of French. I was, however, now bitterly aware that Uncle Nick was neither naïve nor lax. He meant to put me through it, and through it I was determined to go. So I fought my increasing fatigue; stuck to the insatiable Herr Doktor; and talked and translated and summarised and paraphrased till my tongue was parched and my head reeling.

But bondage ended as suddenly as it had begun. About half past five, with the instantaneous change-over from intellectual concentration to Stamm-Tisch jollity for which the German has so grand a capacity, Herr Beck threw back his large head, stuck out his chest and demanded beer. By six o'clock we were in the basement of the old Gambrinus, with tankards of the largest size and a considerable platter of sausage and ham and gherkins. My tired mind quickly revived. The Herr Doktor told endless stories of his student days. He was the dearest person, and I made all manner of promises to call on him when next in Berlin.

We had been in Gambrinus about an hour, when I recognised one of a trio of young men who had just come in. He was a lad I had met in Toulouse just before returning to England, a cheerful, rather raffish being, with whom I had had one or two parties. I begged the Herr Doktor to excuse me a moment, and crossed the room to greet the newcomer.

" Monsieur Loxley " I said over his shoulder. " How goes it ? "

" Well, well " he cried, twisting round in his seat. " If it isn't Dering! Jolly to see you again. Sit down and have one."

" I can't do that. I am in charge of an important Teuton and must go back. But let's meet some time. Are you in town for good ? "

" Both for good *and* evil, old boy. I am starting on a business career, and damned dull it is. But there are evenings. Look here, come and stop a night next week. My people will be away and we'll do a show or something."

The date was fixed, and I returned to my post of duty. The Herr Doktor told one more story, drained a final tankard and announced that he was ready for dinner.   He had been told of a good German restaurant, and thither we went.   I soon realised that the day was as likely to be as remarkable for digestive as for mental strain.   The good man rubbed his hands with such gusto over the Speisekarte that I hastened to plead for something modest, both in kind and quantity.   But his hospitable soul was determined to repay my services in good sustaining German fare, and he proceeded to order accordingly.   It was all excellent, but the amount was staggering.   When at last he bade me a boisterous farewell at the door of his hotel, I was sated with food and talk and heat and noise.   I slept in the train going home, and for most of the next day slumped unhappily.   The day following, Uncle Nick had a letter from his German friend, and congratulated me on having pleased the Herr Doktor alike as guide and companion.   So in German, at any rate, I had qualified; I looked forward to my finals in French with comparative cheerfulness, wondering idly when they were to be.

I had not long to wait.   I think it was the very day after Herr Beck had written his letter of commendation that my Uncle informed me we were going to Paris for two days on the following Wednesday.   He had business there and needed assistance. Now I had arranged to spend the Wednesday night with Ted Loxley and, with a candour which showed I had still plenty to learn, stated the fact, as though it were something of an obstacle to my Uncle's plan.   He looked at me for a moment, with eyebrows slightly lifted:—

" See here, Nick " he said.   " Please get this.   You are no longer a college boy on the loose, nor are you yet your own master.   You're coming to Paris on Wednesday because it's part of your job to do so; and even if you had dated up half a dozen Senators instead of merely another kid like yourself, you would still be putting them off.   Is that clear? "

Wednesday night found us in Paris, and Thursday morning brought me face to face with my individual duty.   This was nothing less than to accompany Uncle Nick to a meeting with the board of directors of a French oil combine, at which a contract was to be arranged. I had to expound his views to them and interpret their counter-proposals. The conference lasted from ten to one and was resumed after lunch for a further three hours. The technicalities were on several occasions too much for me, and I admitted it frankly. But this Uncle Nick did not seem to mind. He knew enough of those himself; it was the more general phraseology of the various clauses which he wanted to understand. At about six the gathering broke up. My Uncle explained that he was attending a dinner offered by the French group, and desired me to spend the evening preparing an English version of the agreement and a summary of the minutes of the meeting. This he would go over on his return from the banquet.

I presented my document about midnight, and for nearly two hours we went over it word by word. At ten the following morning we returned to the scene of yesterday's meeting. My Uncle signed the contract and received a counterpart from the French company. We caught the noon train back to London.

∽   ∽   ∽

It was curious how my relationship with Uncle Nick had become that of a promising but still probationary secretary to his business chief. My Uncle was gay and familiar as ever in off moments; but directly there was any question of my helping with his work or his private engagements, he became authoritarian and impersonal. At first I felt a little injured that he never acknowledged my assiduity in Paris. But gradually I came to realise that, when he was concentrating on his job, he regarded me as an employee whose time and industry were his to command. I had the frankness to admit to myself that he was perfectly right; so I soon lost all sense of injury, and found myself getting interested in that margin of his activities which was my province, as well as full of admiration for the speed and efficiency of his mind.

Then one day he called me into the room which my mother had given him as a study, and for the first time began to talk futures. He said, with a warmth which made me glow with pleasure, that the experiment of sending me abroad had justified itself; that he thought we could get along with one another; that I could be useful to him in his work, and he to me in offering a chance of a career. Was I willing? It meant America of course—Mexico and the United States—but my mother had given consent for the offer to be made, and here it was.

" Uncle Nick " I said, " it's the best thing that ever happened to me. I'd love it."

He seemed pleased. But it was not his way to let pleasure go unalloyed, and he hastened to put a break on my enthusiasm.

" Wait a minute. We are not racing off to Liverpool next week. At least you are not. I can't do with you immediately, and there are plenty of things you must learn before you really get on to the job. My plan is that you go to London for a few months, and by serious study get a line on what oil means and is. I have details of classes you can attend, and there is reading enough to occupy years. Also you will also learn the town; and in my sort of business, the more one knows about all kinds of big towns and the people who live in them, the better. London seems to me something of a back-number; but then I'm a tourist and tourists see nothing. It's a hell of a great city anyway, and all great cities have their lessons to teach. Then in the fall you can cross over, and we'll see what we can make of you. Is it a deal? "

VIII: THE LADY ANONYMA

B Y the beginning of February I was in rooms in Bloomsbury. Three times a week I attended lectures—also a seminar at the Imperial College in South Kensington—acquiring what I hoped were the rudiments of oil technology. The rest of the time I read, and struggled with charts and graphs and equations and whatnot, in my comfortable but slightly gloomy lodgings. Occasionally in the evening I went out with Geoffrey or with one of the various acquaintances I already had or now proceeded to make. I went home for week-ends. I was, in fact, a perfectly ordinary young Englishman preparing to earn his living, with the special good fortune that I had a job waiting for me and a job of unusual interest and possibility.

I want to stress the ordinariness of my life and status, because it throws into relief the peculiarity of the adventure which befell me. Before that bizarre adventure took place I was one of a thousand others. After it had happened I was no less commonplace. The thing itself was merely a fantastic deviation from the path of probability. My personality had nothing to do with it. By pure chance it was I who made a brief and anonymous excursion into the secret places of a stranger's life. But it might equally well have been he, or he, or he. . . .

∽   ∽   ∽

Until this moment I have never breathed a word of this affair to anyone. Obviously, for long enough after it happened, silence was compulsory. When the war was over and a new epoch seemed to have begun, there might have been little harm in discreet recital. But somehow I never cared enough for anyone to confide in him—until you were there. And when you were there, it was waste of time to talk about the past. But now you also are the past, and I am obeying your request to record everything relevant which led up to you, every stage in that moulding process to our brief period of happiness.

Even now I have hesitated as to whether or no the affair really ranked among my formative experiences. My feeling was that it was something so outside myself, that it could hardly claim to have contributed toward my romantic education. But on second thoughts I was less certain. The episode may have had no direct influence; but it dispelled one particular illusion, and made me conscious of personal advantages in the casual contacts of life. And then, on third thoughts, I saw myself writing it all down with solemn complacency for you, of all people, to read. That decided me. We always enjoyed making fools of ourselves to one another; and I would go on enjoying it, until this—our final tête-à-tête—was ended.

                 ∽   ∽   ∽   ∽

It was my custom to lighten my studies of oil technology with reading of a more frivolous kind. This reading I obtained from the most convenient circulating library—in those days the central depot of Mudies, close to the British Museum and within a few minutes of my lodgings. You do not know London, so that ' New Oxford Street ' can have no meaning for you. Never mind. Just take the name for granted. It is sufficient to know that the principal entrance to Mudies was from New Oxford Street, and that there was a side entrance from a narrower street running northward from the main road. The interior of Mudies consisted of a large central hall lined with books, which was the headquarters of the lending library. Around it was an outer fringe of small departments —foreign books, children's books, stationery and the like. Consequently, in order to go from the street to the lending library and to change one's books at the various counters, one had to pass through one or another of the subsidiary departments.

As I went to Mudies fairly often, I soon got on friendly terms with one of the senior assistants—a library clerk of long standing with an amusingly sceptical attitude toward current literature and the reading public, formed by his years of peculiar experience. Conversation with this man came to interest me greatly, and I would wait for him to be disengaged, wandering in the meantime along the open shelves, browsing and sampling their crowded mediocrity.

One day, as I entered the central hall of the library from the side door, my friend was occupied with a lady. I drifted away along the book-lined wall. In a few moments I turned to see if he were at liberty. He had disappeared, and the lady was leaning against the counter. She was half turned in my direction and under the broad brim of her picture hat (women wore picture hats in those days), I had a glimpse of a small face, oval and rather pale. I continued my desultory examination of Mudies' stock. But I was conscious of being watched, and glanced over my shoulder. The lady was looking at me. I contrived to stand at an angle, pretending interest in some book of travel, so that every time I turned a leaf I could see her out of the corner of my eye. All the time she watched me— not brazenly, that would have been bearable, but with a subtlety so discomposing that I had an absurd feeling it would be bad manners to move and worse manners to return her gaze. So I stayed where I was, flicking the pages of my book and wishing that the man I wanted would re-appear and distract his client's attention.

At last he did so, and I could almost hear him apologise for the delay in finding what she wanted. She took her book, gathered up bag and gloves, and walked out of the library toward New Oxford Street. I took her place at the counter.

I suppose it was five minutes later that I left the library and, wanting some ink, went to the stationery department. I was feeling for my money before I became aware of someone standing beside me at the same counter. It was the lady of the library, and she was once again looking at me. I felt an acute embarrassment, due rather to the remoteness of her gaze than to its fixity. It was as though she were looking, not at me, but at something symbolised by me. I seized my parcel, laid a coin on the counter and turned to go. But I was only three steps away when the shop girl called to me. Considerably flustered, and still under the calm scrutiny of those disquieting eyes, I returned. Change? Wasn't the ink a shilling? The girl handed me one and six. " You put down half a crown " she said. I thanked her nervously and turned to escape. My foot

touched something and an umbrella slithered to the floor. I
picked it up, knowing quite well whose it was. The lady
received it with hardly a smile, but she looked at me steadily all
the time I was making my apology. I summoned my courage
and gave her look for look. She was beautiful in the wistful
manner of the Botticelli Venus, and her eyebrows rose in arching
lines. The eyes themselves were like a summer sky in ominous
heat. They were blue; but over the blueness was a shadow
which, though the eyes were cloudless, clouded them. In her
gaze were gravity and self-questioning and an impersonality
which suggested that those eyes, for all that they were busy
with a stranger, were in fact turned in upon herself, searching
her own heart.

By next day I had forgotten my strange encounter, and my
visits to Mudies became once more natural and unimportant.
But about two weeks later, as I entered the library, I saw the
lady standing by the book-case at which I had stood on the
first occasion of my seeing her. She did not notice me, and I
had an opportunity to realise the costly sobriety of her appearance.
But appreciation of her dress soon gave place to interest in her
mood. She seemed greatly agitated. She held her chin high,
and was, perhaps, reading the book-titles on an upper shelf.
But I could see that her lips were trembling, and there was a
tautness in her whole attitude which could hardly be caused by
the problem of choosing something to read. At that moment
she turned her head and saw me. She gave me a steady look,
seemed to stiffen to a determination both timid and reckless,
and walked quickly out of the library.

By now I was more curious than embarrassed. Partly her
evident recognition of me and a suspicion that she had been in
Mudies on purpose, partly instinctive sympathy with one who
must be in distress of mind, impelled me to follow her. You
will, I daresay, not be surprised to hear that she was standing
on the pavement, just outside the main entrance to the shop.
But if you are smiling in anticipation of yet another version of

the old story of an idle woman's fancy for an attractive boy, you are jumping to a false conclusion. I did the same thing, Sally; and you will see, as I came to see, that it wasn't that at all.

ᔕ ᔕ ᔕ

She stood on the pavement, looking uncertainly to right and left. It was the lunch hour, and the streets were crowded with hurrying folk but fairly empty of traffic. A taxi passed on the other side of the street. She waved, but the man did not see and the cab passed on. Once again she looked anxiously about her. I had paused in the doorway of Mudies to watch her, so that when she turned to re-enter the shop we came face to face.

I raised my hat.

" Can I help? Shall I get you a taxi? "

She smiled—quite a different smile from the abstracted flicker with which a fortnight earlier she had accepted her umbrella.

" Thank you so much. It would be very kind. Unless you can recommend me a restaurant. I want my luncheon badly, but I don't know this part of town well."

I took a chance.

" It would give me great pleasure. . . . I know a good place. . . quite close. . . ."

She considered both me and my suggestion.

" That would be charming " she said at last. " You are sure you have the time? "

" Indeed " I said. " I was just going to get lunch myself."

Settled in the restaurant she began to talk gaily. I now realised how carefully impersonal her conversation was, although at the time it went naturally enough. She asked practically no questions and gave no information. I think she enquired whether I lived in this part of town, and I know she spoke of books and reading, and that I confessed to using Mudies mainly for pleasure. But there was a complete lack of curiosity in her conversation which debarred me from even hinting enquiries about herself. She did not ask my name.

Sitting opposite to her, with only the little space of table-cloth between, I learnt more thoroughly the facts of her appearance. Although her skin was fair and her eyes blue (the cloud had lifted and they were now full of sunshine) her hair was dark. She was attractive in a very human way, and her loveliness was neither remotely ethereal nor troubling. By the time the meal was ended, I had lost all sense of strangeness and felt that my hospitality, though fortunate, was normal enough.

" I enjoyed that " she said simply, as we rose to go. " It was kind of you to take pity on a hungry stranger."

On the pavement outside the restaurant I offered to find her a taxi.

" One moment " she said. " I'm thinking how I can return your kindness. You are free sometimes in the evening? "

" Nearly always " I replied, considerably startled.

" Then perhaps you will dine with me one day next week. Shall we say Tuesday? No ceremony. Would it be more convenient for you not to dress? In any case only a black tie."

There was a slight note of command in the manner of her invitation. I bowed, murmuring the suitability of Tuesday. Much as I welcomed it, I admit that this very prompt arrangement for counter-hospitality seemed a little unusual. Our luncheon had been the purest coincidence, and quite an ordinary sort of meal at that. But the prospect of seeing her again was exciting, and I wanted very much to know what happened next. Also I began to feel that I was being complimented, that she liked the looks of me.

She settled her furs round her shoulders and glanced up the street. A taxi was coming slowly towards us.

" Here is one " she said, and as it drew to the curb proceeded with what I can only call her instructions. " I will send the

TFT-E*

car for you.   Is there an underground station near your rooms
where it could pick you up?   At least there would be shelter if
you were kept waiting.   Gower Street Metropolitan?   Very
well, please be there about half past seven, and wear a flower of
some sort in your buttonhole.   Now au revoir, and thank you
again for a very enjoyable meal.   Please tell him to go to
Woollands."

I stood with my hat still in my hand, watching the cab gather
speed and turn a corner at the bottom of the street.   What a
funny affair, I thought.   She does not know the first thing about
me, and evidently does not want to.   Yet she asks me to dinner.
And there was the car, and Gower Street station, and a buttonhole. . . . Pure Oppenheim, except that I was not qualified
even to be a pawn in a game of diplomatic intrigue.   As I
walked back to my rooms I began to wonder whether I looked
forward to next Tuesday after all.   I was still a little flattered,
but at the same time slightly apprehensive.

During the next few days I had severe nervous qualms.   At
times I almost decided I would cut the appointment, dreading
the ridicule which might be involved in the adventure.   I had
no visions of masked ruffians using this friendly lady as decoy,
for why waste decoys on me?   But I might be the victim of a
hoax and it was possible that to dare further would be to risk
my dignity.   Nevertheless the romantic sense, when allied to
personal vanity, is stronger in the male even than that of dignity;
and I always came back to the conviction that, when Tuesday
came, I should keep tryst.

∽   ∽   ∽

For the end of March the night was unusually raw.   A bitter
wind blew down the wide rather desolate street on which my
appointed underground station stands.   I stood outside the
booking-hall with a red carnation in my overcoat, and hoped I
was not visibly shivering.   A sparse crowd of home-goers
flitted under the street-lamps.   To my left, in the glare of

Tottenham Court Road, buses thundered. At Gower Street
the trains run immediately under the pavement, and I could hear
them through the shafts which ventilate the station grinding
in and out of the tunnel. The very pavement seemed to shake.
I felt wrought up, wretchedly cold and conspicuous. Yet not
a soul took any notice of me.

I was once again obsessed by the chances of fiasco. Suppose
the hoax had been already played? Suppose that I was destined to hang about this dingy station—a foolish young man
with a garish buttonhole—until I was weary of the game?
I thanked my own discretion for telling no one of the escapade;
at least my shaming would be private. But at this moment I
heard a voice:—

" The car is waiting, sir."

A uniformed servant stood beside me. With the non-
chalance of one accustomed to wait (complete with buttonhole)
outside an unfashionable underground station on a winter
evening until arrangements were made for his removal, I nodded
graciously. A long black limousine drowsed against the
curb, its bonnet pointing west. The servant held the door. I
jumped inside. The door closed sharply, and I found myself
alone in a luxurious motor-car with every window masked
behind drawn blinds.

We began to slip along the road. There was a check which
meant the crossing of a crowded street. We kept straight on,
and flashes from arc-lights continued to come and go. We
were, so far as I could judge, still travelling west. Then we
turned right, and only the occasional gleam of ordinary pavement lamps shone between the chinks of the blinds. The car
was running silently and well. We turned again and seemed
to slide down hill; then turned and up again. I tried to raise
the blinds, but they were fixed in some way and, fearful of tearing
them (I was impressed despite myself by the sombre elegance of
the vehicle), I hesitated to use force. I next attempted to open
the doors, but both were immovable. Returning to the blinds,

I managed to peep through a chink of window-pane. Only unending houses set back behind stucco garden walls and, planted in front of them, the intermittent lamps.

Lying back on the cushions I now began seriously to wonder what was to happen when we reached our destination. I thought of Sherlock Holmes stories, and the idea of a gang (however unreasonable) began to take possession of me. The conflict would be sadly one-sided. I had an umbrella, a small pen-knife, a fairly inexpert pair of fists, and a physique which, while equal to the normal demands of twentieth century London life, would be a poor ally against a group of desperadoes. I began to regret that I had not learnt ju-jitsu at school, or had not, while at Oxford, been a member of the ' Ashtaroths ', a club which dealt in black magic and claimed to fear no man in history save St Francis of Assisi.

The car stopped suddenly. The door was smartly opened and I stepped out on to the pavement. Immediately in front of me yawned an open door in a high garden wall. The footman was at my side, and skilfully edged me into what seemed a covered passage-way. For a moment I thought of making a dash for liberty. But only for a moment; because the outside door clicked behind me, a light went on, and I found myself standing in a glass-roofed and glass-sided corridor—a kind of elongated conservatory, with flowers in pots and trailing ferns banked on either side and hanging from the roof. At the far end rose a short flight of broad low steps, with at their top what was clearly the front door of the house.

The footman with perfect civility moved ahead, inviting me to follow him. At the head of the steps he rang a bell. The door of the house opened and I passed into a dimly-lighted hall. The rugs were soft beneath my feet; in the air was that faint odour of expensive comfort that hangs about the houses of the opulent.

I gave my hat and coat to a young person who by her ambiguous uniform must surely have been a lady's maid. It seemed odd in this impressive hall to be attended by a lady's maid. The man-servant had disappeared. Presumably he had returned to the car, but I did not recall the closing of the front door.

" Will you come this way, sir, if you please ? "

We went upstairs. Our feet made no sound on the pile carpet. The house was silent as a tomb and nearly as dark, for the hall and staircase were only lit by shaded lamps, set here and there high in the corners of the panelled walls. My guide led the way along a corridor and up another stair. She opened a door, switched on the light and ushered me into a bedroom.

It was a room of medium size, with a bright fire burning, a single bed, pleasant but undistinguished furniture. On the washing stand stood a can of hot water with a cosey over it.

" Madam will expect you in ten minutes, sir. I will come back. I think you will find all that you require. If not, perhaps you would ring. . . ."

She retired, closing the door noiselessly behind her.

My extravagant visions faded to normality. This could hardly be a crook's fortress, nor did it suggest the other extreme —that I had stumbled into a twentieth century Arabian Night. I realised, with a mixture of relief and disappointment, that I was probably neither the victim of a dangerous conspiracy nor a hero of romance. I had been asked to dinner and a car had been sent for me; I had arrived and had been shown upstairs to wash my hands. Actually they did not need washing, for I had decided on a dinner-jacket and was already clean. But my hostess would not know that. She had left the choice to me. In the circumstances it seemed only civil to wash again. I did so, feeling ever more scornful of my own excited fears, and at the same time secretly disgruntled by the arguments of common sense.

The minutes passed. The silence of the house was extraordinary. I pulled aside the blind and peered into the darkness. Below me was a garden, of the kind common to big London houses in certain favoured quarters. I could dimly see the square of lawn, the shrubberies, the bare, stiffly-moving branches of the trees. Beyond the boundary of the garden lay more trees, and then darkness. Only to the extreme left, on the very horizon of my vision, I could see the pale gleam of a few lighted windows, evidence of other houses.

Ten minutes to the second from her vanishing, the maid reappeared. We went downstairs again and along other corridors. Then she stood aside and ushered me into the presence of my hostess, who crossed the rug-strewn boudoir floor with welcoming smile.

" Well " she said, as we shook hands. " So you have got here safely. I hope they gave you all you wanted."

" Everything, thank you."

We moved toward the fire.

" Come and get warm. It is a shame to drag anyone out this bitter night."

We played at small-talk. The lady was perfectly at ease, and seemed unconscious of anything unusual in her guest's presence or in the manner of his coming. Elaborately I trained my voice and manner to the technique of unconcern. I risked a leading question:—

" Do you use Mudies regularly? I do not remember seeing you there before that day, when I knocked down your umbrella."

" No. I hardly ever go. They send out. But I wanted something special and it seemed easier to call. And then my chauffeur misunderstood and left me there. And then you rescued me."

That, I said to myself, is not all of the truth; for I now knew enough of the lady's competence in planning to be sure that she would make her orders to her chauffeur both clear and precise. However I would believe what she wished me to believe, the main thing now being to get on with this mysterious party. In a few minutes the same ambiguous serving-maid announced dinner. As I followed my hostess into the next room, I tried to think out lines of conversation which would lead to a comparison of her way of life and mine. Obviously she meant to keep her anonymity; to attempt to pierce it would be a test of ingenuity.

But over dinner (and a most admirable dinner it was) the situation changed. Whether thanks to the pleasant influence of food and drink, or to the silent luxury of the room and service, or to the strange—and this evening, disturbing—loveliness of my companion, curiosity faded. I no longer wanted to know anything about her save what I could see; I no longer cared who she might be or why I was here. Here we were—the two of us; and when dinner was ended would come the evening.

She sat quite close to me, dressed in a plain black gown which set off the fairness of her throat to most disquieting advantage. I had never seen flesh so delicately pale, yet faintly rosy with the warmth of health. As she raised a wine-glass to her lips, I remembered Mary Stuart's legendary loveliness, and almost looked to see the red glow of the wine shine through transparency as she drank it down. I think I sat through the meal in a growing drowse of wonder at her whiteness.

" We will have coffee in the other room " she said, and led me to the boudoir where she had first greeted me. Coffee and liqueurs stood ready at the sofa end.

" Perhaps you would help yourself. I must ask you to excuse me for a few moments. There is something I have forgotten to do."

The door closed behind her. Thoughtfully I regarded the leaping flames, the glass and china glimmering on their tray. But my state of mind made me restless. I wandered about the room, appraising the faded glow of the painted furniture, the varied exquisite bibelots, the carefully chosen pictures hanging sparsely here and there. Long windows, behind the soaring lines of full rich curtains, and, opposite the fireplace, a doorway also heavily curtained, broke the dull gilded spaces of the wall.

Tired of prowling about, I settled in a corner of the sofa and, having drunk my coffee, fell into a reverie, half-torpor, half-anticipation. Surely there could be but one ending to such a situation as this? Even to my inexperience the writing on the wall was in words of one syllable. The house was as soundless as ever. The atmosphere of the boudoir was very warm and faintly perfumed. Now and again the fire hissed or fell in with a little crackling rush.

Perhaps this was the moment of the hoax? Perhaps she would not come back at all? Worse, perhaps not she but someone else would come back? Or more than one? I remembered waiting in the Hattons' flat for Ruth to come back, and how she had come and what had happened. Restless again, I left the sofa and began a tour of the room, trying to get my bearings, trying to throw off the lassitude caused by the silence and the sweet stagnant air.

I found myself near to the curtained doorway that faced the fireplace. I wondered what room lay beyond. Should I explore? Curiosity at war with prudence, I stood and stared at the hanging. At that moment the curtains parted, and she stood before me.

The black dress had disappeared; she wore now a white gown, clinging and yet loose, as white as her own neck and arms. She looked at me lazily, and smiled a queer taunting smile.

All fear of a hoax vanished, and with them my abstraction and lethargy. Instinct told me the moment of crisis had arrived, and I think it was instinct also which made me step forward and, bending over her hands, cover them with kisses. Then I stood straight again, still holding both her hands, and looked her in the eyes.

She moved backward, drawing me after her. With a soft swish the curtains fell to behind me.

~   ~   ~

When, stumbling a little and fighting against the sleep that lay heavy on my eyelids, I had found my way once more to the small bedroom on the second floor, I plunged my head into a basin of cold water and turned unwillingly to face reality. My watch showed that it was only a few minutes after eleven. A man can, then, in four short hours, live all that I had lived of wonder, of rash hope, of reckless fancy, of delirious fulfilment, of abrupt and cruel disillusion?

In these first moments after the fever's passing, it was the disillusion that remained most vividly. I could have cried to recall that abrupt and terrible dismissal.

With a cold finality, galling in its very courtesy, she had slipped from my arms, and huddling the clothes around her, turned her back upon me.

" You must go now " she had said quietly. " The car will be at the door in a quarter of an hour. There is a dressing gown on the chair beside you."

There had been no light in the room save that from a dying fire. I could just see the back of her head, dark against the pillows. Her voice came oddly from the shadows. Stupidly I stared toward the mound of bed-clothes, neither moving nor speaking. She repeated impatiently:

" You must go! At once! The room you were first taken to is just above here—the second door to the left at the stair-head. Go, please! "

Then even the blackness of her hair vanished. She had buried her face under the piled sheets; and I became miserably conscious of being an unwanted intruder in a lady's bedroom. I groped for the dressing gown, bundled my clothes haphazard in my arms, and crept away.

Those moments of humiliation and dismay were with me vividly, as I fumbled uncertainly with studs and tie. But my head was clearing and I felt my temper begin to rise. The basin of cold water had restored more than mere sanity; it had brought back my spirit. Simply to be shown the door like that

F 2

was intolerable. The act of love, even between lovers who do not know one another's names, gives rights to both. " I'm damned if I go! " I told myself. " She must explain! "

Afraid of losing this mood of indignant bravery, I finished dressing and made my way downstairs. By luck rather than by skill, I found the door of the bedroom which had witnessed my victory and my defeat. It was empty. A reading-lamp had been turned on beside the bed and shone warmly on the tumbled coverlets. I felt my determination waver, and was turning to leave the room when something gleaming on the carpet caught my eye. It was the bracelet which she had worn at dinner. A devil whispered in my ear. I was about to slip the thing into my pocket when, through those well-remembered curtains, entered the very person I was seeking. She was fully dressed in her black gown and her face was white and strained.

She frowned angrily when she saw me.

" What are you doing here? " she demanded. " I told you to go."

I felt suddenly calm. I closed the passage door, by which I had been standing, and walked across the room toward her.

" I came to return your bracelet " I said. " Here it is."

And I held it up between finger and thumb.

She flushed.

" Give it me, please."

I shook my head.

" No, not yet."

She darted forward, but I whipped the thing behind my back and stood my ground.

" How dare you! " she cried. " Give it me at once."

The imperious insolence brought a spice of temper to my sense of mastery.

" No, not yet " I repeated. " Not without some sort of explanation."

She stared at me, and I saw fear at war with fury in her eyes.

" Don't be absurd " she said quickly. " Imagine any explanation you fancy. Put it down to a sudden passion for your beauty, if that flatters you."

I shook my head.

" You should have thought of that sooner. I might have been just that kind of idiot, if you had—well, if the last few minutes of our—our conversation—had been a little different. But it won't do now."

She changed her tactics.

" You are right to be angry " she began humbly. " I see now how—how ungrateful I must have seemed. But— but—circumstances were a little odd, weren't they? I was not quite myself. If I ask you—beg of you—to go quietly away, will you not do me that one further courtesy? "

" I will go quietly and instantly when I *understand*; but not before."

She clasped her hands and, with her head drooped, turned away. After a moment's thought she faced me abruptly. Her mouth was twisted and she was frowning unhappily.

" I don't know . . ." she muttered. " I don't know what to do. . . ."

" Just tell me " I said. " Tell me enough to let me under-stand."

" What shall I tell? " she asked in a faint voice; then gave a little cry: " Oh, unlucky I am! "

" Not so unlucky " I corrected, " for I am not curious as to details. I only want to know *why*. You are not afraid of my —my making use—— "

She shook her head, but did not speak. She gazed about her with eyes already filling with tears.

" Oh, please! " she begged and stretched imploring hands. " Please do not press me."

" I am only asking what I have a right to know " I insisted. " Presumably I have rendered you some service by coming here tonight—— "

She interrupted:

" And have you had no pleasure in return? " she flashed.

This pierced my guard, and I could only bow my head.   For a moment I felt a stirring of the passion of an hour ago.   But I was immediately ashamed, and answered her with humility.   " I had forgotten that " I said.   " I can only beg your pardon. Here is the bracelet.   The car will still be there, I hope? "

She took her bracelet and looked at me with woman's sweetness, loving to yield in her hour of victory.

" Yes " she said.   " The car will still be there."

But she did not move nor take her eyes from mine.   Then suddenly she spoke again, and with pathetic shyness:

" I will tell you just this.   We—my husband and I—have an old name, which we must hand on ourselves or see go into strange, bad possession.   We have no child, and—" with a pitiful smile—" a childless wife is not a lucky one.   My husband is angry and cold, and so unhappy. . . . And you are very like his family. . . . Do you understand now? "

" Yes " I said.   " I think I understand.   It was all for love of him——? "

She covered her face with her hands, standing motionless. At last, barely perceptibly, she nodded.

ᔓ   ᔓ   ᔓ

I have not, I am thankful to say, actually seen that desperate lady again.   I wish I could as truthfully declare that I had not learnt her name.   I did my best.   I tried to avoid such chance information as might tell me what she would not wish me to know.   And for a long time I succeeded.   But one day just after the armistice, I opened a picture paper in the club smoking-room—and there she was, unmistakable and little changed. And by her side was her son.   I suppose in the photograph he was a child of four or five.

IX: THE ABBESS OF ST JOHN'S WOOD

I SAID that the adventure just related dispelled one of my remaining illusions.   It would perhaps have been better to say
that it replaced an illusion belonging to adolescence by one
characteristic of the cynicism of early maturity.

I had grown up properly subject to the British assumption
that no nice woman, even in the secrecy of her own mind,
would attempt to disengage the idea of sexual intercourse from
the sacred mystery of married life.   I accepted with docility
the doctrine that an interest in the process *per se* was part of
the regrettable grossness of masculine nature and, as such,
should be carefully concealed from a society conducted in
accordance with feminine predilections.   As a result, my
earliest approaches to girls of my age had been made in the conventional mood of romantic inferiority—a mood of wistful
humility and of shy gratitude for the smallest courtesy.   Ruth
had deliberately turned wistfulness into optimism, but encouraged the sense of inferiority and the gratitude.   In consequence, when she rounded on me, I was left in bewildered
unhappiness amid the ruins of what had been a genuine idealism.
The appearance on my horizon of Denise had seemed to offer
a chance of reasserting myself to myself.   Here was a girl of
whose moral principle at least I need not stand in awe.   To let
animality have its head would, I thought, do something to
balance my sex-account, which showed at the moment an em-
barrassing deficit.   Also it was high time to discover what the
whole pother was about.

Up to a point, as you know, everything went splendidly
with Denise, self-assertion and experience joining hands in a
triumphant saraband.   But at the end came a new discovery
and a new humiliation.   Not only could a ' nice girl ' lead you
up the garden and there make a fool of you; a girl of the other
kind could take you right into the potting shed, and then leave

you to buy your way out. It was all very difficult and discouraging.

For a while, naturally enough, I went puritanical, and decided to give up this girl-business altogether. The Loxley lad made very merry at Toulouse because I refused to go with him to one of the *maisons*. But I was still scared of the whole subject, and would much rather Loxley thought me a prude than risk another disgrace of any kind.

By the time I had got settled in London the mood of general renunciation had passed, but no desire for enterprise had yet taken its place. Also I was very nearly where I had started as to faith in the delicate pudicity of British womanhood; for I had by now decided that Ruth did not really count. She had lived abroad so long, and in conditions so different from the majority of her kind, that she could not be regarded as representative.

It was, therefore, with this major illusion still dominant that I had encountered in Mudies the Lady Anonyma. A woman of beauty and breeding, she was the sort of person in connection with whom any laxity or calculated irregularity of behaviour was prescriptively unthinkable. And yet what happened? She deliberately planned, and carried through in detail, an elaborate sexual initiative. Her motive was of the noblest; but there is no blinking the fact that, for her own purposes, she determined to give her body to a stranger, and not only did so, but took pains to make the ceremony as luscious and provocative as possible.

Well, if *she* could do that, any one of her sex was capable of doing the same; and I reacted so violently from my conventional belief in the natural austerity of virtuous women that in its place came an exaggerated conviction of their opportunism. I told myself that I now understood my dance partners; I registered as an axiom the belief that women are far more familiar than men with the potentialities of sex, and are liable to use their knowledge quite ruthlessly for their own advantage.

Oddly enough this over-generalised and rather elementary discovery brought with it a delicious sense of release. All the mumbo-jumbo which is made to surround the fact of physical love could, I felt, henceforward be ignored, and the experience valued for what it is—one of the major exhilarations of human existence. As for its social complexities, they were—and would remain—real enough; but they should be respected rather than feared. Never again need I hover between desire and apprehension; wonder if I dare; dare; succeed or fail. The thing would just happen, or it would not. And if it should not happen often enough, there were places where it could be agreeably arranged, places which specialised in side-stepping gentility.

In connection with one such place, I am reminded of a remarkable episode. It is not strictly relevant to this story; but you always took a malicious delight in the way that pure chance will sometimes challenge the pompous pretences of society, and I can vouch that this really happened. One immediate effect of the adventure with Anonyma and of my emancipation from previous inhibitions, was that I occasionally joined my friends in their more intimate relaxations. Ted Loxley was something of an authority on under-London, and he introduced me to a house in St John's Wood. It was a nice house in a good neighbourhood, managed with discretion and less rapacity than is usual in such places. The lady in charge was a great character, wholly without illusion or prejudice, and with conversation unsuited to the squeamish; but she was a good-hearted genuine old outlaw, and her stories of the gaslit dissipations of Victorianism were as dangerous as they were fine, and as robust as they were racy.

It is no exaggeration to say that I got quite fond of Mrs G., and consequently was shocked and sorry when one day Loxley rang me up:

" I say, Nick " he said. " The abbess is in trouble. Meet me at six at Preston's and I'll tell you about it."

It was the usual story. Whether a neighbour had complained or the police had pitched on that particular district for one of their periodical clean-ups, the house had been raided about midnight the day before, names and addresses taken and poor G. marched off to the station. She had given the necessary sureties and was at liberty again; but the case was to come up in two days' time.

" Damned busybodies! " concluded Ted (a little unjustly—unless he meant the neighbours—for after all this was one of the things the police were meant for). " We must give the old dear a hand."

So we prepared to stand by.

The magistrate was unusually severe. He fined G. two hundred pounds, and had a great time blowing about social purity and the canker of corruption gnawing at the heart of British youth. The landlord of the house turned her out on the spot, leaving her with a lease on her hands and no immediate chance of anything except the faint possibility of a furnished let for the summer. The papers were discreet but unctuous; and the world was given to understand that the honour of London had been avenged. So a good time was enjoyed by one and all—except G. herself, and those of her friends who were fond of her and disliked the idea of a caretaker snuffling in the basement of that once hospitable house, now dark and empty and to let.

It was at this point that ironic fate took a hand, and showed that coincidence has a sense of humour, even at the expense of social hygiene.

Among our group was a young soldier, who was engaged to the daughter of some rather correct people living abroad. The date of his wedding was suddenly advanced (I think the girl had worked on her father and got a promise of more money out of him) and fixed for a day near the end of May. The show was to take place in London, and the bride's parents were renting a furnished house for the month. You can imagine

our feelings when we each received an invitation to the wedding
and to a reception afterwards at, of all places, the very house
from which G. had been driven!

It sounds fantastic, I know; but I assure you, Sally, it's
perfectly true. The unfortunate young man had known
nothing of the plans made by his in-laws, who had done the
renting from abroad through their solicitor and were very
satisfied to secure at a moment's notice so pleasant a house for
so reasonable a rent. We could not help ragging him a little,
but promised to behave with decorum on the day itself.

And on the whole we did so, though that reception was the
queerest social palimpsest imaginable. Ostensibly it was an
ultra-conventional version of the conventional wedding party,
with large gracious women in feathered hats, unfurling their
teeth and talking a deal of nothing in the unfinished, gargling
voices of educated London. They swept here and there over
G.'s carpets, sat elegantly on G.'s chairs, and every now and again
surveyed the bride and bridegroom with genteel but none the
less obvious anticipation.

Watching them, I felt that at those moments the past loomed
through its garish overlay, and the ghosts of G. and her girls,
in all their shameless candour, began to move in and out of the
chattering crowd. I wandered up to the first landing. There
was the huge wardrobe which had played a noble part in many
a game of ' sardines '; there were the heavy curtains over the
glass-walled alcove which looked on to the garden behind;
that room on the right, that other room on the half-landing
above. . . . I wished I dared revisit the place in detail; but
with something of an effort I remembered it was no longer a
house *où on se couchait à porte-ouverte*, and returned sadly
downstairs. In the hall I met one of my friends.

" I can't stand this any longer " I said. " It's macabre."

He agreed. We took leave of the happy couple and hurried
away. A week later the Archduke was killed at Serajevo;
and though I heard presently that Mrs G. had set up somewhere

else, I had no opportunity to renew acquaintance with her. Nor did I get out to America to join Uncle Nick. There were so many other things to do.

X: ENGLISH ROSE: WAR-TIME MODEL

I CANNOT bring myself to tell in any detail the story of my official engagement to marry Janet Earle. There would be no satisfaction either for me or you in a lengthy description of the quite commonplace opportunism of a young lady on the make, and the equally commonplace disillusionment of a Temporary Gentleman who mistook base metal for gold. Indeed I would gladly pass over the whole affair. But it was too influential to be ignored. It cured me once for all of susceptibility to *vierges à l'anglaise*, and produced what I know to be an overwrought dislike of the generalised girl-flattery which during recent years has pervaded press, pulpit and publicity.

So here are the facts in summary—and ill-natured summary at that.

I fell in love with Janet during my first home leave, early in 1916; and when I say " fell in love ", I mean it, for by the improvised standards of the war-years it was true.

She was barely nineteen when I met her; belonged to a good family though not a wealthy one, and had a pin-money job of some sort in an emergency government office. This is equivalent to saying that, having passed two of the most impressionable years of her life in the atmosphere of war, she had been rushed into a spurious maturity; and that her so-called work placed her in as efficient a forcing bed for snobbery as even Great Britain, that specialist in snobbery, has ever devised. It is only fair to bear all this in mind. It is only fair to realise that Janet had little chance to be anything but a typical specimen

of war-time femininity.   It will then be permissible to say that
what little chance she had, she failed to take.

In appearance she had to the last detail the chic peculiar to
her date.   She mirrored to perfection the type of young woman
popular with drapery advertisers in any particular season; and
her eager smile was as readily available as that which, in the
judgment of copy-designers, is still the best recommendation
for motor-cars, cigarettes or patent foods.   Her mentality was
equally topical and to pattern.   She was the soldier's sweetheart, the gallant little stoker of home fires.   There was no
disturbing originality in her modernism, no excess of prudery
in her wholesomeness.   In short, her finish and her responsive-
ness combined to create precisely the illusion required by those
to whom England and serenity and clean linen and gay feminine
companionship seemed heaven and earth together.   When I
add that in conversation about her colleagues she would refer
to this one as ' frightfully efficient but of course hardly—well,
you know ' and to that one as ' not quite top drawer ', you will
appreciate that she had all the qualities which made for social
success, and could not fail to be admired, save by the wrong-
headed few.

To this negligible minority I did not at that period belong.
I suppose that the war, which swept most of us into a temporary unanimity of ideals, activities and clothing, acted also,
and inevitably, as leveller of taste.   Into the bargain, ' home '
and its products became precious merely for their own sake;
and Janet was so perfect a show-piece of the shop-window
England of her day, that it would have been strange indeed if
she had not shared in the glamour.

Of course, all these spiteful things I am writing about her are
wholly retrospective; and at the time I should have been furious
if anyone had hinted that a fraction of them could possibly
be true.   I thought she was beyond criticism.   And she thought
I was—if not beyond criticism—at any rate good enough to go
around with, and to have first claim on her vivacity and stylishness.

I was more than satisfied, and believed that no pleasure could equal that of her company. Nevertheless, thinking back on it, I cannot recall that we ever talked about anything except money and her personal attractions, apart of course from the theatre or dance or other amusement of the moment. Certainly I never told her anything which really interested me, or looked to her for advice or encouragement or direction. Still, I did not notice that at the time; and so thoroughly did I enjoy the privileges which she accorded me, that, by the time my third leave came and I was lucky enough to be transferred to " Intelligence ", I decided I would like to prolong their possession all my life.

It sounds idiotic, and it was idiotic. But you have to have known the longing of those days for some sort of security; the passionate desire to settle *something*, and to dwell, even without really believing it, on at least a pretence of a future, to understand how easily this idiocy (which was one of ten thousand) could come to pass. Anyway, justifiably or unjustifiably, I asked her to marry me; and she said she would.

There was a preliminary twitter of aunts and gush of girl-friends and baying of fellow-men. My new job claimed me with spasmodic secrecy, and Janet preferred starring in public in the popular rôle of war-fiancée, to making a round of friends and relations with the timid but joyful smile of a virgin marked for sacrifice. So even the settling influence of family absorption was denied us; and we mostly saw one another wearing party frocks and party smiles, which certainly created an agreeable illusion but did not help toward mutual understanding.

It was not unknown, as the war dragged cruelly on, for certain non-combatants who tolerated bloodshed but disapproved of sex, to raise eyebrows at war-weddings (with which were included war-engagements), on the ground that lack of restraint led to premature embraces, young people having no thought beyond satisfaction of their immediate lusts. This may have been a true view of certain isolated cases, but it was in the main very unfair. On the one hand, it ignored the romantic impulse of men on foreign service to make sure of some individual fragment of home, to secure a continuing share in a country they themselves might never see again. On the other hand, it exaggerated the complaisance of the smart young women of the day. There were, of course, many girls who felt that the least they could do was to give a soldier-lover anything which made his life (while it lasted) more tolerable. All honour to them. But there were others (and I regret to say Janet was one of them) who took (and got) great credit for keeping their heads, which sometimes meant keeping an eye on the main chance. These ' sensible ' girls wanted, first a good time, and in due course an establishment. To get the former, it was necessary to be attractive and ostensibly accessible; to get the latter it was necessary to check up on income and not really be accessible at all. In effecting this difficult compromise, an engagement to marry was found of great utility. It kept other girls away; it legitimatised a certain degree of intimate fondling; and it secured a period of comparative calm, during which the final decision could be taken. If that decision were for marriage, well and good; if not—there was no real harm done and still plenty of fish in the sea.

Please do not think I am scarifying Janet as an outsize gold-digger. She was nothing so purposeful as that. Her impulses were as automatic as her clothes and her sprightliness. She was more like a taximeter than a woman. While the initial distance was being covered, she was alluring; the clock ticked over and she became romantic; it ticked over again, and she became practical. In our case she had not been practical for very long, when a permanency more promising than I hailed her from the pavement. I found I had come to the end of my trip. The flag went up; the new fare got in; and presumably off she went again—this time all the way from titillation to settlements.

I'm being beastly, aren't I? But that's how I feel; and after all she got what *she* wanted, which was always the only thing she ever really cared for.   So let her keep it and let me sneer at it.   She won't mind.

Our engagement lasted for the better part of a year.   I thought I was perfectly happy, not realising I did not know what happiness can be.   Such free times as I had were spent in her company; at other times, when I was away on this or that mission, she glowed in my mind with the warmth proper to the girl I left behind me and (in the words of an almost contemporary song) " lighted the road leading home ".   Then the son of a war-peer turned up, with offers of more lavish entertainment and a future of greater splendour than I could hope to provide.   It was difficult for her.   Or rather it wasn't. She had no choice but to jilt me cold—which, on my return from impersonating a German importer negotiating for nickel in Stockholm, she most efficiently did.

Yes, " efficiently " ; for it is due to her to record that she played the jilt no less perfectly than she had played the fiancée, and with the same satisfactory modernity.

According to her lights, she had indeed done the fiancée with thoroughness and skill.   Primarily she had taken pains to be a ' good sport '.   This represented the majority ideal of the young men of the day (myself included); but to say in retrospect exactly what the process involved is oddly difficult. Roughly speaking, the affianced of a female ' sport ' expected perpetual zest for outings, great skill in dancing, a lot of ready laughter about nothing in particular, some emancipated chat about underclothes, and a fraction (though only a fraction) more freedom of caress for himself—the juvenile lead—than for the male chorus.   All this I got.   Into the bargain, by way of further concession to man's fleshly nature, I was given my lion's share of inadvertent displays of leg, and frequent opportunities of appreciating those V-necked blouses, in which one can so effectively lean forward over a lunch or dinner-table.   On occasions, I was even allowed to wait in the sitting-room of the little flat which she shared with a friend, while she finished her bath. This meant much shouting through the door, and finally a tantalising glimpse of tousled head and bare shoulder, when she peeped out to say 'nearly ready'. But it was clearly understood that these rousing privileges were sufficient unto themselves, and without any implication beyond the terms of a well-ordered engagement.

Then came the problem of how to get rid of me. Janet's virtuosity rose nobly to the occasion. I was treated to a blend of starry-eyed hesitation and downright camaraderie, the whole flavoured with bravely mastered tears:

"We've had some perfectly lovely times. . . . I can't tell you how sweet you've been. . . . But it's better to be frank . . . isn't it? I shall always be very fond of you—and I hope you will in time be just a teeny bit fond of me again. . . . But you know how things are . . . don't think worse of me than you can help."

And so on. It was all very affecting, but manifestly final.

I can write in this disagreeable way now, because, having since observed other Janets doing their stuff, I understand that being a typical product of her period, she cared for nothing in the world except herself, and that she was encouraged in her greed and vanity by silly newspapers and the hysteria of a war-worn society. But when it happened, I was wretched. In the mob-atmosphere of war-making and war-mongering I had, I suppose, reverted to type; forgotten what an earlier Europe had taught me; and become just another overgrown schoolboy, willing to take 'a perfectly topping girl' at her own valuation, and spend all available leisure and cash in helping her to show off. For that was what my engagement had really amounted to.

At the time, however, so extraordinary is one's power of self-delusion, I felt that all prospect of delight had disappeared. It is literal truth that I took Janet's jilting very hard. Not only did it end a period of pride and excitement, but it destroyed hopes on which I had begun to build. Thank heaven it did.

Those hopes, if I imagine them fulfilled, hardly bear thinking of. But the actual engagement was different. Fake though it was, it had glamour; and that, even now, I can recapture. I remember moments in her company when a sort of magic seemed to surround the two of us. The dim streets of war-London will always connect in my mind with her presence, or with anticipation of seeing her, or with the ache of leaving her. My tune-complex also plays its part. There was a musical show to which we went more than once. It had two outstanding songs—one a telephone duet, the other about Chu Chin Chow; and I cannot hear either of them without once again walking at her side through the streets off theatreland, while occasional shaded lamps throw bleak rays on to the pavement, while overhead the searchlights stroke the sky, while all about us is the furtive whispering of a generation which grasped at every chance of pleasure lest to-morrow it died. I hope I shall always be a little grateful to her for such moments, even though their enchantment were of my own imagining. But it cannot be more than a little, for my main gratitude is for the jilting.

That is enough about Miss Janet Earle (who is now Mrs to an honourable), and the meaningless engagement into which I blundered, from which I was so mercifully ejected. It is time to pass on to the Peace Conference, to the Paris of early 1919, where, after all this shadow-play, something real happened.

SHE AND I

I: MISS LASALLE

IT is very much the thing nowadays to execrate the Treaty of Versailles, and to blame on the selfish stupidity of those who drafted it the ills of the post-war world. God forbid that I should defend what was done, or deny that its main legacy was one of trouble. But virtually every hostile critic shows (or at any rate pretends) an ignorance of the difficulties involved, which robs a slapdash judgment-after-the-event of even the trivial value of polemic journalism. Only Harold Nicolson, in his book *Peacemaking*, has described the conference and its work as they really were. In that book, as nowhere else, are made clear the infinity of detail to be coped with; the constant race against time, made the more exhausting by sudden, unpredictable gaps of compulsory idleness; the perpetual thwart of different languages imperfectly understood; the utter impossibility for any one section of the whole to visualise the drift or ultimate importance of its particular deliberations. We were so close to what we were doing, that we could see nothing ahead. The only horizon we could even imagine was the end of our immediate job, after which would develop another and yet another. We were always frantically preparing something in time for something else; and each rush held up the routine-work of another section, just as our own routine would be held up by another section's delay. Finally, we were always at grips with the vast machinery of French bureaucracy, whose guests we were and whose way of doing things was not always like our own. Probably I had a keener appreciation than most of the last complication, because I owed my place in the British Delegation primarily to my knowledge of languages, and only secondarily to such experience of German economic conditions, need for raw materials, and influence in neutral countries, as special missions for ' C ' had given me. Certainly contacts were at once my chief and most harassing duty. It is not easy, without friction, to assess the values of secret reports from half-a-dozen sources of different nationality; to agree memoranda and minutes with French and Italian secretaries; to dispute interpreters' versions of things said and things written. Yet such jobs had to be done all the time, and in a manner acceptable to our hosts. Consequently those hectic months in Paris now stay in my memory mainly as a time of continual adjustment—mental and verbal; of continual compromise, circumspection and tact; and only a little, either of solid achievement or of healing carefree leisure.

One evening, at a small dinner-party given by my chief to certain members of allied delegations, I found myself next to an American officer. His name was Abbott, and he told me so much about himself that by the end of the meal I felt I had known him for years, instead of having seen him officially a couple of times and dined in his company this once. He had been, it appeared, a lawyer in civil life; was now attached to the drafting section of the United States Delegation; and, being familiar with France and (presumably) a man of means, had preferred to take a flat near the Pont de l'Alma and settle there with his wife for the period of the conference, than to live in or about the Hotel Crillon with the companions of his working hours. Before we parted he had invited me to lunch on the following Sunday; and I found myself greatly looking forward to seeing him again, and to a meal in a private dining-room after so much of the genteel bonhomie of the Delegation headquarters and the rather strained continentalism of our occasional visits to restaurants in the city.

I suppose it was my eagerness not to be late, which brought me down Georges V well ahead of time. The sunshine of an early Paris spring flattered the river and made pale filigree of the

already budding trees.   I chose a seat on the terrace of the corner-
café overlooking the bridge, and for practically the first time
since this tormented conference started, was conscious of being
in France.   The traffic slid to and fro across the square; the
sun was gently warm; I liked my drink and my cigarette.
Life, in short, was for a moment not merely a calendar of duties
with periods of relaxation at stated intervals, but something
static and serene.   I wished I had a friend who enjoyed sitting
like this, watching nothing and everything, and after half an
hour neither boring me nor getting bored.   I wished, if such
a one could be found, that we might be free to wander off into
France and only be seen again in our own good time.   A simple
enough ambition, one would have thought; but at the time as
hopeless as most others.

The Abbotts' drawing-room seemed full of people, but
contained in fact only five.   It was not a large room, and French
salon furniture can make even emptiness over-populated.
Abbott greeted me with the warming hospitality of his race and
made presentations.   I met Mrs Abbott—plain, brisk and immediately engaging.   I met two young men, who looked like
two young men.   And I met a Miss Lasalle.

We went in to lunch.

The Abbotts were delightful.   He was a solemn, rather
slow-mannered man, with a large creased face, and dewlaps
like a friendly hound.   She had a sharp questing nose with
pince-nez perilously perched and a quick slant to her ready
smile.   They clearly adored one another—Abbott ceaselessly
delighted by his wife's rapid satirical mind, she happily reliant
on his measured good sense, and loving to tease him as much as
he loved to be teased.   The two young men were, I soon
decided, about as tiresome as young Americans could be—
which is no more tiresome than young Britons, but in a different
vein.   They clearly laboured under the delusion that the
United States had bought Paris; that no previous visitors had

really got the hang of the place; and that as authorities on food, drink, cafés, night-life and sophistication generally they were *hors concours*. I had observed their type more than once in restaurants and elsewhere, but this was my first, as it were, ' domestic ' experience of it. The Abbotts were too charitable and too courteous to react visibly against the ill-bred (and frequently inaccurate) ostentation of their young guests; but Miss Lasalle, who sat opposite to me across a narrow table and whom I found myself watching with increasing pleasure, was clearly working up for some sort of disciplinary action.

Fledgling One treated us to an account of his adventures in Montmartre two evenings before. Actually they only ceased to be very traditional adventures when they became sheer bad manners; but he took great pride in them, particularly in a scuffle with the door-man at Zelli's who objected to his not wearing evening dress, and in having poured half a tankard of beer from the gallery of the Bal du Moulin Rouge on to the dancers below.

Fledgling Two criticised the cellar at Fouquet's, and told us how he dealt with the wine-waiter for bringing vin ordinaire under a reputable label.

" These dam Frenchmen think they can palm off anything on Americans " he concluded.

Abbott interposed.

" I think you must be confusing two restaurants " he said gently. " Such a thing would never happen at Fouquet's."

Fledgling Two waved his hand and shook back the lock of fair hair which fell painstakingly over his forehead.

" Maybe I am " he agreed airily. " I can't keep the joints apart. Anyway the bozo got what was coming to him, whoever he was."

" Do you know a lot about wine, Mr Markham ? "

With a twinge of satisfaction I realised that Miss Lasalle had mobilised.

She spoke in a low rather husky voice, turning her broad white forehead and sleepy eyes toward her neighbour.

" Why, yes " he replied cheerfully. " I think I may say I've gotten a notion or two since I've been over here. But I'd still as soon have a shot of good rye as anything else, and I guess you feel the same? "

" I? Oh, I just don't know the first thing about it. I come from way down in the south and think myself lucky to be in Europe at all. I don't even live in New York, as I suppose you do? "

The lad was momentarily out of countenance. He had a mouth like that of a vacuum cleaner, and the lips pouted disagreeably under stress of irritation. Then he decided to bluff:—

" No mam! " he said with spirit. " My home-town is Tiffin, Ohio, and I'll have you know I'm proud of it. But I've been around at home, let alone over on this side."

Abbott turned the conversation to the progress of the conference, and we spoke of the natural bitterness of the French and, by inference, of the hideous slaughter of war. Something reminded Flegling One of a story he had been told about the collapse of Gough's Army in March. It reflected unfavourably on British military capacity, and may have been none the worse for that; but the wording was crude, and I could see that poor Abbott and his wife were greatly embarrassed by the possible insult to their English guest.

Once again the cool husky voice of Miss Lasalle relieved the momentary silence.

" That is a very interesting story, Mr Todd. And very amusing too, if one is far enough away. But there's one thing I have always wanted to know about our American front, and I'm sure you can tell me—you were in the Argonne, of course? "

I felt almost sorry for the luckless youth, raw little bounder though he was. He coloured scarlet, and muttered that he had only been drafted just before the armistice and had reached

France with Markham about November 20. Then he also rallied, and said with a pertness I could not help admiring:—

" But if you tell me what you want to know, Miss Lasalle, I'll sure make it my duty to get the information and pass it on."

" That's real nice of you " she replied. " Well, you know of the confusion there was in the American sector—especially the block in the transport? I've been told it was largely lads with money back of them, playing cat's-cradle behind the lines where their fathers had pushed them into good safe jobs. Can that be true, Mr Todd? "

Mrs Abbott felt the time had come for desperate measures.

" Sally dear " she said. " Let us have our coffee in the *salon*. Will you lead the way? "

I was left with my host (surely flustered, though he showed no sign of it) and the young men, now sulkily silent. In a few minutes we rose to join the ladies.

Todd and Markham seemed disinclined to linger, once coffee was finished. On the ground of an early date elsewhere, they took leave rather constrainedly of their hostess, jerked a bow to Miss Lasalle and to me, and were seen to the front door by Abbott, whose wise and melancholy face remained impassive to the end.

As they left the room, the girl laughed softly.

" I'm sorry, Alice " she said. " I just could not help it. Where *did* you raise them? "

" You were very naughty, Sally, and I'm ashamed of you. And of them also. I do hope Mr Dering will pardon . . ."

" Oh, please, Mrs Abbott! Don't think of it again. I didn't mind in the very least. Put a little differently, the statement would have been largely true and very salutary. And I wouldn't have missed Miss Lasalle's counter-offensive for anything."

" It's her Carolina blood " said Abbott, coming back into

the *salon* as I spoke. " No self-control at all.   They are all
alike, these southerners . . ."

" Now, Moreton; I won't have you giving Mr Dering the
idea I'm a sort of dragon!   I really have the sweetest nature.
But those two lads!   Who are they, anyway? "

During the half-hour's conversation which followed I
decided that I did not want to lose touch with Sally Lasalle.
I planned to find out what I could from the Abbotts and let
luck and ingenuity do the rest.   But as it happened, luck did
it all, and more promptly than I could have dared to hope.

It was about three o'clock when she got up from her chair.

" Gracious!   Alice, I must *run!*   I've promised to visit an
old lady who used to know mother years ago.   It's some place
way over by the Place d'Italie, and I know I'll never find it.
No one seems to understand me when I ask the way."

" If you will allow me——" I said, with considerable presence
of mind.   " I have to go in that direction myself.   I'm sure
we'll find it . . ."

" That's very kind of you.   I'd be glad of your help."

Mrs Abbott glanced from one to the other of us, and I thought
there was a flicker of amusement behind her pince-nez.

" Good hunting to you both " she said.   " And Mr Dering,
do come and see us again.   If that stupid Moreton forgets to
ask you (as I'm sure he will) just ask yourself.   Now, you will,
won't you?   I'll be *very* careful with my other guests next
time.   Good-bye, Sally darling.   You'll be round again soon?
Why, of course, we are going to Marcelle, aren't we—to-
morrow morning! "

And she sped cheerfully toward the hall, where Abbott in
immutable calm was hovering to open the door and say farewell.

" What charming people " I said, as Miss Lasalle and I started
down the hill toward the Trocadero.   " Have you known them
a long time? "

She nodded.

" For years. Alice was at college with me and I went through the whole stormy period of her engagement—right in the thick of things."

" And were they thick? "

" Were they thick? She wouldn't look at poor Moreton for a year, and went on so about being persecuted. . . . It was real funny, because she meant to have him all the time though she won't admit it even now. Then she said yes, and then changed her mind, and said she didn't think so, and so it went on."

" He looks a determined man " I said.

" That's just why she treated him that way. She wanted to make him mad. But if he'd shown any sign of taking her caprices seriously or being scared when she said no, she'd have acted very differently. Imagine Moreton Abbott looking scared, even if he were! He just stuck around till the ball had stopped bouncing, and then picked it up and put it in his pocket. Of course it's worked out fine. They're as happy as can be."

" Any children? "

" No " she said. " No children."

Enough of the Abbotts, I thought. What about us? So I became business-like.

" Now how much time have you? It's three-thirty; here we are at the bridge; and a taxi will get us to wherever it is in twenty minutes or so."

She stopped and gazed across the river towards the Invalides.

" It's such a wonderful afternoon. I'd like to walk around. But I ought to be there by four o'clock. It's a long trek for a half-hour duty call."

Without any sense of temerity, I made my second coup within an hour.

" This is what we will do. You shall be driven to your old lady, and while you are with her, I will fix up what I have to do. In exactly three quarters of an hour from delivering you at her door, I will have a nice chair ready for you at a respectable café nearby. We will have a spot and then walk anywhere you want."

This time she laughed outright, but with no trace of annoyance.

" But Mr Dering, if I am to take taxis all over the place, I could find my own way by telling the chauffeur the address."

" Not if he could not understand you—like the others."

She laughed again.

" Touchée! All right then—if you say so. I suppose I've run against that masterful English type, who gets trotted out at home as a sort of bogey-man to us spoiled American girls."

I looked crestfallen.

" Please forgive me. Honestly I wasn't trying to be masterful. But I should so enjoy a walk too—and it *is* a lovely day."

" So it is " she rejoined quickly; and I signalled a passing taxi.

We traced the old lady's house without difficulty, passing through the Place d'Italie for the purpose of fixing the subsequent rendezvous.

In a narrow street running diagonally into the Rue de Tolbiac the taxi drew up at the porte-cochère of a typical Parisian house of the pre-Haussmann era. It was a shabby house, and through the open half of the double-doors could be seen a dingy court, with a few sad shrubs and some washing on a line.

" I suppose this is right? " I said doubtfully.

" It's the number anyway. And my friend is very poor. There *are* poor Americans, you know."

Her change of tone frightened me. She had misunderstood. She thought I was looking down my nose. How was I to explain that I only wanted to see her safely at her destination, yet not to intrude? I had no status whatsoever; but queer things happened in remote quarters of Paris, and the southern area of Arrondissement XIII was not among the more demure districts of the city.

I felt myself blushing with sheer distress.

" I didn't mean that " I said miserably.

She was now out of the taxi and, as she shut the door behind her, looked up at me steadily and then smiled.

" I'm sorry " she said. " Nor did I. I'll be all right, I promise you."

As she crossed the pavement I called after her:—

" And you'll come back—to where we fixed? "

Turning in the doorway she nodded, then waved her hand and disappeared.

For a moment I sat in the taxi, staring at the open door. She would have to ask directions of the concierge, then climb Heaven knew how many stairs. I wanted to stand by in case I was needed, but I was afraid to pester her. Finally I told the man to drive back to the Place d'Italie. There I paid him off, and made my way to the appointed café. The terrasse was crowded, as befitted one of the first spring Sundays of the year, and I saw I should have to manœuvre to get a seat commanding a view of the way she would come. I marked out a suitable section served by a particular waiter, took an outside chair near the pavement, ordered a drink, and watched. In about five minutes a couple at a desirable inland table began gathering their belongings. They had hardly risen when I was behind them, drink in hand. Then I settled to half an hour's delicious indolence, spiced with anticipation.

My self-confidence quickly returned. She had forgiven me, or rather she had realised there was nothing to forgive. The afternoon struck me as even lovelier than before. The Place d'Italie—not as a rule considered one of the show-spots of Paris—impressed me as an admirable Place, tastefully planted with trees (now as sharp and gay as ever were Paris trees in spring), busy with attractive small bourgeois and proletarian families, seasoned with occasional groups of young *filous*, their caps pulled over one eye and the slinking gait of the professional bistro-rat.   I felt I had neglected the Place d'Italie.   I must come more often. The Mandarin, too, was of unusual quality.   And cheap. Indeed, since the morning, life generally seemed to have taken up.   Like the weather.   I felt happy.   I could not remember having been really happy since before the war, and then—I told myself—I was only a silly kid, who thought happiness the same as just feeling bucked about something or nothing.   Now I was *positively* happy;   and began, quite naturally, to think about Sally Lasalle and wonder what she had done to me.   Thinking about Sally made me think of other girls I had known, and of cafés connected with them.   I thought of the Fürstenberg where I first sat with Ruth, and of the other place from which I telephoned to her after my failure over the note-book.   I thought of the café in the old town at Tours, and of Denise, and of the fancy-dress ball and what came after.   I was in a fair way to think of others also, but changed my mind.   The present was more interesting than all the past put together; and, besides, I wanted to think some more about Sally.   I realised I had as yet hardly looked at her—not really *looked*. I knew she had a broad straight forehead and sort of velvety brown eyes set rather wide apart under strong straight brows; I knew she was olive-skinned and that her mouth was long and full;   I knew she stood just above my shoulder and wore her brown hair close to her head.   But was the hair long or short?   I did not know.   Nor did I know what her hands were like.   Nor how she walked.

From where I sat I could see the clock on the Mairie.   It was well after half-past four;   she would be coming soon, and I must be ready.   At a quarter to five almost to the minute I saw her **emerge** from the Rue Bobillot.   I could see her moving through the slowly promenading crowd.   I lost her behind a tramway-shelter;   saw her again;   saw her behind a caravan belonging to a circus which stood at the curb; saw her again—now quite close. She moved easily, but like a woman—no hefty lunge or sports-girl stride—and her breasts quivered a little under her thin frock. She looked about her with interest, holding her head up to the world, but neither self-conscious nor flaunting. When she reached the corner of the terrasse, I was there to greet her. We threaded our way back to the table and sat down, looked one another in the eyes and smiled contentedly.

"Well" I said at last. "How did it go? All right?"

She nodded. A waiter came towards me.

"What will you have?"

She looked at my Mandarin.

"Will I like that?"

"I think so" I replied.

I pushed the cigarettes towards her, and we sat and said nothing. I watched her hands. They were small and brown, and the nails were delicate but unobtrusive. She wore a signet ring on her little finger. No other rings. Suddenly I became aware that she was looking at me from under the brim of her small hat. There was determination in her look. Something was coming.

"Mr Dering" she said. "This ' business ' of yours, which was taking you over here this afternoon—there wasn't any. You have been sitting in this café ever since I left you."

"There was business I wanted to do."

"Do I now ask what it was?"

"You don't have to. I'll tell you. I wanted to see some more of you."

She just went on looking at me, and a slow flush coloured the olive of her cheeks.

"I see" she said at last. "But couldn't you have managed it without telling me a yarn? You did do that, you know."

"Please don't look at it like that. I mean literally what I

say. I wanted to be with you for longer. Just *be* with you. No funny business at all. I admit I misled you a little at one point. But I've behaved all right, haven't I? You paid your call as scheduled, and you have now only to say you want me to take you home or even leave you here, and I'll do it. But in the former case you won't get your walk, and in the latter we shan't get ours."

She took a long drink and groped for a second cigarette. Her eyes were now fixed across the square, but I am sure they saw nothing.

" I want my walk " she said quietly, " but I'd like another drink first."

Again we sat silent. I was inwardly elated by what had passed, and even more so by the satisfactoriness of our sitting here in the midst of a French Sunday crowd, as unembarrassed and as content to say nothing as if we had known one another for years.

" You know " I said at last, " it was lucky you mentioned that your visit would only last half an hour."

She was still gazing at the traffic and for a moment seemed not to have heard. Then a slow smile widened that already generous mouth. She turned her head and, most surprisingly, made a sudden face at me. Then laughed her delicious husky laugh.

" You notice too much " she said.

I think from that moment friendship began.

~   ~   ~

The famous walk started about six o'clock. The light was beginning to fade and I do not think Paris has ever since looked to me more beautiful. Certainly she had not done so before. Her beauty was the more curious in that we took a route commonplace beyond the ordinary. I have known the long uphill drag of the Boulevard Arago to be the dreariest chore imaginable ;

but this evening it was exquisite.   The upper reaches of Raspail are, I should have said, so many blocks of tedium; but this evening their only fault was their brevity.

As we went, we talked—talked endlessly.   I do not know what about—just the things we had in our minds, I suppose, and they happened to interest both of us.

When we got to the corner of Sèvres, she stopped.

" I'm going to turn off here.   I don't say ' thank you ' do I?   But I ought to."

" You do not.   All you need say is: ' You're welcome.' No—two other things.   Say you'll see me again.   Say you'll be free next Sunday.   I'm always on duty in the week—but Sunday——"

" You will see me again and I am free next Sunday."

She spoke like a small child learning responses by heart. But I had my answer, and did some quick thinking.   Presumably she lived between here and the river.   Picture-galleries are traditional rendezvous.

" Could we meet at the Victory of Samothrace at twelve o'clock?   Lunch, and then according to weather? "

" That'll be fine " she said, and put out her hand.

Then she swung about, walked quickly down Sèvres to the corner of Saint Pères, and turned left.

∽   ∽   ∽

The week which followed was an unusually disagreeable one. The members of my particular Commission seemed, not only set on prolonging their meetings till seven o'clock in the evening or later, but also incapable of remembering what they had said to one another, and demanding it in black and white with next morning's early coffee.   This meant, for the underlings, no dinner to speak of; copy-preparation till God knows when; and an embittered conflict with the luckless duplicating staff in the small hours of the following day.   More keenly than ever before I sympathised with the compositor in Printing House Square who, when under notice, enlivened the speech of some pompous politician with an emphatic obscenity. Perhaps, I thought, if that intolerable Italian and that infinitely prosy Pole could read in the official minutes that they had spent an hour of the Commission's time capping one another's dirty stories, with occasional gross interjections from the British chairman, they would talk less in future. But you can't get round an international secretariat with that kind of joke—let alone Whitehall's Roneo Queen, who is by Statute a great stickler for propriety, both professional and otherwise.

The events of the previous Sunday receded into such a faintness of distance that I almost ceased to believe they had happened. When by chance I ran into Abbott on Friday outside the Ministry of Finance, a sudden return of the enchantment nearly jarred me into some reference to his lunch-party and to Miss Lasalle. But the quiet formality of his greeting and the brief-case of conference papers under his left arm brought me to earth again, and I went my gloomy way. Even on Saturday night, though conscious of next day's appointment, I felt sluggish and almost sceptical. It had all been quite ordinary, really; and to-morrow would find me just lunching another young woman, and making bright conversation, and wishing, once the food was ordered, that I had ordered something else.

In much the same mood of peevish disillusion I woke to a Sunday sadly different from its predecessor. The wind was raw, and there were flurries of cold rain. I took the Métro down to Palais Royal, and scudded miserably across the great court to the door of the Louvre. The place was crowded, for in addition to the usual Sunday throng there were hundreds of chilly folk who had hoped to sit in the Tuileries Gardens and were now killing time till lunch. The Victory soared magnificently above a dense mass of persons, some moving upstairs, others just standing, and all damp. As I wormed my way forward, I had an uneasy vision of the girl I had come to meet, isolated at the base of the statue and included despite herself in the survey of the crowd. The Victory was there to be gaped at and admired, but Miss Lasalle was not. I could hardly have appointed a worse place of meeting. She would be furious, and with reason.

Of course, when at last I had forced a passage to the front, she was not there, and foreboding was lost in anxiety. She had not come. Or she had come, seen the crowd and gone away again. Or she was somewhere about and I would never find her. I began gazing distractedly to right and left; then at the stairs; then at the upper floor. She was leaning on the balustrade, looking downward and waving her hand. When eventually I reached her, I was uncomfortable with sweat, and rather breathless with fluster and with irritation at my own mismanagement.

Her greeting was a little subdued. I began apologising for being late; for having asked her to come here at all; for the weather; for nearly everything, in fact, except for what required apology—my own nervous petulance. Exchanging common-places, we ploughed our way out of the Louvre and, under the portico, debated whither and how.

" Place St Michel and walk " she said.

The cold wet tramp along the river had a good effect on my temper. We spoke little; and I remembered how, a week ago, her power of silence had impressed me. By the time we were under cover, with the noise and indifference of a crowded café around us, the trials of six hateful weekdays had been forgotten. I realised, with a glow of satisfaction, that I had not been a mere victim of spring-fever; that the blend of ex-citement and serenity which her company had previously produced was as potent in rain and wind as in bland sunshine; that, in short, fate had offered me one of those opportunities we hear so much about, and that it was up to me to seize it.

The detail of our afternoon is of no consequence. We lunched and went to a cinema and walked along the quais toward Austerlitz when the rain stopped, and sat in other cafés when it began again, and at about six o'clock were in the Place de la Bastille. It struck me afterwards that neither of us had shown the least curiosity about the other. For my part, I was content to know that she was there, to enjoy the warm twilight of her voice, and to relish the interaction of intelligence and sense of humour which seemed to be automatic between us. It was strange, also, how naturally the afternoon had gone by, without talk of what to do next or adjustment of inclinations or polite gropings after individual preference or even—speaking for myself—any thought of the passage of time. When she stopped on the pavement outside the Vincennes station and said that it was six o'clock, I was both startled and vague, like one suddenly awakened.

" Is it? " I said foolishly.

" It is indeed.   And I must say good-bye."

" You can't possibly go yet! " I burst out; then realised the brusqueness of my words and the claims of ordinary courtesy.

" I beg your pardon!   I spoke without thinking.   I am afraid I had lost count of time."

I still felt a little dazed and, I suppose, looked it; for she stood quite still, watching me, with a tiny smile at the corners of her mouth and the patience of sympathy in her eyes.

" It's not that " she said.   " But I have to get back.   It's been a swell afternoon."

" You couldn't possibly have dinner—an early dinner? "

She shook her head.

" Sorry.   I wish I could."

I was now my normal self, and knew that she meant what she said. The vital thing was to fix another meeting, and quite shamelessly I proceeded to do so.

G 2

" When again, please ? "

She laughed.

" Really, Mr Dering. I'll be getting a habit with you—like a Sunday afternoon nap."

I shook my head.

" Not yet. Let me think. . . . It's so impossible to be sure of getting off even for dinner. But Sunday, Sunday, Sunday . . . like a couple of wage-slaves. Which of course I am, a degraded, bureaucratic wage-slave. But you aren't, and shouldn't be treated like one."

I believe she knew that I was afraid to suggest her giving up another whole afternoon, for she said quickly:—

" What is the matter with Sunday—except that it is your only free day ? "

I just looked at her. I could not say any of the things I really wanted to say. They hardly belonged to this stage of an acquaintanceship. Also, her unselfishness and understanding had taken my breath away. So for two excellent reasons I remained silent and looked at her. The next moment I pulled myself together, and in a voice which to me sounded borrowed, said:—

" Please come next Sunday. Could we go out of Paris, if it's only fine—walk in the woods somewhere? "

" I'd like to " she replied simply.

I had a feeling of urgency, as though her consent had to be captured and held. The words came with a rush:—

" Then I will be outside the Gare du Nord—suburban—at nine o'clock. That's not too early? We will go to Chantilly or somewhere, and see what the Boche has been up to. Unless you prefer Fontainebleau. But everyone goes there . . ."

As I was speaking, she had begun to cross the road toward the tramway shelter.

" I must take a trolley " she said. " I'm late already. Here is one coming that will do . . ."

The car stopped, and she jumped on to the step, I stood in the road and looked up into her face.

" Do please say that will be all right."

" It's a date."

As she waved her hand, the tram started grindingly down Henri IV towards the river.

II: SALLY

I WAS ahead of time at the Nord; purposely, in order to be there first. A mild, beautiful Sunday was already drawing early country-goers from their homes, and pairs of lovers, groups of lads, and parties of parents, aunts, uncles and children were passing continually through the entrance to the suburban booking-office. There was not much traffic yet, and I saw the bus turn into Denain and lumber up the short hill toward the station. When she appeared behind the vehicle and started across the street, I was not surprised. Somehow I had known she was on that bus.

What did surprise me a little was the surge of delight provoked by the first sight of her. I had lived all the week for this moment; but now that it had come, it shook me like a sudden fever. I kept my head sufficiently to realise that at all costs my agitation must be hidden. With an effort I prepared a decorous salute.

Her greeting was, nevertheless, more frank and natural than mine. I was still dithery after that queer access of excitement, and an attempt to be normal made me ever so slightly constrained. For a second her eyes clouded, and I realised that she had noticed the constraint; further I knew that she was wondering whether, after all, I was only there from a sense of duty, whether perhaps I had repented a rendezvous made on impulse a week ago. Even in that moment of agitation, I was struck by the certainty with which I interpreted her mind, surprised but convinced by my understanding of her instinctive humility. I struggled with my embarrassment.

" I'm a fool " I said. " But the fact is I was so glad to see you had come . . . you might have . . . well, been prevented. And, like an idiot, I never told you where you could send back word."

" I guess the Majestic would have found you and, if I couldn't make it, my friends the Abbotts could have helped."

I threw up my hands.

" Double idiot! So they would. Anyway here you are, and now shall it be Chantilly or where else? "

" Anywhere in the world. I don't care—so long as it's in the sunshine and doesn't smell of gasolene."

ဟ ဟ ဟ

From Chantilly we found a motor-bus to Senlis, and wandered about that grievously brutalised town until it was time for lunch. After lunch we started to walk southward through the forest, found some food at Ermenonville, walked another two miles to a station, and were back at the Nord again by ten o'clock. Put like that it sounds bleak enough; actually it was very much the opposite.

ဟ ဟ ဟ

Sitting on a wall facing the abandoned church of Saint Pierre in Senlis, I said:—

" I would like to call you Sally, please. I find your surname difficult. My surname is difficult too. The other name is Nicholas, and far easier."

" Yes, I know " she replied. " I asked Alice."

ဟ ဟ ဟ

Later in the day we lay on springy heather, with in front of us the dazzling white sand of the Désert, falling away in billowy slopes.   To the left, behind trees, were the buildings of Châalis, faintly seen.

" Do you know, Nicholas, it was lovely of you never to ask my address either last Sunday or the one before, nor try to take me home."

" My dear—why on earth?   If you had wanted it, you would have said so.   As you didn't, you didn't.   I refuse any credit for that."

" But suppose you had altered your mind about to-day?   Or been unable to keep the date? "

" Silly."

ᔆ   ᔆ   ᔆ

The breeze stirred the birch trees, and set up a tiny rattling among the pines.   She was picking up sand in small **handfuls** and letting it trickle through her fingers.

" Lovely and smooth " she said " like dry water."

Abruptly she stopped playing with the sand, sat up, and with an easy swing got on to her knees.   She faced me, her hands clasped in front of her.

" Nicholas, I've got to tell you something about myself."

" Why?   I know all I want."

" Maybe all you want, but not all you need."

Then, with a rush, " I'm married and I've got a child."

I looked up at her.   Her face was taut with shy unhappiness. I had never seen it other than brave and candid, and the sight was pitiful.   But she remained steadily upright, kneeling before me, and her hands only gripped one another a little more tightly. Before I could say anything she spoke again.   The words came unevenly.

" I'm going to be very immodest and say things women are not supposed to say on their own initiative.   But I can't have you hurt if I can prevent it.   You are falling in love with me,

Nicholas; but "—with a forlorn little laugh—" I am not the straightforward proposition you thought. I'm like an empty house. There is an owner, but no tenant."

The attempt at flippancy was almost too much for me. But I felt that it would be easier for her if conversation were, for a while at least, ostensibly dispassionate. With an effort I took up her metaphor.

" What about an offer for the whole property? "

She shook her head.

" I want my baby."

" The property to include the baby. . . ."

" The owner won't sell—and I can't."

" How ' can't '? "

" Why, because—because—it was my fault, you see.'

Still she knelt stock still, scorning the relief of restlessness, looking the world in the eyes as she made her difficult confession. I sprang up and took her hands.

" Get up, Sally. Now we will walk on, and you shall tell me the rest as we walk, or if you don't want to tell me any more, I will tell *you* things."

" I want to tell you more, but tell me things first."

I took her by the elbow and we went slowly into the shadow of the forest and along the grassy drive toward Ermenonville. She pressed my hand against her side, and I could feel the firm warmth of her body and her heart beating under the upward swell of her breast.

" You said I was falling in love with you. Of course I am. It's a platitude to say that I always have been; but I daresay it's true, though I did not understand at first. Nothing can alter it now—not if you had fifty husbands and rows of babies and adored them all and hated me. The situation is glorious and intolerable. What is glorious is that you can't hate me, or you wouldn't have told me what you have; what is intolerable is that one man has married you, and made you unhappy——"

" Please—I told you—it was *my* fault——"

" Don't interrupt. You have been married and are now unhappy. Have it that way if you like. Because I love you, I cannot bear you to be unhappy. Therefore I shall do any mortal thing to make you happier, and *not* do any mortal thing —however much I may long to do it—which might make you more miserable. So it is not mere curiosity which wants to know more. It is so that I can judge what I ought to do."

She stopped and half-turned towards me. I wondered if she were going to cry. But she only looked at me steadfastly for a moment with her lovely melancholy eyes, gave a queer little strangled sob, and then with head averted began walking again. After a few seconds' silence, she started to tell her tale. Her voice was low but controlled.

She was hardly out of college and back home in the small southern town where her parents lived, when dignified but unmistakable overtures were made to her by a local cotton factor of substance and repute. The suitor was not more than ten years her senior; but he was a severely religious man with strict puritan principles, and was held in some awe by the neighbourhood on account of his grave demeanour and sombre aloofness from the ordinary life of the place. That this dour and prominent citizen should so far compromise with the weakness of the flesh as to emerge from his seclusion and pay court to a young girl, caused considerable interest and gossip; and Sally was both envied and teased by the few young people of her acquaintance, while among her mother's older friends were much whispering and speculation. Sally's father and mother were poorly off, and there were younger children to be educated. So home influence was added to the stimulus of outside chaff; and she soon ceased to be merely flattered by her unexpected conquest and began seriously to visualise the prospect of marriage.

The suitor, personally, was presentable enough, though

rather forbidding. Tall and strongly made, he had a large straight mouth, and an abnormal length of nose and upper lip which gave his face an expression of ruminative gloom and seemed to prevent a smile from spreading upward from lips to eyes. The idea of having him for a husband tended, on the few occasions when she really faced up to it, to frighten her; but to a young girl marriage is as much an affair of new clothes and exciting congratulation as of protracted personal contact; and she allowed parental encouragement, and the delightful certainty of being for a while the centre of the local stage, to distract her mind from forecast of the future. He made his formal proposal and was accepted. The wedding followed after a short interval.

During the engagement he showed himself generous with his money; and the punctilious courtesy with which he treated his fiancée helped further to lull any qualms she might have had as to intimacies in prospect. Even the first few days of her married life brought little alteration in the shy formality of his behaviour. Then, however, something snapped, and he became possessed by a queer brooding passion which at first terrified his wife but gradually came to fascinate her.

" Oh, Nicholas! " she cried, breaking off with a nervous laugh. " I am saying the most dreadful things. But I want to be honest. That platitude about treating women rough— it's a fact, you know, so far as love-making is concerned. I always used to think it nonsense, believing it meant being beaten up and dragged round the room by one's hair which, of course, it doesn't. I was scared, but I liked it—and I believe my liking it caused all the trouble later. Do you hate my talking like this? We are never supposed to admit that we enjoy. . . . I mean, it is always the man who has to be humoured and a woman consents just to please him, because on some refined spiritual plane she loves him. It's not true, Nicholas. I did not love my husband on any spiritual plane. He was nice to me at first and I was grateful to him for giving me a comfortable home and pretty clothes. But I never *loved* him, except when. . . . Or isn't that love? I don't know. I suspect it *is* love all right—or a greater part of it. Anyway that was how I felt; and now you can be disgusted with me and I'll not have to tell you the rest."

Her voice broke a little and I waited for a few moments before speaking. Then:—

" Please go on, Sally. I thought that was grand."

She grew calm again; and, although I could feel her struggling to conquer her embarrassment, the story proceeded quietly enough.

The man's urgency in love-making went as quickly as it had come. The strange stirring of passion had died down long before, within eighteen months of marriage, her boy was born. And with its disappearance, even his everyday demeanour changed. He seemed to regard her less and less as a junior partner in the business of life, and more and more as a feature of his home, like the rest of the furniture and possessions. Although, as her pregnancy advanced, he provided all necessary care and assistance, he did so with the impersonal efficiency of one who from motives of prudence and foresight wishes to safeguard his property.

The sudden quenching of the man's desire first puzzled his wife and then began to torment her. For weeks before her baby was born she worried and wondered, and the nervous fret had disastrous consequences. The child was healthy and of normal weight; but she herself had a bad passage, and was told categorically that she would be unable to feed him. The news that his son must be brought up by hand caused the father bitter mortification. The doctor was astonished at his angry disappointment, and equally at his apparent indifference to the progress of the mother's convalescence. It seemed as though his wife's inability to nurse her baby was an insult to his pride, and, apparently in revenge, he proceeded to bar her from the rest of her maternal privileges. The baby was placed under the supervision of an experienced middle-aged nurse, who was instructed to take complete charge of him and be responsible directly to the father.

To Sally it was as though her baby had vanished from sight, swallowed up in the stifling gloom of a house, which from that moment she began to dread. He did not seem to belong to her any more; and although the nurse evaded instructions as much as she dared and, when the father was away at business, left the child to his mother's care, both women were always anxious and fearful, listening for the return of a man who every month became more shut in upon himself and more unapproachable.

" Don't think I'm forgetting my own share in it all—even thus far " Sally said. " Like a vain silly little fool, I had married for money and position and to be grander than the girls I knew. Then once married, he began to want me and I liked being wanted. Then he suddenly didn't want me any more, and I couldn't understand what I had done wrong. When little Danny came, I thought we would have at least our son in common, and that he would perhaps begin to like me again when I looked the same as I used. But I had to go and fail even to nurse my baby! And that finished it. I know it did. And I was so *ashamed*, Nicholas. I felt I had let him down without being able to help it. I blamed myself horribly, and tried all I knew to make up for it. But he would hardly notice me and, what was perhaps worse, he left nothing for me to do. I *had* nothing to do—not even a baby to care for."

The unhappy sense of being a mere useless superfluity began to get on her nerves. But it was a long while before she began even to consider whether alleviation of her own lonely obscurity were possible. She did not, indeed, think much about herself. Her mind was centred on her son. Her love for him, denied all but surreptitious outlets, developed into ingenious evasion of the jailer's rules, and had no desire to thwart itself by escaping from the jail. Into the bargain the conventional morality of the small-town community and the influence of her own up-bringing were dead against any idea of home-breaking. So, for long enough, the very thought of seeking for amusement on her own never occurred to her.

But as time went by, the terrible dullness of her life drove her beyond melancholy and into fear. Was this to go on year after year? In one of her moods of terror, she went to her mother for counsel. Hitherto she had said nothing to those at home which might suggest that her married life was unsatisfactory. Now, however, she told enough of the story to show that things were far from right.

At first the mother was filled with alarm and begged her daughter to have patience. Then she turned on Sally and started to upbraid her.

" At least you have no need to scrape and moil as I have done for years " she said bitterly. " A pity you have not. You might then understand what a woman's life *can* be like, and not think so much of your own fancy grievances."

Sally was silent and went miserably home. " I'm glad at least I held my tongue " she told me. " It's the only thing in the whole wretched business I *am* glad about. I so nearly referred to the money I used to send mother regularly, to the presents I gave them all. *So* nearly, Nicholas. I was worked up that much. But I didn't. I just went back."

The scene with her mother had one important effect—it caused her to consider her own distresses more critically than before. Were her grievances indeed fancy grievances? Perhaps they were, in the sense that she might try herself to remedy them. She was lonely; her husband ignored her; she had no interests, and was not required to have any ideas or take any decisions. Put like that—and as grievances go—they sounded trivial enough; she might at least see what she could do to acquire interests and company, to find outside her home the stimulus which inside it was denied to her. Unfortunately there was little to be done in the actual locality; her husband would only entertain the few families he himself chose to know; and they were severe old-fashioned folk, who made up the business aristocracy of the place and frowned successfully on all attempts to make the town even the most distant imitation of the abandoned cities of the north-east. Such young people as remained were destined themselves to become repressive elders. The others, on one pretext or another, had got out and away.

She told herself that she had no desire to " get out ". All she wanted was freedom to sample new places and see new people, and then, refreshed, to settle down again. There was no question of leaving home; quite the contrary indeed, because home was now more nearly home than it had ever been. Danny was growing out of babyhood, and beginning to run about and talk and play games. Therefore the barrier between him and her was inevitably relaxed, and he was coming to know her as his mother and to share his secrets with her and run to her for remedy when he fell down or had a pain or broke a favourite toy. Still, when the father was present, she remained a cypher; still she was allowed no voice in the child's training. But at least she could be his playmate, and, in small things, his doctor.

For this she was duly grateful; but the changed régime had its mournful side. If she could now hear Danny laugh and hold him in her arms and know that he was happy when she was near, she had also to watch his natural merriment darken suddenly to timid gravity when his father entered the room or, at table, reproved him for some childish joke. More bitter still was the sight of the little boy under a discipline which she thought wrong and often cruel. Once or twice she ventured a protest, but the man looked at her with cold contempt and either turned his back on her or walked out of the room. He began to show signs of resenting even the casual companionship of mother and son; interrupting their play-time by taking the little boy into town with him or summoning him to his study to be read to at unexpected hours.   So she settled to a strange life of alternating happiness and apprehension; longing with increasing urgency for some sort of a change, which would enable her to tell Danny new things and see his face lighten with interest and, when she was unable to reach him, would give her new things to remember and to enjoy in retrospect.

One day she had a letter in a writing she knew well, posted from the city of Richmond, Virginia.   It was from Alice Abbott, who ever since her marriage had lived on the Pacific Coast.   Her husband, who had had volunteer experience, had taken a commission shortly after America entered the war, and was now in a training camp drilling recruits.   He and Alice had decided, when the war was over, to accept an offer of a partnership in a New York law firm; so she had packed up their west-coast apartment, and settled temporarily in Richmond where she had relatives.   She begged Sally to pay her a visit.

The chance was too good to miss.   Even *he* could hardly object to her oldest college friend; and the prospect of seeing Alice again and talking over old times and, perhaps, pouring out all her troubles, made Sally almost sick with pleasure. Summoning her courage, she asked her husband for permission to go.   To her surprise, he agreed readily enough, gave her the necessary money, and told her to be back in three weeks' time.

" At first " she told me " I was kind of dazed—like a prisoner pulled out of a dungeon after months of darkness, and blinking in the daylight.   I remember wandering around Richmond, looking in the shops and hardly realising anything except that I was free to do what I wanted and need not pull myself together before every meal or make timid conversation or be bored and bored and bored.   Then I came to; and must have romped and chattered with Alice's friends like an excited child. We went to dances, and I found I got partners and that other men cut in, and I began to consider what I looked like—which I just had not thought of for years. And then life began to stir in me again; and I got to look forward to seeing certain people, and one in particular—a sort of cousin of Alice's, who seemed to go everywhere and be liked by everyone. He was always trying to date me up; and Alice laughed at me and called me the Merry Widow and—well, you know how like silly girls silly girls can be! I had told Alice everything by now, and she had looked very grave and not said much, except that I had better enjoy myself while I had the chance—which I certainly did.

" Then, during the third week of my stay, I had a letter from home. He said he had to take a long business trip and would be away another two or three weeks, and that I would do well to stop where I was, if my friend could keep me a while longer.

" My first impulse was to jump at the chance of a time at home alone with Danny; but, when I consulted Alice, she pressed me to stay. She said my husband would be furious when he found I had gone straight back the moment I knew he was away; couldn't I get home two or three days earlier and make it look more casual? The idea of making him angry scared me; more than once I had been really frightened of him breaking out. I'd seen one frozen side of him melt and freeze again, remember; why not another? So what with fear and the fun I was having. . . .

" For I *was* having fun! My flirtation with the man I spoke of was going fine—at least what a girl in my state of mind calls ' fine '. He was well on the string, and took me about and said pretty things to me; and I fancied myself in complete control of the situation. So I was more than ready to keep right on, if only for the pleasure his admiration gave me, and parties, and going about with him, and being noticed. Don't blame me too much yet, Nicholas. Remember I hadn't been noticed for so long."

" I'm not blaming you, my dear.   I'm only interested."

So things went gaily on, till all of a sudden, Sally's delightful game of make-believe was broken to pieces.   She had another letter—this time from her younger sister who lived at home. It said that Danny's nurse had been down in great distress to say that the master had taken Danny away to school—the nurse did not know where, but it was far away.   At first Sally just stared at the letter in horrified amazement.   Then she went up to her room and locked the door.

" I sat there an hour; and during that hour queer things happened to me.   First I was in despair, and planned to hurry home and track Danny down and throw myself at his father's feet and beg and implore him.   Next I went all cold with rage. He had lied to me about his business trip—this virtuous, censorious, self-complacent brute had lied deliberately, in order to steal my child.   I realised then that I hated him more than anything in the world.   I suppose I had been too much afraid to hate him up till now.   But I was not afraid any longer.   I would have my revenge—though how I had not the least idea.

" And as I sat up in that room and hated him, there came back memories of the few months during which I had really belonged to him.   It was extraordinary to think back to what had passed between us, and then forward again to my present mood.   And —do you know—the things I felt, and what he looked like, and—oh, all of it—rushed back at me with such force and tumult, that I went burning hot instead of cold, and was so steamed up with a mixture of fury and excitement, that I believe if he had walked in at that moment, I would first have forced him to take me and then have tried to kill him. . . ."

She broke off and turned to look at me with eyes wide with horror.   Then, as though she had suddenly heard herself saying those last words:—

" Do I really mean that, Nicholas ? "

" Not now, you don't, but I dare say you did—then."

" But it's dreadful. . . ."

" Only dreadful as a sign of your misery. Please, Sally, stop telling this over again. It only brings it back."

She began to blush, and the colour, as it flooded up from her neck, turned her skin to a rich rosy brown.

" I can't stop now " she whispered. " I'm just coming to what I *must* tell you."

But the pause lengthened and I could almost hear the choke of her embarrassment.

" I'll tell it for you " I said. " I think I know what happened. You went out that evening—or afternoon—with the Richmond Casanova."

" Now, Nicholas! Don't say that. He was really a nice boy."

" No, he wasn't. He was terrible. Anyway I think he was terrible. And let me go on. You went out with him. . . ."

Suddenly she gurgled.

" Oh, my dear, aren't you just sweet! How I like you being jealous."

" Jealous? I'm not jealous of a man who flukes into heaven on a rebound! "

I had spoken hastily, and noticing that her amusement had turned to apprehension, went on more quietly :—

" I'm sorry, my dear. I suppose I am jealous. Never mind. You went out with him. You were still all keyed up— partly starved, partly out for vengeance." After a pause: " Well? Isn't that what happened? "

She walked on, and said nothing. Then she nodded. " Yes " she said gently. " That is what happened."

Those few moments of silence had given me a chance to collect my wits and self-control. I realised I had taken more for granted than I had any right to do, and into the bargain betrayed an element in my feeling for Sally which I had not admitted even to myself. I was ashamed; and the more so, when on the heels of shame followed a thrill of anticipation. I pulled my mind away from dangerous thoughts and concentrated fiercely on the immediate present.

" And after that? " I asked.

" After that, the deluge. You see I was being trailed."

I stared at her in astonishment.

" You were being what? "

" Trailed . . . followed around."

" But, Sally, why? "

" He wanted to be rid of me. I suppose he hated me as much as I hated him—and had been doing so for years. He had his son. That is what he longed for—a son. But he was not going to do anything about it himself. That would harm his reputation. I must do the slipping-up, and he waited for a good chance to make it easy for me. He reckoned I was sure to break out sooner or later. He knew no girl could go through the extremes of heat and cold that I had gone through, without some time swinging back again. So he fixed an opportunity, and gambled on his knowledge of human nature. He is a clever man. He deserved to win."

Pity and indignation bewildered me. For a moment I could not speak; then knew that I must speak, and said, lamely enough:—

" But did he win? At least you were free."

" If you call exile ' freedom '—and losing my boy."

This silenced me again. The implication that this dusky wood, to me the threshold of Paradise, was to her ' exile ', was discouraging enough; the lament for her child came from a privacy I could not violate. I managed just to find my tongue.

" And then? "

To my surprise her voice became jaunty and a little cynical.

" Oh, then he just wrote me the kind of letter his sort has always written. . . I had deserted my home, broken my marriage vows, dishonoured his name. . . . You know, all the clichés. . . ."

The jauntiness had gone shrill; then cracked. The pathos of her pretence restored my self-esteem—or rather transformed self-pity into pity for her.

" Oh, my dear! . . . And was that all? "

" Not quite. He said he did not wish to see me again; that he had instructed his lawyers to pay me a small allowance through any bank I chose to name; that I was to write to them and not to him; that he had already suffered shame enough, and I must remember that I was still his wife. . . ." Her voice dropped to a whisper . . . " Still that man's wife."

" He won't divorce you then? "

" Oh no! That would be against his principles. He is a very *virtuous* man—a cruel, lying beast, but *moral*. And here was a chance for cruelty and morality to go hand in hand. What more could he ask? "

" And was *that* all? "

" Finish. I have not seen him since."

" Nor Danny? "

" Yes. Danny I saw—once. With great difficulty and thanks to my sister's help, I did find out where he was. I went down to the school. Alice came with me and played the potential parent. She did it so well that we were invited to watch the junior school playing games. And there I saw him."

" Well done! Did he see you? "

" He certainly did. I took care of that. As the game ended and our visit was nearly due to end, I just went reckless and sent poor dear Alice to ask for him by name, on the ground she knew his parents. He came—and—and I believe he was as glad to see me as I to see him."

She was near to breaking down again, so I asked no further questions and we walked some way without speaking. Then I ventured.

" When did all this happen? "

" Only last fall."

" And what came next? "

" Oh, I went all soft again.   Seeing Danny did it, I suppose. I wrote to my husband; confessed that I had been a wicked woman; begged him to forgive me; swore to slave for him and Danny all my life, and asked for leave to come home and take my punishment."

" Did he reply? "

" Not directly.   His lawyer wrote that his client did not wish to be pestered with unwelcome letters; and unless I promised never to trouble him again, my allowance would be cancelled and would I, please, send the necessary undertaking in writing."

" But what did you *do*? "

" Oh, I just gave up.   I sent the undertaking.   Then I stopped on with Alice for a while.   She and Moreton were just heavenly to me.   I don't know what would have become of me, but for them.   I'd no money; and until I could get a job, had to have the allowance.   I *had* to, Nicholas—do believe me."

The fierce pleading in her last words startled me.   " But, Sally, of course you had to!   Who says you shouldn't . . .? "

She seemed to crumple into sudden fatigue.

" Oh, I don't know.   I was afraid you might be thinking I made a heroic gesture; and then I would disappoint you again."

" Again?   When first? "

" When I told you what a mess I had made of everything."

" Oh, Sally, Sally!   Will you not be a bit conceited and selfish for a change—just with me?   Do I have to tell you that anything you have done is right for me, because you have done it?   But let us get back to the subject.   What about Danny? Is the father fond of him? "

" Oh, yes, he's fond of him—sort of obstinately centred on him, as part of his own scheme of life."

" Then he won't ill-treat the child ? "

" Heavens, no! not intentionally—particularly with me out of the way. But he'll crush the childhood out of the poor little soul."

" There's no hope of his agreeing to hand him over to you ? "

" ' No hope ' is understatement."

" So you can do literally nothing to make life easier for the kid ? "

" Not unless thinking about him helps—and wanting him."

" And about you—is there a job ? "

She nodded.

" There is—and I don't know that I care for it much, now that I'm face to face with it. I went with Alice and Moreton to New York. He sailed with the Conference delegation almost at once and I helped her settle in her new place. Then I had a piece of luck—or what seemed luck then. I was offered a job by some period decorators and furnishing people. Back at home some people have all the money there is—you knew that of course—and a lot of profiteers are going ' old family ', which means sending their sons (like those upstarts at lunch the other day) to give Americans a good name in other countries, and themselves a stock of traditions. They want heirlooms and armorial china and chairs belonging to Diane de Poitiers and Madame de Maintenon's escritoire and tapestries and what-all. This firm argued that France was hard hit and, now the war was over, would part with anything for cash. I had taken French at college, and had spent some of my endless hours of married leisure studying French history and architecture and costume and style generally. So they suggested I come over, hunt out the distressed aristocrats and dangle the dollars. Dandy, isn't it ? "

" Poor Sally.   I wish I had some heirlooms.   Do these folk pay you well? "

" They will do—well enough."

" What do you mean by ' will do '?   Are you on commission merely? "

She ignored my question.

" Let me finish.   Once again Alice saved my life—or my reason, anyway.   I liked a lot the idea of getting away from America.   I'd got to kill the longing for Danny and try to drive all that had happened out of my head.   So I jumped at the firm's offer.   But then I went panicky and lost my nerve. I was like a crazy thing.   I just couldn't face sailing to France by myself, and forcing my way into strange and probably un-happy homes, and all that.   So Alice took charge.   She cabled to Moreton she was tired of waiting about New York for him, and was coming over, and would he have somewhere for her to live.   He did, of course, the angel that he is, and she and I travelled together.   That's all."

" Not quite all.   You didn't tell me what these people are giving you to live on."

" Nick, don't ask any more.   I would like to forget it all for a bit and just enjoy *now*."

" You will remember I love you, Sally?   Don't forget that too."

" Do you still, Nicholas.   Then that is the ' now ' I want to enjoy."

" It will last beyond now."

She took my hand and held it firmly, but said nothing more. When we came out of the forest it was quite dark.

∽   ∽   ∽

We were in the train going back to Paris.   It was a stopping train, made up of all manner of miscellaneous coaches, and it swayed and rattled over the neglected tracks.   We had a decayed first class compartment to ourselves, its dove-grey cushions stained and torn, a dim lamp flickering in the roof.

" Sally " I said, " I must say one or two things about you and me."

She nodded; and I went on:—

" By sending me away you won't help your boy. Your husband has shut the door on you; and, except to marry again, you are free to do what you like. I cannot lose sight of you now, Sally—*cannot*, do you understand—unless you tell me I have to. Are you going to tell me that? I want to be with you, and, if I can make you a little happier, have a chance to do so."

She was about to speak, but I checked her.

" One moment more. So long as the conference is on, we shall merely be like two people in different jobs, who meet after hours at intervals and sometimes go out of town for Sunday. That is not what I mean by ' being with you ', and that is not going to help you through a bad patch. But when the Treaty is signed—as I suppose it must be sometime—I will get some leave. I would like to spend it with you. May I? "

" Nicholas, you must not get affiché with an outcast wife."

" May I, Sally? "

" But I don't know where I'll be. . . ."

" *May* I, Sally? "

She began rocking herself gently to and fro. " Oh my dear " she cried at last. " Make it happen! "

The train jerked over the points at the Pont Marcadet and went clattering through the cutting.

" We are just in " I said. " I will write to you care of the Abbotts."

She did not answer, until we were walking along the platform to the ticket-barrier.

" I would rather you wrote me direct " she said. " Have you time to take me back? The address is 6 Rue de la Petite Falaise—behind the Institut. A pretty name for an ugly street. I don't mind, now, your knowing that I live in a slum. I was afraid both other times."

In the taxi I just held her hand. My mind was a confusion of happiness and distress. That physical discomfort should be added to her suffering spirit was grievous. I guessed that her employers gave her travelling expenses, and promised payment by results. No one could offer her money—I least of all. The only thing I might do was to put her in the way of buying things. I thought of all the friends I had ever made in France. Two or three were possible. . . .

We turned right, into the Quai Conti.

" Tell him to stop here."

I had already told him precisely this when we got in, and, as she spoke, the cab drew to the curb.

" So you thought of that also " she said, half to herself, as we crossed the road.

The narrow street was not actively sinister, but airless and shabby. At her door I took her hands, kissed them and let them fall.

" Goodnight, Sally. I think I know where you may be able to find some of the sort of things you have been sent to look for. I'll write you about them. And about other things. Let's meet very soon again—and thank you for a perfect day."

She stood still for a moment, her head a little bowed. Then raised it and smiled faintly.

" Goodnight, Nicholas."

III: BRANDY FOR ONE

I TACKLED immediately the job of verifying the names and addresses to which Sally might be referred, and wrote to her as promised. I also secured a fairly reliable guarantee of freedom for the evening of Friday, and asked her to dine and spend the evening with me. It seemed even more desirable than before to break the cycle of Sundays, although I had no intention of giving up my prolonged weekly sight of her—merely of embellishing the intervals with as many emergency meetings as possible. Indeed I decided, by way of variation, to suggest that the next Sunday afternoon we pay a joint call on the Abbotts, thus simultaneously discharging a social duty and advertising the fact of our companionship. This latter seemed to me important. I wanted the Abbotts on my side.

I posted my letter on Monday. When by Thursday evening I had had no answer, I was in more than half a panic. She must be ill. Who was looking after her? Who *was* there to look after her? I did not know. Somebody, however, obviously ought to do something. I even played with the idea of myself invading the Rue de la Petite Falaise, and forcibly taking charge. But instinct told me this would be a mistake. It would introduce a discordant element into a relationship which still astonished me by its swift inevitable blossoming and the inherence of its emotional harmony. I felt I had a right to every intimacy a man could have with a woman, and yet no rights at all. The next stage would come when it was due to come or when she wanted it.

The only solution seemed to be Alice Abbott. I must pay my intended call, alone, and with quite another purpose. Also as promptly as possible. The first opportunity would be the sacred Friday evening destined for Sally and now indeed to be devoted to her, but very differently.

On Friday morning there was still no letter. At what I hoped was a convenient time I telephoned the Abbotts' flat. Could Mrs Abbott see me any time after six o'clock? Her maid answered me. Mrs Abbott had been out of Paris for two days, and was to return that afternoon. The maid was not aware of any engagement for the evening. I rang up the offices of the American Delegation. After some delay Abbott was located,

and I heard his deep " Hullo " with such relief that I nearly
began to laugh wildly into the telephone. Yes; Alice would
be at home for dinner. Would I join them? There was no
time to reckon pros and cons. I accepted gratefully; but hung
up wondering what he was making of my sudden wish to see
his wife, and whether I should have to explain myself under the
disconcerting gaze of those shrewd and serious eyes.

It was, however, immediately evident that the Abbotts knew
something, if not everything, of the purpose of my visit. I
arrived a little after seven and was shown into the salon. Alice
Abbott was sitting alone. There was no sign of her husband.
She greeted me with genuine but embarrassed kindness, and
began forthwith :—

" Mr Dering, if you had not already been due to come here
tonight, I should have written to you as soon as I reached Paris—
and sent you this."

She handed me an envelope—sealed, and bearing my name
in handwriting I instantly recognised although I had never
seen it before.

" Moreton asked you to dinner " she went on " knowing
nothing of this letter. All he knew was that you wanted to
come and see us. I am now in a difficulty. You will surely
want to read your letter at once, and it is possible you may
want to talk to me after you have read it. Or maybe not. I
don't know. I have not read the letter, but I know what it
is about and why it was written. If I say that you would do
well to dine elsewhere, and either come back here or not, it
sounds as though I don't want to have you. That I promise
you is absolutely not so. If I urge you to stay—leaving you
to read the letter now—and you want nothing more than to get
out of here, it puts you in a jam."

All the time she was speaking, I stood holding Sally's letter
in my hand, bewildered questions falling over one another in
my head, half-hearing what Mrs Abbott was saying, half-

listening to the noisy confusion in my own brain. When she stopped talking, I must have looked at her in obvious perplexity and distress, for she put a hand on my arm and said gently:—

" I hate to have to do this, but I couldn't shirk it. I am sure you had better leave us now; and if I can be of any help—any help at all—come right back when you want."

I rallied sufficiently to take the meaning of her kindliness and tact, and to mutter a few words of thanks. Then I put the letter in my pocket and went out into the street.

∽   ∽   ∽

It was nearly half past seven, and through the side windows of the café on the Place de l'Alma I could see the place was practically empty. The night was chilly; and as I stepped to the main door between piled tables on the unused terrasse, I remembered sitting out in the sun less than three weeks ago, killing time before my first lunch with the Abbotts, before my first sight of Sally. And now I was here again—before what was to have been dinner with the Abbotts, before reading what was, in fact, my first letter from Sally. Would it also prove my last? My heart turned over, and almost sick with apprehension I found a corner table, put the envelope face downward in front of me and stared at it, until the waiter had brought me café-cognac and retired to his interrupted newspaper.

When at last I summoned my courage, I slit the envelope carefully with a pocket knife, drew out the contents and began to read. There was no address on the plain sheet of rather cheap paper with up-and-down ruling, French fashion, in pale blue.

" *Nicholas, dear, dear Nicholas, will you try to believe that I write this only because I love you? Try hard, my love. I would never lie to you, and I think you know it.*

" *Last Sunday was the most perfect thing that ever happened*

*to me, and I want you to understand that I shall live on the
memory of it so long as I live at all.   But as I thought it over
—and still more when your letter came and I saw that you had
done all that worrying about me, with everything else you have
to do—I began to see that I must run away.   Yes! run away,
like the little coward that I am—from everything I want most in
the world.*

   " *It's not fair to you, Nicholas, to let you get all involved with
a girl who cannot help you to get out of life whatever you want
to get.   I don't know what that is, and I don't care.   I only
know that if you want it, I would want it too—and spend my
life doing anything I could, so you got it.   And I can do*
nothing, *just* nothing.   *I am useless to a man who expects
more of me than any girl can give to any man.   And you* do
*expect more.   It is so like you to have made no single pass at
me, never to have asked where I lived (I said that before!) and
at my door—the night of that lovely, lovely day in the forest—
just to kiss my hands and say goodnight.*

   " *So I am disappearing.   You will be hurt at first—oh,
God, how I hate to hurt you!—but it will be best for you in the
end.   You will forget about me ; and, once free of this conference, go right ahead with whatever is your job.   Sooner or
later I'll hear something you've done or read your name somewhere.   And then I'll tell myself—' One time that man told me
he loved me . . . and I believed him . . . as I still do, because
it was true.'*

   " *Oh, my darling, whatever happens to you, remember that
one woman loved you so much that she left you ; that she did
not dare to see you again, because she would never again have
the strength to do what is right.   What I am doing is right,*
right, RIGHT.

   " *Goodbye, my love.*

                                          Sally."

I read the letter through a second time, put it carefully back in its envelope, and replaced the envelope face downwards on the table. The lower edge was not quite parallel with the rim of the table, so I straightened it. Then I sat in my chair and just stared in front of me. I was aware of the ticking of a clock, and of the occasional rustle of a newspaper as the waiter turned a page or flattened a fold. There seemed to be no other sound.

I had no coherent thoughts about anything. Thought is exhausting, and I felt too tired to attempt it. And anyway there was nothing to think about; or so much to think about that it was no use starting. I began to smoke, and the taste of tobacco reminded me of my coffee. I had drunk one mouthful only and the cup was three parts full. These three parts were stone cold. I took a sip, replaced the cup, and decided that coffee—even coffee-cognac—was one of the drinks I most disliked. I was considering a substitute, when my eye caught the upper edge of the envelope containing Sally's letter. I had opened it neatly with a knife, but not so neatly that the line of it was as sharp as the three other edges. There were tiny irregularities where the paper had parted crookedly to right or left. One such, in particular, offended me. I got out my knife again, and began to restore symmetry. But I found to my surprise that my hands shook so badly that I only made matters worse. I held my hands in the air and looked at them. They went on shaking. Hell! I thought, I might be drunk. And why not? At least a drunk man finds himself interesting and amusing, and I found myself neither the one nor the other. I will get drunk, I decided; and rapped on the table.

After two Mandarins I felt warmer and more comfortable. I had eaten nothing since lunch and it was now nine o'clock. Of course I was not yet even exalted; merely a little encouraged. I felt I had been long enough in this particular café and that Sally's letter had lain long enough on this particular table. In my mind I ran over the cafés she and I had visited together on

our two Sunday outings. First of all was one on the Place
d'Italie; then one on the Place St Michel; then one near the
Odéon; then one behind St Germain; then one on the river
opposite the Ile St Louis. Was that all? No—there was one
near the Châtelet, not an attractive one, but handy after the
cinema. In the Place de la Bastille we had not sampled a café;
only a tram. At least she had.

This enumeration of cafés suddenly bored me. I paid for
my drinks, put the letter into my breast pocket and went out
into the dark street. There had been a shower of rain and the
pavements were wet. It was still chilly. At the corner of the
bridge I hesitated. Hardly anyone was about. The trees in
the Cour Albert Ier were dripping softly on the gravel; the
lamps planted among them made the shadows deeper and the
whole avenue dank and uninviting. I walked over the bridge
and turned east. Opposite the Invalides station I hailed a taxi.

Place d'Italie. Here, at any rate, was a certain animation.
The cafés were not full; but there was traffic in the square and
the night-crowd of the neighbourhood was coming and going.
The terrasse of Sally's café was in use, for it was a large café
with enough depth to let the end-partitions shelter at least the
inside row of tables. I had two more Mandarins and smoked
six cigarettes. The clock on the Mairie was lighted from inside.
Last time I had looked at it, the sunshine had lighted it from
outside. I felt myself intimate with the clock on the Mairie,
familiar with its habits both day and night.

At ten-thirty I went inside and bought some more cigarettes;
came out again and had a third drink. The terrasse was empty,
and several of the parties inside had looked curiously at me
when I came in for cigarettes and went out again. They
evidently considered it too cold to sit out of doors. They
knew I was doing so, because I had been compelled to rap on
the window when I wanted a waiter. This, for my third drink,
was unnecessary, for I ordered it on my way out. I felt that

this showed foresight and competence. So many people would never have thought of it, and would have had to start rapping again. I carried efficiency still further, for when the waiter came I paid him off. Another rapping saved.

I drank my third Mandarin with flagging enthusiasm. I had hitherto thought it a good drink, with all the kick of Picon and more sense of humour; but now I found it cloying and over-decorated. I wished I was drinking something else. Nor did I like the look of the Place d'Italie, now that I surveyed it once more. Its details were not very clear; but it struck me as overstocked with huts and kiosks and statues and monuments and urinals. Also such local citizens as passed within my view seemed physically unattractive and of dubious honesty.

There appeared to be two Métro stations in the square, one to my right, the other further away and almost opposite. This was provoking. One should not be confronted with alternative Métro stations. I had a feeling that the one across the square was probably the more efficient. Anyway, in order to reach it in comparative safety, I should have to make a considerable détour, and a walk would do me good. The journey involved two important street-crossings, but they were not serious so late at night and I arrived unruffled at the ticket-guichet. I then proceeded to walk all the way back again through a tiled passage. When I found myself at the foot of the stairs leading down from the other entrance, I was amused. That would learn them to go building stations all over the place and confusing the public. There were several notices on the walls—Direction this and Direction that. I decided to go north. This re-visiting of places connected with Sally was silly. Besides I was tired of the south side. Nevertheless, when the train rasped into Bastille, I got out. The cold air of the square was pleasant and it was not raining. I leant on the wall overlooking the canal basin, and felt almost cheerful. It came into my mind that Alice Abbott might be expecting a call from me and be sitting up. But surely she would have realised before eleven o'clock that I was not coming, and it was now nearly a quarter past. " A thousand apologies, madame " I said to myself in French. " Two thousand in fact, but what would you? " I shrugged my shoulders so vigorously, that one elbow slipped off the wall and I nearly knocked my chin on the stones. Little Tich, I said, and giggled.

Still chuckling, I began to walk toward the lights of a café on the west side of the square. As I crossed Henri IV a south-bound tram stopped at the halt. I recognised the lettering. For a moment I thought of getting on board, but it was clearly more important to get something to drink. Besides at some point I should have to get off; and there would be the worry of getting all the way back to Bastille again. So I decided to ignore the tram. There would be a later one.

The cognac in Bastille was not very good, but at least it was neither sweet nor sticky. After my third, I told myself that for really good brandy one must go to a really good bar. It was useless to sit around in Bastille and expect to have brandy as good as one could get near the Opera. I hated those bars near the Opera, but at least they had good brandy. There were no taxis, so I went back to the Métro. I had forgotten about Sally's tram; but as no trams were in sight, it did not matter. At Palais Royal I had intended changing trains, but thought I would come up to street-level again and take a taxi. Across Rivoli was the great block of the Louvre. If only the galleries had been open, I would have gone in to see the Victory of Samothrace. I wanted particularly to see the Victory of Samothrace. Why they shut galleries just at the time busy people can visit them, I could not understand. Typical bureaucratic stupidity.

I put a black mark against the Louvre, and started to walk up the Avenue de l'Opéra. There were plenty of people about, and beautiful cars were purring up and down the street. I concentrated on the problem of good brandy, and remembered a bar in the Rue Daunou where it was very good. At least someone had told me of a bar where it was good. I had never been there, nor could I remember the name. The Rue Daunou is not a long street, but contains more than one bar. I must take them in order, as otherwise I might miss the one I wanted.

In the first one several men turned round as I entered, and one of them greeted me.

" Why, it's Dering! Come on, my lad. What'll you have ? "

They were newspaper men, and I knew two or three of them in the way one got to know newspaper men during the Conference.

" I'm looking for some good brandy " I said.

" You shall have it old son. Harry, give the gentleman some real brandy."

We talked of this and that, and I stood the company a round of drinks. Then it was someone else's turn. They were large brandies, too.

" You look a bit chewed, Dering " said one of them. " Anything wrong? "

" I'm tight " I said.

" Naturally. So am I, more or less. So are we all. But that's nothing. You look as though you'd seen a platoon of ghosts."

" I've seen the Place d'Italie " I replied. " That's bad enough."

" Sorry. I didn't mean to be inquisitive."

" Nothing to be sorry about. And you might well be right. Perhaps I did see some ghosts . . ."

" Pink rats more likely " one of the group whispered to his neighbour. I had that curious long-range hearing which, at a certain stage of drunkenness, brings small sounds in from a distance and gives them clarity. I heard the whisper distinctly. It amused me.

" No, not rats " I said.   " Just ghosts."

The two men looked confused and began brushing ash off their coats, as one does in embarrassment.

" I must get on " I said.   " I have to try the brandy up the street.   Someone told me there was a bar in this street which had really excellent brandy, but I've forgotten the name. Perhaps this is the one after all."

" Well, it is good, isn't it? " asked the man who first greeted me.

I nodded.

" Very good.   But up the street it may be better."

" There are girls up the street " said someone.

I was irritated.

" What the hell——" I began; then realised that I was too weary to be cross, and spoke patiently.

" I do not want girls—or ghosts; I have had enough of girls *and* ghosts to last me for months.   Damn the lot of them, the twisters.   I want brandy.   You know where you are with brandy."

The room was swaying a little before my eyes.   I wanted badly to shut them, but was afraid to do so.   Anything might happen to the room if I shut my eyes, and then where should we all be?   Still, it was important to get them shut somehow, and perhaps the best plan would be to go to bed.   To shut one's eyes in bed was quite in order.   I could come to-morrow and settle the question of brandy.

" I think I'll go to bed " I said suddenly.

The man I knew best took up his overcoat and hat.

" Good plan " he said.   " I'll come along.   I go your way."

By a freak of memory I knew this was not true.

" You don't go my way.   Your hotel is just across the street there.   It's waste of time to go by the Étoile to—to—Capucines when you are so near.   And journalists mustn't waste time."

H 2

He laughed.

" Quite right. Nor they must. And just so as to be quicker on the job, I have moved my hotel. I'm now close to you. Goodnight everyone. Come along, Dering."

I did not believe him, but felt incapable of argument. Slumped in the corner of a taxi, I had to give my whole attention to controlling the dizziness and worse which sought to master me. My stomach stirred ominously; my eyes drooped and drooped, but every time they closed, I felt a surge of nausea and I forced them open again. My companion said not a word. At my hotel he collected my key, saw me into the lift and into my room. I tried to tell him several times to go away, but the exertion of speaking was too great. Once in my room, I made a supreme effort. He was helping me with my overcoat, and I had a horrid feeling he would want to take off my shoes also. No time for that. No time for anything, but to get him out and take what was coming to me. I managed to say quite clearly: " I'll be all right now. Goodnight. Thanks."

At last the door closed behind him.

IV: FRIEND AND RELATION

SATURDAY found me more than chastened. I was, candidly, a mess. As against my acute and complex suffering, ordinary head-and-mouth disease—the conventional hang-over of music-hall and comic-paper—was a mere childish ailment. By mid-day it was still painful to move my eyes, and a red-hot stiffness from ears to shoulders and half-way down my back made anguish of every incautious gesture. I was not at all sorry for myself in the sense of having a grievance, having enough reason left to realise that I had only got what I had asked for. But the discomfort was extreme, and as a member of the British Delegation I was utterly worthless. At about one o'clock I replaced in my tray a bulky but peculiarly tedious file dealing with steel-works at Burbach-Eich-Dudelingen and its war-time operations, and teetered out into the Champs Elysées. It was sunny and milder, and I thought a solitary half-hour on a seat might be gently curative. Actually I went to sleep and, waking at half past two, felt undoubtedly better. Back in my office I found a note lying on top of the Burbach dossier.

Moreton Abbott wrote to express his wife's regret and his own that I had been unable to dine with them the previous evening. They hoped that luncheon tomorrow (Sunday) would be possible. Looking forward to seeing me, he was, cordially mine.

Even in its relaxed and wayward condition, my mind managed to read between the lines of this carefully commonplace little note. What dears they are, I thought; and sent a polite acceptance.

∽   ∽   ∽

Abbott himself opened the door of the apartment and greeted me with his usual calm solemnity. He was wearing his hat.

" Come in " he said. " Glad to see you. I hope you are not too hungry for anything, as lunch has had to be put off half an hour. I have been called out unexpectedly. But you will find Alice in the salon."

She welcomed me with less constraint than at our last meeting, and I decided to make no bones about the real purpose of my visit and (obviously) of her invitation.

" I owe you an apology about Friday night " I said. " I do hope you did not wait up for me."

" No later than I wanted. And now sit down and listen to me. Or shall I listen to you ? "

" Where is she ? " I asked bluntly.

" But, Mr Dering, if she didn't tell you where she was, I'm

not sure if anyone else ought to. Anyway, she's away on the
job at present, and busy."

I sat and thought for a few moments, staring at my hostess
with what must have seemed sombre stupidity. Then anxiety
overcame shyness and, jumping up from my chair, I made a
desperate appeal.

" Please, Mrs Abbott, you *must* help me. I have *got* to find
Sally, and no one in the world but you can put me in the way
of it. I don't know whether she told you how much she told
me; but you already know everything she might have told me,
and I will assume she told you most of it. Even if she didn't
and there is twice as much again, it makes no atom of difference.
She has run away for my sake, and equally for my sake I am
going to catch her. That sounds selfish, I know; and it is
selfish. But not until she tells me straight out to leave her
alone, can I do so—and I'm not sure if I can then. Please,
Mrs Abbott . . ."

" Perhaps she did not like to tell you in so many words to
leave her alone " she replied. " A woman always tries to spare
a man who—who has been kind to her."

" Did you see the letter she wrote to me? "

" I told you before that I had not seen it. But——"

" Mrs Abbott, would Sally, even in an attempt to spare my
feelings, write lies to me? "

She shook her head.

" No. That never."

" Very well, then. If what she said in her letter is true, she
is not sparing my feelings. She is trying to prevent something
she is afraid I may later be sorry for. I want a chance to convince her that I have not merely lost my head like an excited
college-boy, but know quite well what I'm doing and what I
want."

" And what do you want, Mr Dering? "

This brought me up short.

" What do I want ?   With Sally ? "

" Certainly—with Sally.   You've just said you know quite well what you want, and I would like to be told."

She spoke almost sharply, and her usually mischievous face was prim and severe.   The change frightened me.

" I'm talking at random " I said miserably.   " I only want Sally to be happy, and I think I could make her a little happier than she is at present.   If I'm wrong, then. . . . But wouldn't she have told me so ?   Wouldn't she ? "

" A moment ago you said you had to find her for your own sake.   Now it's for hers.   You are a little contradictory, aren't you ? "

I burst out again :—

" Of course I'm contradictory.   I'm suddenly cut off from the person I want to see most in the world, told it is all for my own good, and then not even given an opportunity to plead for myself.   Wouldn't you be contradictory, Mrs Abbott, if you had been thrown overnight from heaven to a sort of bewildered hell ? "

She looked up at me with pursed lips, and her eyes behind their crooked pince-nez began to twinkle.

" I should indeed " she said quietly.   " Now sit down again, and let me think what is the best thing to do."

I sat down.   There was a short silence, during which I bit my nails and resisted the temptation to scratch various small itches which, for no reason whatsoever, started up all over me. Then she began to talk.

" Sally, as I think you understand, has had a wretched time. She is my best friend, so I do not mind speaking well of her in her absence.   She is the most genuine and the least conceited person I know, and that type suffers worst of all from the sort of life she has led.   Someone with more self-assurance—I don't mean self-command; I mean wish to assert oneself for one's own sake—would have fought with that horrible man long ago. Sally forgot her own troubles in worrying over the way her little boy was treated; and for his sake she would be holding on and submitting even now, if it hadn't been for what happened when she came to stay with me. That, as I know, was part of what she told you.

" Now the effect of all she has gone through has been to make her humbler than ever—too humble, I think—and her inferiority complex is seriously oversized. She came to see me the day after you had been in the woods together, and broke down badly. I could not get her to discuss anything from her own point of view. She insisted that she was just no good to anyone and was not going to tangle you up in her own troubles. Only when I tried blackening you, did she show any spirit— no! don't interrupt—and so I blackened you some more. I said that any man who fancied himself in love with a girl and had such a story told him as she had told, would instantly think her easy money and try to take advantage. That made her really cross, and she started to tell me—oh, lots of things. But before long she was back again at her old self-distrust, and declared that she was leaving Paris and going back home."

" But where *is* home? " I broke in. " She has no home. She can't just go back all alone to America with no one to look after her. . . . And, Mrs Abbott, did you *mean* what you told her about my thinking her easy money? "

" I kept an open mind, Mr Nicholas. How did I know? Men *are* like that. But " she added " I don't mean it any longer."

" Then you will tell me where she is? "

" Not actually, no. She asked me not to. And besides, at this moment, I am not very sure. But this much I will tell you. She has gone in search of stuff for her people in New York—and is travelling from place to place, including the places you suggested to her. That sounds like a clue; but it isn't, because she is dodging about—on purpose. She will end up in Marseilles and take a boat back home from there.   That, at least, was what she told me."

" Is there a boat ? "

" Presumably.   But I do not know.   I remember she reckoned it would be three weeks before she was through with her work."

" And is she set on going home—whatever happens ? "

Alice Abbott got up from her chair, as the sound of an opening door came from the hall.   She gave my arm a friendly squeeze.

" I think that depends on what does happen " she said. " There's Moreton.   I will go and see about your lunch."

∽   ∽   ∽

Monday was full of incident.   I was down at the American Express when they opened, and found that there was indeed a boat from Marseilles to New York in just over three weeks' time.   Nothing was scheduled within a fortnight either before or after this sailing.

Back at the Astoria, I found the head of my section had not yet shown up, so I called up Alice Abbott.

" I am very sorry to trouble you and shall be equally sorry each time I do, but I shall have questions to ask."

" Let us hope I can answer them.   What's this one ? "

" Have you some sort of an address where you can be sure of Sally getting a letter between now and her leaving ? "

" A letter from whom ? "

" From you."

" Yes."

" Thanks very much.   That's all.   Goodbye."

" Hullo there!   Nicholas (pardon my using your first name, it's quicker)—no enclosures allowed, you know."

" Not even a message ? "

" What kind of a message ? "

" I hardly know yet; probably one of those casual sort of ones, disguised as a bit of news. ' By the way, I saw so-and-so today and he said so-and-so.' That kind of one."

" Well, I'll decide when the crisis comes. Of course I may not be writing at all."

" True. Nor you may. Goodbye again, Alice, and you're an angel."

I had hardly hung up when the telephone rang again.

" Mr Dering? " said the girl at the private exchange. " You want to speak to yourself."

I knew well which one she was—a pretty little affair and well aware of it, with whom I had danced at the Majestic more than once and liked for her frank flirtatiousness.

" Say it again, Miss Connor."

She giggled.

" Mr Nicholas Dering to speak to you."

" Put him through."

It was indeed Uncle Nick, speaking from the Continental:—

" Hullo, hullo " he said. " Yeah, it's me in person. Are you fixed for lunch? . . . Call for me then, when you're free. I'll wait around."

The next thing was to see my chief, so I rang through and, finding him arrived, asked for two minutes.

" In ten minutes " said his secretary.

Once more the file devoted to Burbach-Eich-Dudelingen was pulled from its tray and placed hopefully on my blotter. At the end of ten minutes I left it there, and went along the corridor.

" I want to apply for leave, sir, in three weeks' time."

Sir George looked at me over his glasses.

" When does the Commission report? "

" Well, sir, we expect the first draft this week."

" And who do you suggest should take your place, if the final document is not sent forward within three weeks? "

" Stevenson could do that."

He drew a small picture on his blotting paper, while I stood in silence.

" Must it be in three weeks ? " he asked.

" Yes, sir.   That is essential."

" How long since you had leave ? "

" Eighteen months—apart from three days getting things together before we came out here."

" Very well.   I agree in principle.   But you must see that Stevenson is competent in case he is required—and of course leave is always liable to cancellation."

" Of course, sir.   Thank you very much."

ᔕ   ᔕ   ᔕ

I sent for young Stevenson and told him what was afoot.

" But damn it, Dering!   I don't know the first thing . . ."

" Quite time you started to learn, then.   And so you shall, this very day.   The second committee meet this afternoon at two o'clock to agree their report to the main Commission.   I have a lunch date and shan't be along till three.   That gives you an hour on your own.   You'll only have to listen, probably— unless old Driffield wants yet another copy of some paper I've already given him three times.   Everything is in my folder there.   Better take it away now, and read up our past delibera- tions.   Great minds, the lot of us, particularly the Italian and the Pole."

Rather ruefully the lad withdrew, and I settled down to dispose, once and for all, of those Luxemburg steel-works.

ᔕ   ᔕ   ᔕ

Uncle Nick was in the lounge of the Continental, with a newspaper and a drink.   I would not like it thought, just because I have not mentioned him, that I had not met my uncle since before the war. This story is only concerned with its particular theme, and makes no pretence to maintain continuities of an irrelevant kind. Actually Uncle Nick had been in England two or three times during the past five years, and twice I had had a glimpse of him. On the other hand, our present meeting was the first for two years, and also the first to take place within sight of a re-established normality; so that, whereas during the war he, like everyone else, had spoken only of the present, I was not surprised when over lunch he broached the question of the future.

" I suppose you have considered what to do when this show is finished? " he asked suddenly.

I shook my head.

" No—but I must do—some time or other."

" You were coming to me once. Remember? "

" Of course I do. But that was long ago. Is there likely to be another chance? "

" I guess so; in some form or another. Naturally things have changed; but I'll be glad to have you with me, for a while at any rate. We can see how we get on."

" That's very good of you, uncle."

" Plenty of time for thanks when we've tried it out. Besides I'm in a hurry."

" How—in a hurry? "

" I'm sailing next week and I want you to come with me. I go to London tomorrow, and get off from Liverpool Thursday week."

" But, Uncle Nick, I'm all tied up with the delegation! "

" Resign, my boy. A life's job is more important than a few weeks of Treaty-making. And it's now, or—maybe—never. I am going back to re-construct my whole show, and there are only too many young men able to take any place I can find for you. The war's over everywhere, remember, and jobs are going to a premium."

" So if I don't sail with you from Liverpool, on Thursday week, you won't want me at all? "

" I haven't said I won't want you. But later on I may not be able to do with you. Come, Nick, it's an opportunity; and I thought you were the sort to seize an opportunity. Was I wrong? "

" I'm sorry, uncle. But I can't come to America with you on Thursday week."

He was very displeased.

" Can't—huh? All right; please yourself. But I thought better of you. We like men to jump to things over there and take risks. Still, if you prefer to stick around and play for safety in a government office, that's O.K. with me."

" It's nothing to do with any of that. I've got to be in Marseilles in three weeks' time."

" For the love of Mike——" he began; then looked at me intently. " What's all this, Nick? A date? "

I nodded.

" A sort of date—on my side, anyway."

He turned sideways in his chair and beckoned the waiter.

" Wait a minute; wait a minute. We'll have some brandy and take this slowly. I was an old fool not to think it might be a woman—as it is, I suppose? "

" It certainly is."

" Fine! " (to the waiter). " Leave the bottle on the table, please. Now then, son, tell me all about it."

I couldn't help laughing at his sudden change of mood. Not only had his displeasure vanished utterly, but his ordinary manner as between uncle and nephew had given place to the attentive eagerness of one man expecting a good story from another.

" There's not much to tell " I said. " It's all so lop-sided and incomplete. You'll be bored stiff."

" I'll judge if I'm bored. You go ahead and tell me the story."

" All right " I said. " You've asked for it."

∽   ∽   ∽

When I had finished, I looked at my watch. It was well after three o'clock.

" Good Lord, I must run! I'll lose even my safety-first job if I'm not careful, and then what? "

He stood up, hands in pockets, jingling money and keys " Forget that safety-first business. I'm sorry. I got sore for no reason. Can you come to the hotel to-night? I want to think all this over. Dinner? "

" I can't be sure " I said. " I'll either come to dinner about eight or look in much later. I'll leave word with the porter."

And I hurried to the rescue of the luckless Stevenson.

∽   ∽   ∽

Late that night I followed Uncle Nick to a retired corner of Viel. The world's most efficient half-world looked us over and knew at once that we were of no professional interest. My uncle, with his hat tilted over his eyes and his long legs stretched out, waited till the drinks came before uttering a syllable. Rather to my surprise I began to feel nervous, and to wonder for the first time whether I was in for trouble. Then he spoke, and with a harsh precision which confirmed my fears.

" I realise " he said " that what you told me at lunch was in confidence, and I shall of course treat it accordingly. Also I admit I've no call to dictate what you should or should not make of your own life. But I want to be sure you understand exactly what you are proposing to do. For the sake of a girl who can never be anything to you but a doxy——"

I got up.

" If you are going to talk like that, I'm going."

He looked at me from under the brim of his hat.

" Sit down, boy " he growled. " No offence meant. I'm

a poor hand at fancy speaking, and probably say things crudely. You know what I mean.   Put it any way you like."

"Well, go on " I said ungraciously " I'll listen some more."

He seemed a little disconcerted, and hesitated how to begin again.

"Hell! What'll I say?   For the sake of a girl who cannot marry you and may not even want to see you again, you first apply for leave from official service and then throw down an offer of a job from the man most willing and likely to give you one. Is that sense? Of course it isn't. It's just crazy. What will your government pundits think if they find out what you have gone off to do? What will your folks at home make of it—if they hear what you've been up to? And, finally, what kind of an idea does it give *me* of your probable usefulness?   How do I know you won't go cavorting off after a whole string of girls when you're supposed to be working for me? "

I had now recovered my temper, and was further encouraged by a feeling that the crescendo of my uncle's rhetoric was ever so slightly artificial.

"You've not got it quite right, uncle " I said.   "I've not worked out this Sally business even to myself.   It doesn't need working out—yet. I have just got to see that girl again and get things straight between us.   What will happen, God knows. But I know what has happened; and I no longer care a damn about anything else on earth except finding her.   What you call the ' government pundits ' can be trusted to look after themselves. If they spin me, they spin me. I can't stop to think about that.   As for the family—well, I'd be sorry to cause them distress, but I've done nothing they can object to so far and may never. If I ultimately do, I'll stand for it.   You and your ' string of girls ' are all—well, let's say ' off the point '.   This is not just an ' affair '.   I'm old enough to know the difference, and I tell you my feeling about Sally is so special that it can't be compared with anything which ever happened to me before. I've *got* to go through with it. It may end altogether in three weeks' time; but that I shan't know until the three weeks are over, and until I have seen her (or failed to see her). I can't *not* go to Marseilles. Therefore I can't go to America with you. I can see how ungrateful and obstinate I must seem; and how foolish from a practical point of view. But I can't help it. I'm not ungrateful. I'd find it hard to say how much I am the other thing. I'm not really obstinate, except in the sense I'm so set on this trip to Marseilles that I can see nothing else. That leaves folly. I'm chucking away my best chance of livelihood because I've lost my head over a woman. Well, I suppose that's true. But I'd be no use in any job without my head, and it's a fact that I've lost it over Sally. So from every point of view I'll be wise to try and get it back. If I can't get it back, I'll manage some day to grow another one."

With the end of this long speech I became confused, and took refuge in my drink. When I looked at my uncle again, he had removed his hat and was gazing at me enigmatically. Then the familiar smile creased one corner of his mouth.

" Thanks, Nick " he said. " I enjoyed that. Sounds like you mean every word of it, and you certainly know well enough what you're doing . I hope you find your girl. I guess you will. I'd like to come and help you look for her, but that wouldn't do, would it? There's one thing, all the same, I can do—which I doubt if you've thought of."

The relief of knowing I was forgiven was overwhelming. I suddenly understood that I had recently walked a tight-rope without even realising it. One slip and I would have been done for, so far as my uncle was concerned. I now knew that I would rather stand well with him than with anyone else— except Sally. It was nothing to do with a job or with money. He was a shrewd man and a just one, and to satisfy him was something worth doing. That I had made no slip was no credit to me—only to Sally.   She filled my mind and had chosen my words.   Thank heaven for her.

Uncle Nick saw my abashment and probably read my thoughts.

" One thing I doubt if you've thought of " he repeated.

I looked enquiry.

" What's that? "

" How long leave will you get? "

" Well, I was going to ask for a month."

" No hope of longer? "

" Not much."

" And at the end of your month? "

" Back to London and work—until they tell me to clear out."

" But if by any chance you do find your Sally; and if by any chance she is glad to see you; and if by any chance she cancels her passage and you decide to spend some time together, of what use will even four weeks be, except to torment you with going so quick? "

" I know, I know!   But I don't think of that."

" That's where I come in.   You don't have to think of it."

" What do you mean? "

" Just this.   Earlier to-day I told you to resign.   I tell you so again.   Instead of merely going on leave three weeks from now, you will have said goodbye to the whole turn-out.   Then go to Marseilles.   If things fall out badly, you cable me when you'll reach New York.   If things fall out well, take your time and cable or write me when you want to come.   I have fixed a job for you in my mind right now, and the salary.   You'll start being paid on the day you leave your present position."

" But . . . Uncle Nick . . . it's a fairy-tale."

" A true one, anyway.   What you feel for that girl gets me, and I'm more dumb than I think, if it doesn't get her too. There's little enough of that sort of romance in the world, and

I want to be in on the edge of it. Go to it, Nick, and have just one hell of a party."

∽ ∽ ∽

Monday, as I said before, was full of incident.

V: LOVE PLAYS SUCH FUNNY GAMES

FROM the terrace of the Gare St Charles in the sunshine of a May morning, I saluted the vast panorama of Marseilles. A chaos of pinkish-grey, like the stones of a moraine, the houses tumbled down the hill at my feet, stretched away in an untidy huddle to right and left. The basin of the Vieux Port was a jostle of small craft, with the Pharo and the Pont Transbordeur signalling dot and dash across its mouth. To south-eastward were the cranes and warehouses of dockland, beyond which could be seen the spars and funnels of ships. The horizon was the sea. Journeys end, they used to say, in lovers meeting. Was this my journey's end?

The possibility made me a little breathless, but I was hopeful as seldom before. Ever since the night when my uncle had played deus ex machinâ, things had gone gloriously right for me. The Commission had duly reported; my resignation had been received with just the amount of disgruntlement necessary to give it dramatic quality; and I had paid a final visit to Alice Abbott.

Actually these events occurred in reverse order. For obvious reasons my call on Mrs Abbott had to pre-date my departure by several days. I told her when I was leaving and when the boat sailed.

" I shall have no address " I added " except care of the American Express, Marseilles—and, of course, the passenger gangway. I thought I would come and tell you. It seemed friendly. And you have been very kind."

" I appreciate your thoughtfulness " she replied gravely. " Have a good trip."

ᔓ   ᔓ   ᔓ

Like a swimmer about to dive, I lingered a moment longer on the station steps before taking my plunge into the city. It was about half-past eight. The boat was due to sail at five in the afternoon. Eight hours in which to go the rounds, to make a plan and change it, to make other plans. I started down the stairway and walked quickly toward the centre of the town.

The office of the Fabre Line could trace no booking in the name of Miss Lasalle. The American Express had no letter for me. All this I had more or less expected. Now what?

It was not my first visit to Marseilles: but it was the first under the conditions necessary for the sort of exploration I wanted to make. Before, there had been other people, and a rush, and either the forced jollity of a gang-binge or the solemn historical curiosity of older relatives. Now I was alone, with hours to play with and, at the end of them (or so I hoped), fulfilment. Conditions were ideal and, when one came to think of them, very unusual.

Normally, to a traveller in a hurry, the city of Marseilles is not a city at all; it is merely an interruption. Either he is about to embark, or he has just disembarked, or he has once again succumbed to the Riviera, kidding himself that possibly on this occasion it will not be such a garish snobbish bore as last time. To the eager outgoing traveller, or to the jaded seafarer home from the East who longs only for Paris or for London, the Port of Marseilles begins or ends at the steps of the Central Station. A huge city lies to right and left; but he is merely conscious of it as a noise, a scurry and an extra mile or two between himself and either the high hopes of a voyage to come or the final stage of a journey of which he is weary. Even if he has to stay overnight, his mind (like his suitcase), is not unpacked, but merely opened for his immediate convenience and as soon as maybe closed again. As for the Riviera addict, the place to him is just a station where one waits interminably or, sometimes, has to change.

Today, therefore, was special. With eight hours on hand and only myself to please, I would walk the town and get the feel of it. An able-bodied being with a taste for pavement-walking and none at all for sightseeing can cover a deal of ground in eight hours, can sample many different strata; and, if he has a sense of direction and a good memory for a street map, will not seriously go astray.

During the morning I was in high spirits. There was stimulus in the polyglot masculinity of Cours Belzunce, where knots or pairs of men bargained with shouts or in whispers, trafficking in every commodity from a newspaper or a collar stud to those which may not publicly be bought or sold. There was exhilaration in the flowery brilliance of Cours St Louis and under the great plane trees of Cours Pierre Puget, with the sunlight thrusting through their leaves to trace a filigree of gold on the sombre trodden earth. There was the laughter of sheer excitement in the vast confusion of Rive Neuve, the tumult of carts and lorries and barrows and tramcars, the silver and blue-black glitter of piles of fish and mussels, the torrents of oranges bumping down their wooden gangways, filling the air with the sharp sweetness of ripeness and decay. I climbed through the gardens of La Colline to the fortress church of St Victor, whose square battlemented towers have for a thousand years faced and defied the mistral. Though nowadays sunk in neglect and loneliness, St Victor remains the symbol of the true Marseilles, the Sailors' Church, the guardian of the Port. Traditionally the town is strident, mannerless and blind to beauty. It let Monticelli die in misery; it only gave posthumous honour to Daumier because the generous zeal of Bourdelle was stronger than the tasteless apathy of Bumbledom. But the genuine Marseilles remains what it has always been—one of the great ports of the world, dependent on nothing but its own strength and energy, owing no allegiance, temperamentally as violent as its climate and its colouring.

On the hill opposite St Victor stands the pretentious vulgarism called the Cathedral. It cost fifteen million francs, and is built on the very edge of the maze of alleys which constitute Europe's largest knocking-shop. Fifteen million francs spent on a neo-Byzantine horror to the glory of God and, within a quarter of a mile, how many million earned in His despite? There you have the other Marseilles—outwardly pompous and suave, at heart mean, material, cynical and gross.

Highly pleased with this sonorous generalisation, which I worked out over a couple of aperitifs and an excellent lunch, I started off for my afternoon of exploration, telling myself that in three hours I might have found Sally, and that to have read the riddle of Marseilles and traced a fugitive girl well within twelve hours would be pretty good going. My self-esteem, in fact, was well up to scratch. But I had hardly gone a hundred yards before an uneasy depression began to cloud my good humour. The golden sunshine took on a tinge of copper, and I became conscious of a dark spirit, beating up from hidden recesses of the city.

Under the surface of the busy modern town, with its café-terraces and handsome shops and sauntering crowds, there seemed to lurk a menace of evil and cruelty. It was broad daylight, and the time of day was of all times the least sinister. During the morning, subject to a general direction, I had wandered more or less at random, turning this way and that with no feeling of a changing atmosphere save that which arose naturally from the differences of district. But now, as I left a populous street, I had suddenly a sense of something in ambush.

The sense would pass as quickly as it had come, but before many minutes it was back again.

Whole areas of the city must have been built on haunted ground. One just turned a corner and passed from civilisation to outlawry, from the ordinary hazards of modern life to a state of affairs in which, without rhyme or reason, anything might happen. Things were no different after a clearance of bad property. The huge open space behind the Bourse, where slums had lately stood, had not the atmosphere of an open space in any ordinary city. It seemed to be shunned even by its own people. All round it, propped with great scaffoldings to prevent them toppling backward into desolation, the houses lining surrounding streets turned windowless and scaling backs upon its loneliness.

Not the least extraordinary feature of this strange and disquieting experience was the suddenness with which one could strike a bad patch. It seemed that I had only to turn east off the Rue de Rome, or north off Meilhan, or the Rue de la Republique, or indeed in almost any direction off any main thoroughfare, and I was involved in horrid little empty streets, running this way and that, up and downhill, intersecting at sinister cross roads where murder could be done at high noon and no one interfere. Certainly from the tiers of windows on every side eyes would be watching; but in the rooms behind the windows other crimes were afoot, and why should dog eat dog?

Sometimes the little streets were merely sordid and forlorn. Their inhabitants were too tired or too spiritless to kill or to violate or even to rob. The grey walls seemed to sweat squalor from inside. There would be found tolerance of any outrage, but neither the skill nor the pluck to join in it. I suppose the men-folk—struggling shop-assistants, clerks or what not— were away at work; for the only persons I saw were women, and three at least of them stood at a half-opened door and called or gestured to me with a significance half-hopeless, half-insolent.

" If you *want* a woman. . ." they seemed to say, " but probably you don't. . . . Half an hour. . . . Just a few francs. . . . Not? Very well; to hell with you." And one could imagine the shrug with which they turned into their miserable homes, muttering " It was worth trying."

At about four o'clock I made my way to the entrance to the dock. The liner lay alongside; but I was assured that no passengers had yet been allowed on board nor would any be permitted on board for another hour. I made as thorough a search as was possible of waiting-rooms, customs-sheds and other available lurking places, and then decided to kill what remained of my time by walking through the old town. I had been there before; but it had been after dusk, when the lights were flaring, music tinkling from every bistro and bawdy house, and girls of every colour and kind calling and clutching from the open windows. Now I would see it by daylight, and in the sleepy heat of mid-afternoon.

The result was interesting. In contrast to those sour, uncanny areas of secret crime or wanton lassitude which I had visited earlier, the sensational canyons between the Rue du Panier and the Hotel de Ville had the freshness of normality. Here at least were life and bustle; and if the life were only the life of a flesh-market and the bustle the bustle of brigandage, both were candid and vigorous.

There were a number of people about, and the district was open for business, but without great urgency and evidently working on a skeleton staff. To be left alone it was only necessary to keep your wits about you and know enough of the tricks of the trade. I would like to have lingered longer, noting the decrepitude of the fine houses of the aristocracy of old Marseilles (to spite whose memory the bourgeois rulers of the town, under Louis Philippe, deliberately turned these streets into a harlot's ghetto) for there are few ironies more dramatic than the fate which has overtaken them. But it is unwise, even in mid-afternoon, to stand and stare in the corridors of the Grand Lupanar, unless you are in the quarter for the quarter's purposes. So I made a steady pace to St Laurent and back up the steep gorge of the Rue de la Prison to the Grande Rue, with its jostle of shopping women elbowing one another, chattering and shouting, as they moved from one to another of the open-fronted displays of ribbons and lingerie and fish and tripe.

Well before five I was back at the dock and settled down to wait. In due course a few people began to climb the gangway; others followed at intervals. There were not many intending travellers, and I could see each one quite clearly as he or she approached. It was nearly five-thirty, and the ship was preparing to leave. A late-comer scrambled on board. Officials went to and fro; bells rang; men shouted. Then the gangway was lowered, and the few people waiting on the dock began to wave farewells.

So she had not come. I was not so much disappointed as gloomily resigned. I doubt if I had been very hopeful, ever since the shipping office had failed me and there had been no letter at the travel-agents. But I had had to go through with it, because there was no alternative. Nor, unfortunately, was there one now. I felt miserably at a loss; then pulled myself together. An alternative must be found, and I must have time to consider where to find it.

I decided to collect my bags from the station and take a room for the night. I would then go and have dinner on the Corniche and look at the sea. On the way up town I noticed that the American Express office was still open, and, acting on a sudden impulse, went in. To my surprise they handed me a letter. It was addressed in Sally's hand, and had been posted in Clermont-Ferrand. I was so excited I could hardly tear the envelope. Then, standing in the middle of the floor of the American Express office, I took it straight between the eyes.

> " *Nicholas, I have just heard from Alice that you are waiting to catch me in Marseilles. She had no business to tell you anything about me, but that does not matter now, as I have altered my plans. I do not want to be hunted about France, and I do not want to see you again. I know I am partly to blame for all this, because I wrote a silly hysterical letter and said a lot of things I should not have said. So I ask your pardon for bringing you a long way for nothing. But I am not hysterical now, and wish to make it plain that the only service you can do me is to leave me alone.*"

I do not quite know what happened next. But I suddenly became aware that the clerks behind the counter were eyeing me uneasily. I must have been standing for two or three minutes, stock still with the letter in my hand, oblivious of where I was or what I looked like. I suppose they thought me either sick or mad. I pulled myself together and went out into the street. In a café I had a quick drink and read the letter again. It was not my own imagination. That was what she had written.

I had to struggle to fix my mind on the consequences of this thunderbolt catastrophe. Something, I told myself, would have to be done; something deduced as to her change of plan. But as I was trying to fight off the angry desolation which threatened to overwhelm me—to fight it off just long enough to *think*, if only for a few seconds—I seemed to hear a whisper in my ear, proffering mandragora. The secret voice of Marseilles had broken silence. The next moment the city's mingled fascination and terror swept upward and engulfed me, and I felt myself battling with wave after wave of evil, assailed—in the manner of some legendary anchorite—by fancies atrocious but alluring. At first I was frightened. I felt my lovely eagerness to find Sally and to hold her, disintegrating into a sort of purposeless unconcern. I tried to recapture it, but it slipped further and further out of reach. Then, with a slow exhilaration, I knew that it was swiftly taking shape again, reforming into something demoralising but seductive, until, where had been an ache for Sally and a wish to love and serve her, was a vengeful impulse to debauch. Again the voice of Marseilles murmured wanton encouragement: " You have only to choose " it said. " I offer you everything."

It was a strange and, in retrospect, a humiliating experience; yet it was logical enough. For weeks I had lived with the idea of a woman in my mind, with the face and gestures of a woman before my eyes; during the last nine hours I had been keyed to the highest pitch of hungry anticipation, counting, if not on an immediate sight of her, at least on the certainty of seeing her within two or three days, of convincing her that we were fated to be lovers, of achieving the perfection of passionate companionship. And now, not only anticipation and certainty, but even hope lay lifeless at my feet, murdered by the very hand that raised them. While I had been in quest of Sally, spirit and body had craved for her in harmony; now spirit, cut down from exaltation to despair, had withered away. Love, I told myself, has died, and lust reigns in its stead. Le roi est mort. . . .

I made my plans calmly and, I confess it, with relish. I had noticed during the morning an ostentatious but forlorn hotel, off the beaten track of Anglo-American tourism but clearly in its day a place of comfort and consequence. I now went in search of it again; and in the empty bar, made a few discreet enquiries. Before the war the place had been the favourite rendezvous for German visitors and residents; now that there were no Germans, it stood virtually empty, trying for other clientèle but handicapped by its reputation and by its shabby splendours so unmistakably of an earlier age. I now understood the tarnished vulgarity of the hall and lounge (how they brought back Imperial Berlin of long ago!); the showy badness of the wall-paintings; the faded patches behind the reception

desk, where doubtless in former days hung pictures of the
Hohenzollern and German time-tables and notices about money,
and this and that.

The place chimed perfectly with my new mood of cynical
resentment toward the present.   This melancholy pile of brick
and plaster had once been happy and confident; it was now,
through no fault of its own, a place of ghosts.

I took a room and bath·; asked for my things to be fetched
from the *consigne* at St Charles; and returned to the bar, where
I drank listlessly but with caution, talking to the *concessionaire.*
When at last I went upstairs, I found that, though the room was
a fine one and well-furnished, the bath-waste was out of order,
one bedroom light needed a new bulb, and that the cord of the
Venetian blind snapped in my hand.   These trifles were quickly
put right, and with pathetic eagerness.   I was careful to make no
complaint.   Indeed I liked the place the better for its inefficiency,
which was not ill-will but the slow paralysis of hopelessness.

In due time I went out to find my dinner, for neglect, however
acceptable in furnishings, makes havoc of a kitchen.   Dusk had
come and gone, and a warm, soft darkness lay upon Marseilles.
Throughout the meal I looked forward to my night's adventures
with zest and appetite.   Deliberately I nursed my sensuality—
a sensuality born of bitterness, and therefore part desire for
vengeance, part longing for escape.   And so I sat till dinner was
done, rejoicing in my freedom and my solitude.   Then I left
the restaurant, and plunged into the shadows of a city which
knows no taboos.

                ∽   *∽*   *∽*

Next morning's afflictions were wholly spiritual.   I awoke
late and in perfect health, free of aches or pains, unconscious even
of fatigue, but with a memory only too vivid of everything I had
seen and done during my hours of madness.   I was horribly
ashamed of myself.   Madness of a sort it must have been,

I

which had transformed me, though perfectly sober, from a rather unadventurous hedonist into a reckless and exigent voluptuary. In old days, they would have described me as possessed of a devil. The phrase may stand; for indeed, having succumbed to a joint assault by instincts I hardly knew I had and by the pandering genius of Marseilles, I had passed under their control and run amok. For a while I brooded miserably over my degradation. But at last I stifled self-reproach, by telling myself that there were important decisions to be taken, urgent arrangements to be made; that the first item on the agenda was to get out of this city, and at once.

I dressed and packed, swallowed some coffee, and within three quarters of an hour was out of the hotel and driving toward the station. Much as I disliked doing so, it was necessary to stop at the American Express office and make a final enquiry. To begin with, I braved the very assistant who had handed me yesterday's fatal letter. Was it imagination that he gave me a startled glance, and that I heard him whispering to a colleague as he hunted the pigeon-holes of the poste-restante? Probably; but the fact or the fancy gave me a nasty twinge. There was nothing for me. Why should there have been? But I had been right to ask, if only because I hated doing so.

I crossed the office to the shipping counter. On the ground that I had just missed yesterday's boat to New York, I asked for alternative routes. The man shook his head. No further sailing from Marseilles for three weeks. I had better go to Paris. Thence to Cherbourg or to England. It would be quicker. That, I said, was out of the question, except as a very last resort. He began turning over a pile of papers. Genoa, perhaps; no, nothing for several days. Spain? Further than via Paris. Wait! There might be something from Bordeaux; the Transatlantique ran an occasional service. He consulted a bundle of coloured sheets, looked at the wall-calendar, and then pursed his lips.

" You're in luck, maybe. *La Bourdonnaise* sails from Bordeaux to-morrow night. But she may be booked up. You can make it all right, leaving this evening; but we must telegraph a reservation."

I did some quick thinking. The man's suggestion was obvious common sense; but I was determined not to spend a further unnecessary hour in a town which had become a *musée secrète* of infamous recollection. I pretended to weigh various business obligations.

" Bordeaux. . . ." I muttered. " Let me see. . . . Tell you what—if you would be good enough to telegraph about a passage, I'll collect the answer from the shipping office. I could use a day in Bordeaux better than one here. And if there's nothing doing, I'm no worse off."

I paid for the telegram, thanked him for his help, and returned to my waiting taxi. At the station I found that a *rapide* left in under an hour to Tarascon, where was a connection to Sète, due to arrive during the late afternoon. I then retired to the buffet and, until the train came in, sat and read with concentration. I wanted to feel that my journey had already started.

In the train, partly for self-chastisement, partly from policy, I re-read Sally's letter. It was every bit as shattering as I had remembered, and the last words were perhaps the worst of all. " The only service you can do me is to leave me alone." It came back to me that I had used almost the same words to Alice Abbott. I had said I would not give Sally up " until she tells me straight out to leave her alone ". Had she not now done so? What telling could be straighter? But I had added that I was not sure, even if she did order me to leave her, that I could do so. I was still ' not sure '. I must try once more. And if I failed again? Well, I should fail; but not for want of trying.

I turned my mind to the procedure of this final attempt; and as I thought back and forth, I had an idea. We reached Sète more or less to time. I borrowed an Indicateur and consulted the hotel-advertisements; then hurried to a post office and telegraphed Alice Abbott:—

> " *please wire her married name hotel marivaux bordeaux very important* ".

Waiting for the night express, I considered the chances of an answer to my telegram. It seemed curious that I should never have heard—nor indeed have cared to know—the name of Sally's husband. And yet my ignorance was natural enough. To have asked her would have been irrelevant curiosity on a distasteful theme and, seeing that she was travelling under her maiden name, slightly impertinent. In my conversation with the Abbotts the point had never arisen. Now, however, that there was reason to regard Sally as a fugitive, she might well seek a disguise; and the most obvious disguise would be the use of her other name. In fact it was possible that she had used it already, when booking for Marseilles. I had asked for ' Lasalle ', and if there had been a recent cancellation in that name, I felt almost sure the American Express would have remembered and told me. They had shown themselves friendly and competent, and I knew the boat had been far from crowded. I wished I had thought of all this sooner, but admitted there had been no real reason for doing so. At least I had thought of it now. But would Alice tell? She had, in all likelihood, been reprimanded already for telling too much. Suppose she shut down on me? In that case I must do the best I could. Sufficient unto the day.

The Hotel Marivaux is opposite the Midi station in Bordeaux, and I was there before eight o'clock. No telegram so far. Anxious to lose no time, I hurried into the town and, after swallowing a cup of coffee and a roll, tackled the city office of the C.G.T. Yes, *La Bourdonnaise* was due to sail that evening. No, there was no reservation for Lasalle. They were unhelpful people; and although they answered point-blank questions, did so with ill-grace. If they had been different, I might have enquired as to the fate of my own unwanted application, and so have taken them more or less into my confidence. But as they chose to be stuffy, they could stop stuffy, and get into any muddle they liked over an unclaimed reservation ordered from Marseilles.

Hoping that the quayside office would be more amiable, I toiled down to the docks, but there found the same spirit of surly indifference. No access to the boat would be allowed before seven p.m. Only intending travellers might go on board at all, and entrance tickets would be necessary even to reach the quay. Where, I asked, could one get an entrance ticket? Here at the dock. Then, please, I would like to have one. What passenger did I propose to accompany? There was no answer to this question, and I said curtly that I had an idea a friend of mine would be travelling. The clerk smiled nastily, and regretted that tickets were only issued to bona fide applicants.

In flustered irritation I returned up-town. It was midday. There was still no telegram from Paris. Half-aware of the futility of doing so, I began looking up trains from Clermont-Ferrand. Why on earth, because two days ago she had posted a letter from Clermont, should I assume she was still there? For no reason, of course. I stopped looking up trains. I went across to the station, and stood for well over an hour at the main barrier watching the stream of passengers. At two o'clock I left the station, telling myself not to be a damned fool. I took a tram back to the central office of the Transatlantique, hardly knowing what I wanted to do or say when I got there. The office was shut, and did not reopen till three o'clock. Hot and impatient I went to a café. I had had no lunch and only a small roll for breakfast, with the result that one drink made me muzzy in the head and hotter than ever. At three o'clock I was about to cross the road to the C.G.T. when I realised that I had not been at the hotel for more than two hours and that a telegram might be waiting. Evidently I was losing my head and running round in circles. On leaving the station I had gone straight to the shipping office, though the hotel was just across the way. Idiot, idiot and idiot! But there was no telegram at the hotel and the porter told me, rather tartly, that anything which came would be promptly put in my room. I said I had no room, which seemed to annoy him still further. How, he enquired, could I use the hotel address, if I had no room? I stared at him, while the implications of his remark penetrated my bemused intelligence. Did he mean to say that anything addressed to the Marivaux in the name of someone who had not booked a room would be refused? He shrugged his shoulders. Who could say? It depended who was on duty; a message might be refused; or it might be pigeon-holed in his lodge. But as he had already told monsieur, there was nothing here. And he left me to attend to a new-comer. I was now both distracted and angry. " Damn and blast this town! " I thought. " Of all the lousy, ill-bred places. . . ." But I had enough sense left to realise that I should only make matters worse by showing temper. When the porter was free again, I tackled him firmly but civilly. " I must ask you to help me " I said (and slipped twenty francs into his hand). " This telegram is important. If it comes, please keep it here for me. If it has already come and been refused, please find out about it and tell me. I will be back in an hour." He took the money, and grunted ungraciously. I wanted to hit him, but felt that this might come better later on.

At the C.G.T. they were even more unaccommodating than before. I asked if I might see the passenger list of *La Bourdonnaise*. In which particular passenger was monsieur interrested? It was a temptation to give my own name, but the prospect of subsequent complications was so alarming that I refrained. I explained that I was trying to intercept an American lady, but did not know for certain in what name she would be travelling. Had this lady, then, more than one name? She had a maiden name and a married name. And what were they? With a great effort I kept myself in hand. I explained that I only knew one of them, and had already learnt that no one of that name had booked a passage to New York. Then if I did not know the other one, of what use would be the passenger list?

This finished me, and I stamped furiously out of the place. I was at the hopeless disadvantage of anyone who, without a coherent story, is up against official pedantry. Besides I had to admit, even to myself, that my enquiries were illogical and absurd. But I could at least have explained to a sympathetic clerk that the passengers might have been so few that their names would recall something, or in some indirect way have helped me. I could have got him to see that I was catching at straws and far beyond reasonable argument. But to those people I was just a suspicious nuisance, and would have become more of one, the longer I had stayed.

Before four o'clock I was back at the hotel. For an hour I fidgeted in the hall, waiting for a telegram which never came. At five I decided that my only hope was to watch the gateway to the dock, and that I must go down there at once. The fact that I had been told it would not open till seven mattered nothing. More than likely the fellow had lied to me out of sheer cussedness. But some ninety minutes of intolerable waiting proved that, whatever his faults, the man had told the truth. Ninety minutes! They seemed nine hundred. There was nowhere to sit. The wall was sheer, and not even the most squalid café enlivened the dreary street. It was dusty and hot and I had a bad headache, part from hunger, part from rage, but mostly from torturing anxiety. The small dockside office of the shipping company was presumably open. At all events it looked as it had looked earlier in the day. But, miserable though I was, I could not bring myself to face that clerk again, and not only be indebted to him for a place to wait, but betray the very fact that I was waiting.

When at last the big gates opened, I found I could only get into a long cobbled yard, between two huge sheds. In one of these sheds was the entrance leading to the quay. It was guarded by a man in a peaked cap. He looked a more agreeable man than my experience of the Bordelais had led me to expect, and I asked him politely whether it was permitted to enter the shed. He pointed up the yard, and explained that entrance tickets were obtainable at the bureau just outside the main gates. I knew that bureau only too well, but simulated gratitude for his information and walked drearily back towards the street. I took up my position beyond the gates, on the side furthest from the bureau. Taxis and cars and barrows and people on foot began to arrive. When the first taxi drove right in, I realised I could hardly have chosen a worse place to wait. I tore up the yard after the cab, and, when it disgorged a numerous French family, had to pretend that running up and down cobbled enclosures on warm evenings was one of my eccentricities. I was conscious that the whole proceeding might have ruined my status with the man in the peaked cap and even finally alienated him. But there was no alternative.

Time passed. My head ached more than ever; my feet were red hot and very painful. Then, during a pause in the arriving traffic, the man came over to me and asked what I was waiting for. I told him. To my incredulous delight, his eyes wrinkled into roguish amusement. At last, in this God-forsaken town, I had found someone with the traditional French sympathy for a romantic escapade. " She will come " he said. " Never fear. And I will place you where you cannot fail to see her. Hurry! If anyone from the bureau saw, there would be trouble." I slipped through the sacred doors into the gloom of the huge shed. At the far end, the bottom of the liner's gangway sloped into sight. Behind it was the cliff-like side of *La Bourdonnaise*

herself.   There was a group of people round the foot of the
gangway, and over to the right two customs-men were busy
examining trunks and bags.   My friend motioned me to get
behind the sort of sentry-box which served him as office.
" Between this and the wall, you can see who comes " he
whispered.   " I will put on the light."   And he switched on a
lamp which hung low just over the entrance.   I waited in deep
shadow and, by flattening one ear against the corrugated iron
wall, succeeded in scrutinising each face as it passed under the
light.   One after another faces came and went, till they seemed
a procession of strange masks.   My head was dizzy with
alternations of hope and disappointment; my neck ached, and
I could feel that my ear was slowly filling with flakes of rusty
iron.   I began to despair, for there were signs of bustle and
finality away to my right, and I could guess that sailing hour
was not far off.

And then she came.   All alone, in a little brown felt hat, she
stepped into the cirle of light to show her ticket to my friendly
janitor, and passed on into the dim vastness of the shed.   For a
moment I leant against the wall trembling from head to foot,
overwhelmed by the very sight of her.   But the seizure passed
and, as she moved towards the douane, preceded by a man
with one trunk and a valise, I moved from my hiding place and
followed her.   I caught up with her before she reached the
customs-counter.

" Sally! " I said gently.

She turned quickly and I could see that she looked pale and
thin.   Then her eyes opened wide in horrified recognition.
She put her hand to her throat and began to take little backward
steps, staring at me with such fear and sadness as I hope never to
see again.

" Sally—forgive me.   I had to find you."

" No, no, Nicholas, you must go away.   Leave me; please,
please leave me! "

She spoke almost in a whisper, but there was no anger in her eyes, only the sorrow and the fear. I realised I must act first and argue afterwards. She was paralysed with confusion and alarm, and there was not much time. I signalled to the man with the luggage.

" Bring that back. Madame is not sailing. Take it to the door, and if there is no taxi there, wait till I come."

Then I turned to her, who still stood staring, hand to throat.

" Sally, darling, I am not leaving you now—if ever again— and you are not taking this boat. Come. We will go up into the town and get some dinner. I promise that you shall do just what you want, when I have put my case to you. But we are both too agitated to talk now, and talk we absolutely must."

Her head drooped, and for several seconds she remained motionless. Then, without raising her eyes:—

" You were at Marseilles?"

" I was."

" Did you have a letter from me?"

" I had it."

" Then why——"

" Because I couldn't help it. That's why."

There was a short silence.

" How did you know. . . ." she began.

" I didn't know. I just had to try anything. But come with me now, you poor tired baby, and I'll explain it all. Oh, Sally, I need you so badly."

She gave a great sigh, and her shoulders slumped with sudden exhaustion.

" I'm through " she murmured. " I can't do any more . . . and I tried so hard."

Then very slowly she began to walk toward the door by which she had come in, while the douaniers stared after her in silent astonishment.

I: LOVE IN BLOOM

A ND that, Sally, is enough about you in the third person.
Maybe, from your point of view (and inasmuch as you
know most of what follows as well as I do) it is enough about
everything. But I am not stopping just yet. Even if this were
one of those stories of pursuit and capture, of search and discovery, of courtship and surrender—at the end of which he and
she lived happily ever after, I should still go on, choosing my
memories for the mere pleasure of doing so. As things are, I
have a motive more urgent than pleasure.

∽   ∽   ∽

Over dinner at the Chapeau Rouge we were almost silent.
On the surface it was the silence of embarrassment, but underneath I think both of us felt that peace had come. I remember
that, as the meal went on and the realisation that you were
actually sitting opposite took hold of me, I was content just to
look at you; and that you kept your eyes on your plate, because
every time you raised them, I was staring at you. I remember
watching the worst of the fatigue fade from your face, and a
little colour creep into it; and I remember very vividly how at
last you pushed away your plate, and sat back and looked
straight at me, and for the first time really smiled.

When the coffee came, I knew that I must no longer shirk
the problem of the immediate future. With a conscious effort
I managed to overcome the queer shyness which throttled
me.

" Sally, I am beginning to be frightened of what I have done.
I have made you miss your boat, and here you are stranded in
Bordeaux. It sounds awful, put like that."

You just smiled again and said nothing; your eyes were gentle and the lines had vanished from the corners of your mouth.

I struggled on:—

" I am about through as a dominant male. You must say what you want me to do, where you want to go now."

" I don't mind. Anywhere."

" But, my dear, I have upset all your plans. . . ."

" They weren't plans, they were panic."

" You will really stay, then? We can be together? "

" Unless you walk out on me, Nicholas, we'll have to be."

You were sitting on a fixed settee against the wall, and I was opposite, with my back to the restaurant.

" I want to come and sit by you " I said, getting up. " There's not much room, but that doesn't matter."

You moved a little to one side and I settled into my new place. I could feel the warmth of you all down my leg, and our arms were touching.

" Squashed? " I asked.

" Yes, please."

I stubbed my cigarette in the ash-tray, and sat silent for a moment, content to tell myself that all this was true. Then I began to think what to say next and what to propose.

" Sally, that letter at Marseilles. . . . Why? . . . like that? "

You were sitting with your left elbow on the table, chin on hand. By merely turning your head, you faced me at a foot's range. It was so like you, when a difficult question had to be answered, to answer it face-on to the questioner.

" I couldn't trust myself to be indefinite or even polite. That's why."

" But had nothing happened except a letter from Alice? "

" Yes—one other thing had happened. I had heard from home."

" How—from home? "

" From my sister.   She told me some of the things they were saying about me—things he had put in their minds, I suppose."

Your eyes were steady all the time you were speaking.   I could almost feel your fierce determination not to seek any kind of cover.   As once before, in the woods near Châalis, I marvelled at your courage and adored you the more for it.   You were always a better man than I, Sally; and about the only thing to be said for me is that I knew it.

" Oh, my dear. . . . It doesn't matter what they say."

" No.   Now it doesn't.   But it did then.   It made me see just how much of an outlaw I was—just what kind of a thing I looked to the folks back home.   And I wanted you to be free of it all, Nicholas—free for always.   Do you understand? "

I understood, but did not trust my voice sufficiently to say so. We sat close, and for a while did not speak.   At last:—

" May I make some plans? " I asked.   " Or will you? "

" Not I.   I've said I don't mind what happens or where I go. And that's true—so long as you come with me.   You make all the plans, always.   Then just tell me."

I began tentatively, thinking as I talked:—

" I know you are very tired; but I believe, if you can stand being tired a little longer, it will be better in the end.   I want us to get out of this place.   It has been a hateful place all to-day, until I found you; it did nothing to help me find you, and it does not deserve an hour more of you than is absolutely un-avoidable.   I would like us to go and get a train and start to-morrow somewhere quite fresh.   I know it's monstrous to ask you to do a night journey; but I believe we'll be glad.   Can you bear it? "

" I'd like it, my dear.   I'm not tired any more.   Where'll we go? "

We sat in the now empty restaurant with *Chaix* in front of us, and studied trains.

ↄ   ↄ   ↄ

There was an hour at Villebourbon between the early morning arrival of the express from Bordeaux and the departure of the north-bound stopping train.

" Too soon for a barber to be open " I said ruefully.

You laughed; and I realised that I had never heard you genuinely laugh before, not even the first day I saw you, when we fenced with one another on the Place d'Italie. There had been a moment near Châalis when you gurgled and chipped me for being jealous. That had been a lovely but isolated moment, for melancholy had set in again. Yes, there had always been a shadow somewhere.

" Don't spoil it Nicholas. It's cute."

" I think it's horrible " I said. " It feels horrible anyway. And I'm dirty and scrumpled. How do you manage to sit propped in a corner all night and come out looking lovelier than ever ? "

" I'd tell you, if I did. Let's have some coffee."

The buffet was just open; and I thought of the fate of a traveller changing trains at a provincial town in England at half-past five in the morning. God be praised for France; and for bad coffee at the right moment; and for the early sunshine on untidy tracks; and, above all, for you, with a smut on your face and your plain coat and skirt, and your vagabond hat with the dark hair alive and tousled beneath it.

" I like your hair all funny and straggly " I said.

" There now! And a moment ago you were playing me up to fancy myself a postiche d'art."

" I wasn't. I said you were lovelier than ever."

" Then properly clean and tidy, I'll be just tolerable, and really dolled up a sort of ghoul."

" Have it anyway you like, darling. All I know is that you look adorable at this moment. I'll give you a definite schedule when I've had a chance to study the model at every stage."

I said this without thinking, and the final implication took me unawares. As it did you also, Sally. You may not know it, but you blushed.

∽   ∽   ∽

We were in the hotel at Valentré before nine o'clock. The sun was already warm in a cloudless sky, and the day promised great heat.

" You are now going to sleep " I said. " I will come and tell you when it is time for lunch."

" Don't I unpack, please? "

" No—only just what you need at the moment."

" And what are you going to do? "

" Get shaved. And then walk about."

You looked at me curiously, and I knew that you were hesitating between amusement and bashfulness. Then you bobbed a half-curtsey.

" Just as you say, sir."

∽   ∽   ∽

It was not difficult for me to read the riddle of your glance, because I had precisely the same mixture of feelings myself. The fact interested me, and as after leaving the barber's I wandered slowly up the broad central street of Valentré, I pondered the immediate future of our relationship.

This business of sexual intimacy is at the outset a shy-making affair, even for close acquaintances who have been able to see it coming for months and know that it is expected of them. You and I had not seen it coming and no one expected it. Nor were we closely acquainted; we were just in love. On the other hand, we were old enough and experienced enough to know what we were doing, and there had been no doubt in the mind of either of us, when we had set off the night before, that this was a lovers' journey in every sense. We had gone away together, put up at a hotel together and intended to sleep together. All that was implicit in the very fact of being here. So the embarrassment which had driven me out of the hotel and rushed into your eyes as you looked at me, had not been due to uncertainty as to the other's attitude nor to fear of the unknown nor to dread of mismanagement. Why then was it there? Why, though we were fully aware of being embarrassed and were both amused by it, were we unable to throw it off? It was a curious state of affairs, and I wanted to understand it.

But although I thought back and forth, I could not get easy in my mind. The situation was altogether an unusual one, and the more I considered it, the more delicate it appeared to be. Any sort of a wedding creates its own calendar which, whatever the terrors and perplexities inherent in it, goes through according to plan. Conversely a coherent love-affair, even the most irregular, has a mounting rhythm of passion and desire, of which the climax comes at its own time, usually when a long-sought opportunity offers or some stubborn obstacle is at last overcome. But we had neither time-table nor the urge of sudden opportunity to help us past the barrier of our diffidence. We had not even to pit our wits against a spying world, for we were perfectly free to do what we liked and go where we liked.

By the time I had passed the Barbican, descended the steep path which slants down the cliff toward the river, and, sitting on a solid slab of stone, was gazing at the grandeur and beauty of the stream, I had worked through the stages of our problem and unhappily decided I must give up seeking a solution in advance. All that high falutin about taking love in one's stride and being released from inhibitions and the torture of shyness, which I had thought to be great truths revealed to me by the coming of maturity, was no help at all. Which is not surprising, seeing that it was just beautiful nonsense. Indeed I felt fuller of inhibitions than ever before.

Finally I just threw in my hand and hoped to goodness that

matters would work out. They would have to work out. Twilight and darkness might help ; they often did. But until evening came things promised awkwardly, and it was with some trepidation that about noon I returned to the hotel.

I suppose I ought to have known that by now you would have taken charge of the whole situation. When I got upstairs, you were sitting by the window in a clean linen dress, darning away at something and looking as fresh as a May morning. I shut the door and looked at you. The love I had for you came welling up from where all my foolish worries had driven it, and began bubbling and purling in my ears. I suppose I stood there in stupid bewilderment over my own happiness. Certainly I have no memory of moving towards you. But the next moment you were in my arms, your mouth first battling with mine, then yielding gloriously. We clung together and I knew that my doubts and hesitations had been born of lack of faith. Between you and me was already an understanding beyond the stage of shyness and uncertainty. We had no need either of urgency (lest love escape) or nicety (less love take flight). As you strained against me, I could feel your heart beating.

At last you leant away and, with hands on my shoulders, lifted a flushed and smiling face.

" The first time you ever kissed me, Nicholas. Did you realise ? No—not again just now. I want that one to stand alone. Oh, my darling, isn't it incredible ? And all the after-noon and all to-night and to-morrow and to-morrow. . . ."

Your hands tightened a moment and then slid away. Suddenly matter of fact, you moved toward the middle of the room.

" Listen. I have unpacked all your things and put them away—there and there. Various buttons are missing and two pairs of socks still have holes in them. I can't find the collars of one shirt. You'll want to change, and I want to send a word to Alice. You'll find me opposite on the café-terrace. I'll

order your drink. Don't be long, my love, I'll want to see
you again—so badly."

~   ~   ~

As the afternoon passed, an invisible mist crept over the sky.
The sun still shone, but dulled and rayless behind a faint film of
murk. The air was motionless and very warm. We went in
search of buttons and other material for housewifery. We
bought you a hat—an agreeable white straw hat, with a pert little
red feather like a question-mark sticking up at one side.

We sat in the cool gloom of the vast jumble of styles and
reconstructions which is called the Cathedral. Braving the heat
again, we struck across the town to the great bridge and, leaning
over the parapet, watched the wide stretches of the river. Then
back into the town again, through a little public garden and under
the heavy chestnut trees of a large desolate square. There was
a café at the corner, with shade on one side. We sat and smoked
and sipped at drinks. It was the perfection of life—peace,
freedom and companionship.

"I'd be purring if I were a cat" you said.

"You'd be a lovely cat, but I like you better as a woman."

"Oh, but you'd be a cat too. Then you wouldn't."

"True. Which wall would you choose to yowl from?"

"That one over there, with the flowers behind."

"There'd be other cats, yowling too."

"There would *not*."

Silence again and contentment. Every few minutes I had to
touch you—your hand or your knee or your foot or whatever
was in reach.

"Sorry about it" I said at last. "But I'm still not quite sure
you're here."

You turned round, suddenly serious.

"Nick darling, I am so terribly much here that I don't believe

I'll ever think to be anywhere else.   That frightens me.   I must
not be a sticker.   I want you to promise, if you wish to be free
of me, that you will say so."

"That's an easy one" I said cheerfully.   "I'll promise all
right."

"No—I mean it.   I know you want me here now.   I can
tell when you are happy; and while you are happy, I am.   But
I shall know the moment anything is troubling you, and get a
panic that it is something to do with me.   If I can be sure you
will tell me, I won't worry.   Promise, Nick."

There is only one kind of remedy for such a mood as this;
but a café is a public place.   I took your hand and pressed it
tightly between both of mine.

"Sally, Sally—if I started to tell you what it means to me
having set eyes on you at all, I'd take an hour.   And as for the
miracle of our being out and away together—that would take
days, if I could find words for it at all.   But I will do a deal with
you.   I promise to confess as soon as I want you anywhere but
just where I am, provided you promise the same."

"I can't do that" you said softly.   "You see, I never
will."

"Very well, then.   Discussion closed."

∽   ∽   ∽

A little later:—
"It's going to storm" I said.
Indeed the murk had thickened, and the sky had gone from
bluish grey to a faint coppery orange.
"I hope it does" you said.   "It should be a fine sight.   And
I want to be frightened, now I'm not frightened any more."

∽   ∽   ∽

The storm was in no hurry, though undeniably on its way.
After dinner we went into the street.   It was nearly dark, and

the sounds of the passers-by were oddly loud in the breathless silence which seemed to brood over the town.

" It's coming all right. Let's get down to the Univers before the rain starts. There's an orchestra of some sort tonight. I saw the placard."

We tucked ourselves comfortably into an inside table of the café. The place was filling up rapidly. A low stage had been erected towards the back of the room, on which were music-stands. Notices pasted on the wall-mirrors announced the one-night visit to Valentré of a celebrated orchestra of Russian émigrés. The performance would begin at nine o'clock.

Long before that hour there was not an empty seat. Then I remember, above the noise of the crowd, that I heard thunder, far away over the southern hills. Shortly afterward the first rain-drops began to plop heavily on the dusty gravel of the Place. It was hot in the café and smoky. Never before had I felt so keenly the exhilaration of being submerged in the ordinary life of a French town. The tables were set so close that our neighbours were right on top of us. Everyone was sweating and in the best of humours. My right arm lay along the back of the seat behind your head. I had only to move my fingers to touch your ear or feel the soft vigour of your hair.

" What fun this is " I said.

You wriggled happily, and I felt the movement travel all the way down your side and flank. The rain was now falling with a long steady swish.

The Russians made their appearance and were greeted with loud applause. They wore embroidered blouses and loose red trousers tucked into high boots. All were young, and in varying degree their faces showed breeding. To the accompaniment of thunder, the concert went its way. Then quite suddenly the storm passed. The rain still fell, but now gently. A cool air blew in from the square. There was a pause in the music, the players withdrawing for refreshment. Waiters moved among the audience. We re-arranged ourselves so far as space allowed, ordered more drinks, and then leant close again. I doubt if we spoke at all. I think we just sat in perfect contentment, occasionally looking at one another and smiling vaguely.

After the interval, the musicians took their places once more. As the rustling and noise of the café settled into quiet, the outside stillness, now that the storm had gone, came sweeping in through the open window like something tangible. The air seemed charged with silence, sweet and sedative as an opiate, and I could see that others beside myself had become wrapped in a sort of distant drowsiness.

Whether in pursuance of their programme or because they were skilful enough to exploit the mood of their audience, the musicians skimmed softly into *Fleurs d'Amour*. The tune was new to me, new I fancy to everyone present; and after half a dozen bars it had the whole miscellaneous throng of us by the throat. The Russians drew from it the last drop of aching, wistful melancholy; and as the melody sighed and slithered to an end, one knew that every sort of inarticulate and fumbling emotion was stirring this crowd of ordinary simple folk.

There were three encores; after the third the Russians, opportunists as ever, began mopping their foreheads and, with half-humorous shrugs, pleaded for another rest. The crowd showed willing, content to sit in a dreamy fuddle or shift its feet or have another drink.

" Gosh, that's a grand tune " I said. " It got me more thoroughly than any tune since the Waltz Dream—which I heard in Berlin years ago, when you were still in pinafores."

You snuggled your head against my shoulder.

" You weren't Methuselah yourself " you said. " All the same, I wish I'd been there—pinafore or no pinafore."

" You'd have been an embarrassment, precious. There was a lady there already."

" Was there indeed? Baby-snatcher! A nice lady? "

" Not awfully, no. But a lovely tune—and a good show. All about a dashing young officer called Niki."

" Called Niki? How spell? "

" N—I—K—I."

" Oh, that's cute! Short for Nicholas. Short for you. Better than Nick. Cosier. Did the lady call you Niki? "

" I'm afraid she did—once or twice."

" Then I will too. I'll not be done out of a pet name by some vamp way back in the middle ages. I'll not be done out of anything which has ever happened to you. I *won't*. Will I, Niki? "

" Sally, you are the sweetest thing. . . ."

" Ssh! They're back."

And so they were. But they never (for me) recaptured the enchantment of *Fleurs d'Amour*, which remains—and for always —*your* tune, Sally, your special, inalienable and tragic tune. Better for my peace of mind if it were not. For henceforward I shall never hear it without seeing once more through a lazy film of smoke the mirrors and cheap gilding of the Café de l'Univers at Valentré; the long zinc-covered bar and its motley background of bottles, tier upon tier; the Russians with their lean pale faces and smart white tunics patterned red and blue; the homely, sweltering audience of town and country folk. Worse still, I shall never hear it without feeling again the warmth of you all down my side; without breathing the faint perfume of your neck and arms and hair; without remembering what life promised on that blessed evening, when we were at the beginning of our love-story and were gaily, pitifully confident that it would never end.

∽　　　∽　　　∽

The concert finished at about eleven o'clock. We walked out into the delicious cool of the square and into the dripping

shadows of the chestnut trees.   After pacing up and down a
few times you stopped, faced me and took my head between your
hands.

" Oh, Niki!   To think that life can really be like this! "

For a moment we clung together.   I said:—

" Life can, is, and will be.   It's bed-time, little one.   Let's
go back—quickly."

ട   ട   ട

Light from a street-lamp, slanting upward through the open
window, lay in a pale triangle on the ceiling.   Outside, the
boulevard was perfectly quiet.   No voice or footstep broke the
silence; there were only a faint rustle of leaves and the sound of
an occasional rain-drop shaken to the pavement by the intermittent breeze.

I raised myself on straightened arms.   Propped on my
hands I looked down at you, lying there beneath me, relaxed
and passionate, surrendered and victorious.   Your eyes were
closed; your hair made a disordered halo for that brave calm
face.   Your arms lay loosely outspread; and with your breathing faint shadows flickered over the warm ivory of your throat
and shoulders.

For a moment I wondered and worshipped.   This lovely
thing was all mine—the exhausted beauty of the drooping mouth,
the languid arms, the swelling smoothness of the proud, defenceless breasts.   I bent and kissed their dusky tips.   " Fleurs
d'Amour " I murmured—then whispered in your ear:—

" Is it good, Sally? "

The eyelids fluttered and the long red lips just parted in a
little smile.   I persisted:—

" The best ever? "

You turned slowly on the pillow and opened eyes which,
behind a veil of sensuous dream, shone like jewels.

" Far, far the best. . . ."

Then, tilting back your head, you raised both arms:—
" Come down to me again, Niki! I want you back."

II: THESE FOOLISH THINGS

IT is no good, Sally. I cannot go on as I had intended. How shall I choose what to recall, what to seem to forget; seeing that I recall everything, and everything has the same importance, being you? If you were here, we could range back and forth over the field of common memory, keeping and rejecting at will. We could revive a thousand absurdities, laugh again over a thousand silly jokes beautifully meaningless to anyone else, and even if we ignored all convenient *notabilia*, we should still have the things which really mattered. But I cannot, all by myself, rummage the ruins of our happiness and try to piece together significant episodes, glimpses of history and chatter and nonsense, passages of love. Not only do I refuse to discriminate, but I only know half the original pattern of them, and the other half is lost—because you are lost.

I must let hazard act for me; or providence, if you prefer; or my subconscious. I must empty my mind of everything else but the knowledge that you and I were once together and leave the past, if it will, to declare itself. Whatever it chooses will suit my purpose. Anything, however foolish or trivial, will keep you by me in fancy; and that is the best I can hope, seeing that nothing could keep you there in fact.

ᔣ ᔣ ᔣ

You are sitting in a meadow beside a busy chattering stream. The hay has been cut, and the colour of the short grass is a pale sheltered green. But along the banks of the stream tall grasses, small shrubs and a few flowers have survived, and countless little butterflies fidget and dip from place to place.

I know where this is. Do you remember a valley up in the

Auvergne hills, two hours or more from Le Toit du Monde?
We set off for the day, carrying two rather stale rolls split in half
and meagrely embellished with cold mutton, a few small hard
pears and a bottle of *ordinaire*, and took a path into the woods
just because it was a nice path—as indeed were all the paths
thereabouts. Before long we caught up with an old woman,
wearing a black shawl over her head and carrying a large and
heavy basket. I persuaded her to let me take this for her, and
once she had accepted the idea, we proceeded amiably in company. Her face had the fine drawn beauty which so frequently
shows itself among French peasants of old stock, while her courteous interest in our expedition and the gentle dignity of her
manner contrasted strangely with the noisy exhibitionism of
many of the well-to-do motorists who invaded the hotel at Le
Toit for a long lunch and a short glance at the abbey-church.
When we reached her cottage and I had handed over her basket,
the old woman thanked us with the self-possession of a great
lady and—in a patois none too easy to understand—recom-
mended a desultory path sloping away between flowery banks
and patches of open heath. By doing so, she did service for
service; for a lovelier valley than the one in which the path at
length arrived, I never think to see. It was a deep valley but
very broad, so that the stream, which chuckled down the middle
of it, had space to twist and turn and cut the sloping meadows
into fantastic promontories and peninsulas. On one of these
we chose to sit. Ostensibly we had stopped for lunch; but I
think we were there three hours, lying in the sunshine, watching
the butterflies and bees, dabbling fingers in the little stream to
see the minnows scurry, feeling the warmth and scent of summer
and the peace of this remote elysian place blend with our own
contentment and deepen it.

" Heavenly, Niki " you said. " It's like something beyond
reality—the sort of legendary place that Maeterlinck was always
trying to create."

" I'd rather think of it as William Morris."

" Why? "

" Because Maeterlinck's women are wraiths, but Morris liked flesh and blood."

" Well, I'm going to be a wraith. It's more refined."

" Too late, darling. You're registered as Class A flesh and blood, and you can only get permission to change by producing evidence that you're no longer up to standard. There *is* no evidence."

" You wait. I'll find some, and vanish into air one night; and then you'll know."

You've done just that, Sally; and now I know indeed.

ᔊ   ᔊ   ᔊ

We are under the awning of a crowded café—so crowded that the only table we can find is against the door leading to the lavatory. This retreat is in such demand that my conversation is punctuated with jerks, because every time the door is opened it bangs the back of my chair. We think the banging funny and start a scoring game, one five minutes against another.

I know where this is—on the central square at Clermont, whither I had insisted on our going in order to see the actual post-box from which that dreadful letter had started its journey to Marseilles. I wanted to talk to you about Marseilles; and thought I could do so more naturally if we came to it by way of this ludicrous pilgrimage.

But serious conversation was hopeless within the orbit of the banging door, so we just sat and talked nonsense and got giggles. It did not matter. Nothing mattered. There was always plenty of time.

When the terrace began to clear, we moved to a more tranquil table.

" I want to tell you what that post-box did to me " I said suddenly.

" Post-box? What *is* the man talking about? "

" Sorry. I didn't mean to be cryptic. I was switching back. Let's take it slowly from the beginning. Earlier today, as you may recollect, we visited a repulsive blue box, fastened to the wall of a disagreeable building near the station. Remember? "

" Oh, that? No, Niki darling, don't start that again. Please let my horrible letter be forgotten. I go all shaky, when I think what harm it might have done."

" It actually did some good—at least I think it did. But I'm scared what you'll think."

There was a second's pause before you replied; and I knew from the change in your voice that, during that second, you had sensed my embarrassment and prepared to soothe it.

" Tell me " you said. " I'll not think differently from you."

So I stammered through the sordid story, feeling more of a blackguard every minute but making no excuses and white-washing no sepulchres.

" Why I think the foul show may have done good " I con-cluded, " is that perhaps it got something out of my system—something which must have been there. But you had to know."

I sat unhappily staring at the ground and waiting for you to speak, then felt your hand laid on my knee.

" Poor sweetheart! How terribly I hurt you! But I'm thankful I drove you into the dives of Marseilles and not right away. At least you stayed on the ground, and thought it all out again next day. Was it fun? "

" What?—the night life? Yes—I'm afraid it was, rather, while it was on. But it was bloody next morning."

" I'd like to know what was most fun, Niki—what *you* enjoyed most—if it wasn't all too difficult for an amateur. For, you know, it doesn't have to be bloody next morning."

∽   ∽   ∽

We are racing through an immense pine forest, up and down

paths of trodden needles, rushing to get back to the inn before the rain begins.

I know that this is in the Vosges; and that all the hurry is because I have only got one pair of trousers, having left all the others in our big luggage at Strasbourg. Do you remember how, for the few days we were at Maxensweiler, it poured regularly every evening about five o'clock and how, thanks to those damned trousers, we always had to get home long before it was necessary? On this particular day we had misjudged things badly, and were doubtful whether even by running we could save the trousers from their fate. But it was worth making a real effort; and so we ran.

We just managed it, flopping in the café of the small hotel, streaming with sweat and very, very thirsty. They had an excellent open white wine, with the mild address but forceful character of many open wines. Prudent as ever, we ordered mineral water also, and a bottle of each went down almost before we noticed we were drinking at all. Still thirsty, we called for a second round; and at that moment two uniformed chauffeurs, belonging to the line of motor-coaches which ran tourists through the Vosges, came in for a drink and a game of dominoes. It was their hour of freedom. I suppose they had spilled their cargo at the big hotel down the road, for it was raining cats and even the most determined sight-seer would hardly have gone wandering in the woods. We had started in on our second pair of bottles when you nudged me:—

" Lovely-looking man! "

" That's very nice of you——— " I began.

" No, idiot, not you! The one next me."

" I beg your pardon. What'll I do? Go and play tig with the other one? "

The wine was by now at work on both of us. You always looked divine when tipsy, and at this moment the fact struck me more forcibly than usual.

" You're lovely when a little tight, Sally. Why aren't you always? "

" You must buy me more to drink. Or I'll get someone else to. Perhaps this beautiful man will buy me some. What'll I give him in exchange? "

" What have you? "

" Lots of things. The love of a good woman and a fine fountain pen and a receipt for a Louis Quinze armoire which is awaiting shipping instructions in Nantes and———"

" He won't want any of those. He only wants dominoes and a little rest from yanking a charabanc round hair-pin curves."

" Then it's all no use? "

" All no use " I replied solemnly. " But never mind, this is an excellent drink. Let's have some more."

" Fine. But, darling, I've just remembered your trousers. Are you sure they aren't wet? I could ask my friend here to lend you a pair. It would start a conversation at any rate."

" Sally, I will not have you picking acquaintance with chauffeurs—here, there and everywhere—let alone borrowing their trousers. You'll get yourself talked about. You will now come upstairs, taking the Perrier with you. I will bring the wine. Then you can take off those heavy shoes and that uncomfortably tight jumper, and daddy will read aloud to you."

∽   ∽   ∽

By the time the bottles were empty the costume problem had been solved, and we looked about for some occupation suitable to a wet afternoon. The sight of the feather duvets, lying plump and pompous on the beds, suggested a game of Zeppelins. The Zeppelin player seizes a duvet and launches himself into space. Almost immediately he hits the floor, where he remains, cruising vaguely over Europe and pointing out geographical features and places of interest to any other Zeppelin which happens to be near. Visits may be exchanged between the personnel of friendly Zeppelins, and often lead to much social jollity. Nobody wins or loses, and it is in order for the players ultimately to go to sleep.

∽ ∽ ∽

We are in another forest—a very different kind of forest and in very different weather. The forest around Maxensweiler is wildly up and down, with outcrops of rock which build a sudden small precipice across an incautious path, and turbulent brown streams swirling through miniature gorges at the bottom of deep curving valleys. You leave the tracks at your peril in this sombre region of pine-clad monticles—trivial enough as mountains go, but full of traps for unwary walkers and instant death to a sense of direction, once you have lost your way.

No such dangers in our second forest—a forest of the Ile de France; orderly, chequered by a gridiron of drives with a poteau at every main cross-road, on the whole level, cared for, section by section, by the forestry experts of the government. It was in such a forest, though not in this particular one, that we first walked together and you told me your story, looking me straight in the face with eyes enlarged and darkened by the tears you would not shed. Perhaps the slight claim these gentle and well-ordered woodlands make on one's attention is a large part of their charm. It hardly matters which way you go; you may wander on, absorbed in talk, happily conscious of the soft air and the changing light and the birch leaves shimmering in the wind, but free to laugh over yesterday's jokes or to pursue sham-serious argument.

Near the margin of this forest the timber is large and there are few side paths. Main drives, deep in dust after drought or churned in wet weather into sloughs of folded mud, lead inward toward the central areas where felling and replanting—in meticulous and scientific rotation—are regularly in progress. As we press on, away from the main road, the full grown trees

are fewer and the criss-cross of paths begins.   Here are areas
(roughly rectangular and each about an acre in extent) of birch
and larch and oak at various stages of adolescence, the small
trees carefully wired round, the larger ones freed from tutelage
but not yet ready to go out into the world as timber.   Across
most of the open areas narrow footpaths wind through shrubs
and thorn brakes and small plantations, leading diagonally
from one drive to another of the main network.   A little further
still, and we come to patches of open ground—clearances in the
forest, where the glorious sunshine falls sheer on to bell-heather
in full flower and ling in bud and the slim curling fronds of
bracken.

A felled trunk, a left-over from a former generation of trees
which once covered this scented shining space of heath and
shrub, lies in a shallow depression in the ground.   The moss
and heather have piled up against one side of it, on the other a
cluster of tiny birches, doubtless self-sown and therefore
unregistered by authority, promise a patch of shade as high noon
passes.   The silence is absolute, save for a buzz of insects and
the whispering crackle of last season's drifted leaves, now hidden
among the wiry stalks of the ling.   A mile ago we heard wood-
men at work and caught a glimpse of two of them; but these
apart, there has been neither sight nor sound of human being for
the last hour.   ' Shoulder-strap day ' we called this, Sally.
Do you remember?

In my rucksack were a yard of bread, slices of galantine and
ham, butter, tomatoes (all bought within twenty yards of the
hotel, here and there in the main street of Les Yvelines) and
grandiose strawberries in a glass jar.   Also a bottle of rosé.

" Hungry, Sally? "

" And thirsty. . . . What a perfect place, Niki!   In its way
as magical as our valley near Le Toit."

Turning quickly to survey the extent of your secluded king-
dom you tripped over a root.   You would trip over something,

even in a dust-bowl. Never were there feet sweeter and shape-
lier and more incompetent.

" If Madame will be seated, luncheon will be served immediately. Also she will be more secure."

Like a little girl, with your legs straight out in front, you
flopped down on to the warm springy mattress of heather,
pulled off your big straw hat, shook back your hair and clapped
your hands sharply.

" Hullo there, waiter! Can a girl eat in this two-bit joint
or can she not? I'd have you know I'm a busy woman and
can't wait around all day." Then you remembered an incident
of the previous evening and gave that low gurgling laugh I
loved so much. " D'you know what, Niki? Just now I sat
down like that man in the café when the chair broke. Only he
hadn't heather under him, poor dear. I never saw a chair
break quite that way before, did you? All four legs in different
directions like a star-fish with four prongs. Prongs? Not
right. Prongs isn't right, is it Niki? Ought to be tentacles—
no, they're curly; ought to be. . . . Heaven be praised, food
at last! "

" I am afraid " I said, as I handed you a huge knobbly sand-
wich of ham and galantine (you always liked the knobbly ends
of the long loaves) " that while Madame eats she will have to
stop talking."

So lunch went by, and the level of rosé fell in the bottle, and
the strawberries disappeared, and we came to the last three
inches of wine (kept by tradition to go with cigarettes) and lay
back against the tree-trunk on the cushion of moss and ling,
and smoked, and stared at the blue sky above the tops of the
biggish trees which edged the clearing on the side facing us.
We had the sun behind us, so that the trees were a brilliant
golden green and the sky an almost violet blue.

After a while I got tired of looking at the sky and turned to
look at you. Your eyes were shut and your head, propped on

the empty rucksack, was tilted backward. If you were not actually asleep, you were sufficiently so to serve my purpose, which was to be able to look at you in peace without being asked what I wanted. But I had not looked for very long before I knew what I wanted, and that I could hardly hope to get it without your collaboration. Sooner or later, therefore, I should have to tell you.

It seems a funny thing to say in the middle of this particular reminiscence, but I have never been one for picnics. I am not susceptible to the urge to do out of doors what is ordinarily done inside a room. A meal at a table with the usual cutlery, plates and glasses seems to me a simpler and pleasanter affair than crouching about on cornery rocks or damp grass with one collapsible drinking mug (which usually leaks) between four people, paper napkins supposed to envelop bits of rind and cherry-stones and other tacky débris but in fact so porous that everything soaks through, and continual worry lest the bottle or thermos be upset. Add the local hazards such as ants, wasps or game-keepers, and you tip the balance finally in favour of an indoor meal. And if a chap feels like that about a thing as simple and everyday as lunch, it stands to reason that he feels even more strongly about the more complex and private activities of life between four walls. As indeed I had always thought I did. I have never, when reading a bucolic novel, envied those lusty lads who, during harvest, drag plump protesting peasant girls behind the sheaves at dusk and vigorously enjoy them. Indeed I go further, I suffer agonies on the girls' behalf. Heaven knows, mere stooking is prickly enough. Conversely, I am equally unresponsive to the raptures of that singular type of intellectual who undresses on Wimbledon or Putney or any other near-London Common and gazes with reverent and un-fleshly awe at the physical equipment of his (or her) companion.

But the fact remains that, as I lay there propped on one elbow in the caressing warmth of that remote sweet-smelling

K

forest glade, as I looked at your gentle sun-browned arm and the tilt of your rounded chin and the long easy line of your relaxed unconscious body, I wanted to love you. More than that—I decided to love you. There and then.

And I did, Sally. You were very sweet (when were you ever else?), and lent yourself readily to the slaking of that sudden uprush of desire—until the fever took you also, when it was no longer a question of lending or even of giving. Ecstatic afternoon! And the only casualty a shoulder-strap. It broke at one end during the process of readjustment, and I cut it off at the other with my pocket-knife and put it in my cigarette case. I have kept it ever since, along with other tiny material splinters of our broken love-story. I had a silly romantic notion that they would serve to remind me. . . . As if I could forget! I shall not keep them much longer now.

ᔕ   ᔕ   ᔕ

Forgive me, Sally. I had not realised, when I threw on to hazard (or providence or my subconscious) the control of memory, how greatly photography—and verbal photography most of all—can lie. I am not going to violate, even on pages intended primarily for you, any other of our absurd delicious privacies. The episodes just described had at the time the lovely extravagance of joie de vivre. They become mere ribaldry in retrospect.

I dare not risk further misrepresentation. Better forget than travesty the peace and sunshine of the grass plot beyond the apse at Vézelay with its sweet wild grass and soaring trees; the pale desolate heat of Provins; the music from an unseen window which strayed across the square at Nancy and set the rain-drops singing in the dark; all the other moments when beauty or contentment, released by sight or sound or scent, took sudden possession of the two of us, so that we caught our breath.

They would, perhaps, suffer as badly in the retelling as the delicious follies of Valentré or Maxensweiler; and I could not bear them to seem mere perfumed sentiment.

Likewise the blazing colour of the formal gardens at the sugar king's château near Nangis, where even the gravel was planned flamboyantly in blues and reds so that from the terrace it was hard to say which sections of the vast parterre were mosaics of flowers and which of real stones; the racket and exhilaration of the circus at Troyes; the sinister walk at evening through the deserted streets of Givors, and how we suddenly turned a corner into a little square and found it packed with silent people, all gazing at a high-lighted window where two men (also silent) fought to kill—these excitements, which when they happened came with the bracing shock of crisis, might, in resuscitation, be rant and melodrama. Better forget them all, than by distortion spoil any one of them. Besides, what is the use of trying to fight off the end? I have not the spirit left even to delay it further. Nothing can stop it now: and it is very near.

W E were once more in the woods between Chantilly and Mortefontaine.

" You know " I said " I believe I ought to go to Paris and see if anyone has written about anything. Even divine detachment has its limits."

" I've been thinking that—and other things—for quite a while; and then thinking of something different."

" Where are the Abbotts? "

" I just don't know. It's shameful. Alice is sure to have written me. But she'll understand—up to a point. That point is about reached."

" Shall we go tomorrow? "

" I suppose so."

∽   ∽   ∽

Several letters were awaiting me at the travel-agents, and there was one for you. This had been written three weeks previously, and two days before Alice's departure for America. It covered several sheets and concluded:—

" *You know the address, and when you come up for air, you may have time to send me a post-card. We may even meet again one day. There's no knowing. Moreton sends his love. He is very shocked by your crazy goings-on and so am I. But we hope it is keeping fine for you.*

Your affectionate

A. A.

P.S. Sally darling—you deserve a break, and I love to think you've got one at last. But start in gradually getting back to normal. It has to happen."

Of my letters only one was important, because only one directly concerned you and me. The rest were vague dissatisfactions and requests for news, which could be blandly ignored. The one, however, was serious. Typewritten on severe headed paper with *REF: YOUR REF:* OFFICE OF THE PRESIDENT, *cable address, telephone number* and what-have-you, it began " *My dear Nicholas* " and ended " *Your affectionate Uncle N.D.*" In between it was authoritative, curiously stilted in style, and devastating. My chief had found it desirable to change his plans. After sizing up his organisation in America, he had decided I should be of more service to him in the office of his London correspondents than in the United States. He anticipated considerable European business, and assumed that my linguistic training would prove equal to the demands made upon it. He would be obliged for an early intimation of the date when I proposed to take up my duties.

I read this letter, sitting beside you in a café on the Boulevard de Temple opposite the Cirque d'Hiver. I handed it over, and sat without moving, trying not to realise that it meant the end of our honeymoon. I had known that this (or something like it) was bound to happen some time. But now that it had happened it seemed like catastrophe, and I could think of nothing except that the world had forced its way into a lovely privacy and shattered it. At last I roused myself to a sense of manly responsibility. I must put a brave face on things, be brisk and commonsensical.

" It will be just as much fun when we get used to it " I said, with a poor attempt at heartiness. " And he as good as says we will come abroad a lot. We'll have to flat-hunt. That'll be amusing. And buy curtains and a cork mat for the bath-room—— " I was getting brisker and brisker.

" Niki—stop."

The tone of the interruption startled me. But even then I had no idea that what I had taken for disaster was in fact the merest preliminary.   Then you began to talk, and the bottom fell out of everything.

"Niki, my darling, listen to me.   I have been realising for a long time that I should have to say what I am going to say.   I have even tried to start it once or twice; but you looked so happy and I was so happy, that I shirked.   I cannot shirk any longer.   This letter of your uncle's is my cue, and I must take it.

"Niki, dear Niki, you and I cannot go to London together. We could not have gone to New York together.   We must say goodbye.   Once we materialise again, and become ordinary people having to do with other people, we shall be all wrong. We shall be an offence to some, a whispering-game for others. (I am not trying to save you from yourself any more, so don't get all chivalrous and don't interrupt.)   Don't you see that what has been spontaneous and natural and nobody's business will immediately become something either furtive or defiant?   Of course you do; and you wouldn't go through with it.   Nor would I.   I won't even try to.   I know perfectly well that I can't face it, Niki.   I just can't.   Besides, the time we have had must be something by itself—something detached.   It must not fray out into half and half.   It has been too perfect—to be—real. . . ."

Your voice trailed off into a whisper, and the change roused me from the confusion of alarm and bewilderment into which I had fallen.   Glancing, I saw your lips quiver and, with the vague idea of helping to stave off tears, began:—

"But, baby, I don't understand. . . . You can't mean . . ."

"Please let me go on.   I—I'm in hand again now.   Sorry to be a fool.   *I must go on.*   Do be patient with me, Niki.   I know that weeks ago—that time when I asked you to say when you were through with me—remember?—and you said you would if I did—that time I said I'd never have to.   I know I said that.   And I meant it then.   But I hadn't thought of all the other people.   Why should I?   There seemed to *be* no other people.   But there are.   Lots and lots of them.   And they'd look sort of knowing and go away, and I would be sure they were talking and asking questions—questions about me. And then *you'd* come up against it and get angry with them and not be able to do anything, and gradually come to see it was my fault.

"And even that isn't all. There's Danny. I can't desert him. It would be deserting him, even though he never knows I'm anywhere around or never hears of me. So long as there is the smallest chance of my being of use to him, I must be within call. I have not been worrying about the Danny aspect of the case because, until just now, I assumed you would be going to the States and that the obstacles to our being together would be only of the other kind. But now it's London, and everything is against us. What was impossible before is doubly impossible now. . . ."

Half to yourself you repeated: "Doubly impossible." Then added: "I—I—I think that is all."

∽   ∽   ∽

Yes, that was all. We trailed back from the Cirque d'Hiver to the travel-agents—I arguing, protesting and at last dully acquiescent; you, with yours lips a tight unhappy line, un-answering save to shake your head or fiercely clutch my hand. I prayed there to be no boat. There was a boat. I prayed there to be no vacant berth. There was a berth. And so the next day to Cherbourg; and our last night together; and our last country expedition, with lunch in a sunny wood and queer defensive talk breaking the silences; and the clouds piling in from the west; and the rain; and back into Cherbourg; and the dock; and the final few minutes by the rail; and the last feel of you under my hands and your mouth for the last time crushed against mine; and the ship's lights blurring into distance behind the rain which fell as steadily on my heart as on the sea.

FINIS